A Few Quiet Beers with God

John Perrier

Title and Copyright notice

"A Few Quiet Beers with God"

By John Perrier

Published by JP Publishing Australia

Copyright 2015 John Perrier

ISBN 978-0-9875694-4-8

Science Fiction/Comedy/Humour/Adventure

Also available as an E-Book

ISBN 978-0-9875694-3-1

Disclaimer

This is a work of fiction. Any resemblance to actual events or persons, living or dead, is entirely coincidental - except, perhaps, for the deficient hygiene habits of the main character Dave, which I have unashamedly copied from one of my university flat-mates.

Please see the end of the book for:

- More titles from this author
- Ways to connect with us.

Being lazy will make you poor,

but hard work will make you rich.

Good News Bible, Proverbs 10:4

It is the Lord's blessing that makes you wealthy.

Hard work can make you no richer.

Good News Bible, Proverbs 10:22

PART ONE

A suburban Australian back street.

Probably a Tuesday or Wednesday, 2034

Chapter One

The pizza delivery drone could have changed everything.

If the drone had activated Dave's doorbell just one more time, it may have roused him from his sleep, but its government-regulated programming ensured that after just two polite rings it returned, pizza *in situ*, to its store of origin. Dave continued snoring.

If drones could think, this one may have wondered: what type of person would order a pizza for breakfast?

*

Dave gingerly opened one eye. He noted with relief that he had, for the third day in a row, slept in his own bed. Carefully, he teased open his other eye, and checked his smart-watch for the time. The smart-watch's screen was not in clock mode, so he spoke to its voice sensor to wake it from its battery-saving hibernation.

"Elvis, wake up," he barked croakily, but the not-so-smart-watch stubbornly refused to spring into life.

"C'mon Elvis," implored Dave in the general direction of his left forearm. "Wake up." But still Elvis-the-not-so-smart-watch refused to blink into service, so Dave tapped its face again, at first then gently, then impatiently, and finally with all the vigour his tired body could muster at short notice, before the watch finally booted itself awake.

"Elvis, switch to clock mode," instructed Dave. However, Elvis simply continued absently blinking as if awaiting further instruction.

Dave took a deep breath; he could feel a headache quickly building in the back of his neck, which was in some part due to the frustration he was experiencing with his smart-watch, but primarily due to the large quantity of beer that he had consumed the previous evening.

Rather than dictating further muddled instructions at his watch, Dave tried a variety of screen taps and an assortment of finger swipes to scroll through different apps, programs, features and functions in search of a simple clock. Despite owning Elvis for nearly a decade, Dave had not yet had the chance to watch the instructional tutorial, listen to the overview audio, or even browse the "Getting started – the basics" picture book, so he had no real idea of what he was doing. Instead of accessing the clock, he stumbled through various apps and screens, including, in order:

1.   The pizza delivery app that he had used the previous evening
2.   Mail-chat (three unread messages, each more than a year old, including one inviting him to watch a tutorial on how to use mail-chat)
3.   Life-Movie Replay (currently displaying an error message as he had not yet synced his contact lens cameras to the program) and
4.   A blood alcohol monitor (court ordered).

Dave became increasingly frustrated as he rolled through dozens of other screens that he had never used and could not identify, until he finally chanced upon "clock mode". When, he wondered, would someone invent a wrist watch that simply told the time, rather than cluttering up his valuable forearm space with so many useless add-ons?

His eyes wouldn't adjust to the small font, so Dave projected the image onto a nearby wall, and was finally able to discern the time. As he did, two sensations ebbed into his consciousness. One was the escalating headache and churning nausea that he now realised were symptoms of his worst hangover so far this week. The other was an even more painful realisation: it was ten past seven. Damn, he had slept in. *Damn*, he would be late for his interview.

After eight years of unemployment, hundreds of job applications, the same number of rejections, and only eight small lies on his curriculum vitae video, he had finally scored a job interview. His *first* interview.

Which was in twenty-five minutes time.

Dave vaulted out of bed and staggered towards the kitchen. He struggled to hitch up his trousers, which were still at half-mast from the previous evening's aborted attempt at undressing, as he instinctively sought what he knew was the quickest antidote to the malaise that he was presently fighting: pizza.

Where was the fresh breakfast pizza, he wondered, that he had taken the precaution of ordering for this morning? Had the delivery drones crashed again?

He grimaced in annoyance. He had always been a faithful and regular pizza purchaser, and felt that his status as a VIP customer warranted service that was more reliable. However he knew that complaining was useless because the entire service - from the robotic kneading of the "home baked" crust dough to the drone delivery of the finished product - was fully automated. The complaints were handled by the same computer program that chopped the pepperoni, so Dave saw little point in being too vociferous. He had once tried to contact the business owner, but he had departed for cruise around the inner solar system and left a message promising to attend to Dave's *important, valuable and erudite suggestions* when he returned. That was three years ago.

As Dave opened the fridge its interior light blinded him, nudging his headache into a higher echelon of pain. He groped around the shelves, and soon located some congealed slices of last week's dinner on the otherwise empty racks. Dave toyed with the idea of heating the leftovers but quickly demurred, as he would need ten minutes to find the griller, which was buried somewhere under the growing mound of dirty dishes that dominated the kitchen.

The dish pile formed a peak above where one would suppose the sink was located, where a milk-stained vase balanced precariously atop a cereal-encrusted ashtray. Dave made a mental note to clean it up when he had a chance.

He gobbled down four slices of cold salami-capsicum-pineapple-anchovy-and-egg pizza. Calmed by the familiar combination of starch and grease, his headache began to subside, and the layers of dough gradually suffocated his nausea. As Dave's physical condition improved, his mind cleared.

Dave glanced down at his watch again. Its display had defaulted to an advertisement for a gambling enterprise, so he again tapped, swirled and dragged his fingers across its face until he mercifully fumbled his way to clock mode, which indicated that he now only had 14 minutes until the interview was due to begin. His frustration and his hangover both gave way to a new feeling: panic.

Galvanised to a new level of activity, Dave ran down the hallway towards his bedroom, hurdling piles of dirty laundry and empty pizza boxes on the way. He arrived at his bedside and threw the mattress off its base. Lying flat on the boards was a clean, white shirt: his lucky shirt.

He pulled it on over his head, and then, while congratulating himself for the time he had saved by not removing his shoes the previous evening, he hurriedly continued his morning hygiene routine. First, a short shot of air freshener under each arm. Then he splashed his dark hair with oil and combed it with his fingers, smoothing out any tangles as he encountered them. He skipped his shave – the stubble made him look more mature, he thought - and to save more time he substituted two pieces of peppermint chewing gum for his usual teeth cleaning routine. Satisfied that he was looking respectable, Dave rushed back down the hallway, grabbing his keys as he went.

Dave was possibly the only person in the country who still carried keys. He had tried to use a UBI Entry Portal – the Unique Brainwave Identifier, which could sense the owner's presence simply by reading their emitted brainwaves – but its system kept crashing whenever he arrived home drunk, which was often. He tried to recalibrate it when he was drunk, but the unit thereafter refused him entry when he was sober.

The old-school Iris Detection Locks has similarly failed whenever his bloodshot morning eyes had confused its scanner. Eventually Dave had lost patience with the new-fangled security and had scoured his grandfather's attic, where he found some turn-of-the-century door keys and locks, and installed them during one unusually productive Wednesday afternoon.

With a certain sense of *schadenfreude* Dave had connected the now-disused Iris Detection System to the body corporate power supply, jammed an old glass marble into the eye scanner, and observed with daily satisfaction as the software endlessly cycled through its identification process, constantly updating and searching its databanks for the owner of this most mysterious iris.

After installing the old locks Dave soon discovered another advantage: modern thieves had developed cracks and hacks to easily defeat the modern high-tech security, but were totally flummoxed when presented with an old brass key hole. He hadn't been robbed since.

With keys in hand, and confident in the knowledge that he still had nine minutes to get to the interview, Dave stepped outside and quickly pulled the door closed behind him. One minute later he was fumbling frantically with the keys to the lock of the same door. First, he tried the right key, but used it upside down. Then he tried the wrong key. After that he tried the original right key, but twisted it the wrong way. In frustration he shoulder-charged the door, which only reactivated his headache. He then reverted to his original strategy before finally chancing upon the correct combination of key, alignment and rotation.

"The address," moaned Dave. "Where did I leave the address of the interview?"

As he looked around the debris-laden room, a deep sense of hopelessness enveloped him. Finding a grain of salt in the Sahara desert would be easier than locating a simple piece of paper in this pigsty. Why hadn't he cleaned it up when he had the chance?

Panic stricken, Dave tried to recall the conversation that had informed him of this quickly dissolving opportunity of a lifetime. After saying goodbye to the managing director of *Fiddlesticks Inc.* he had promised - ugh - not to be late for the interview. The address had churned itself repeatedly in his mind as he tried to enter it into his smart-watch, but as usual his fingers were too clunky to type on the tiny screen, his air-keyboard wasn't working, and Elvis continually misheard his voice entries. And he still hadn't had a chance to sync his Life-Movie contact lenses so that he could replay the conversation. Damn – he would fix all that tomorrow.

In desperation he searched for an old-fashioned pen to write the information down on an old-fashioned scrap of paper. Dave could have sworn that a hundred rarely-used pens perpetually cluttered his unit, always getting in the way. Except, of course, when he needed one. Why was a pen never about when he needed it?

In a last desperate measure before the address slid its way out of his mind forever, he had used an old toothpick, dipped into some leftover red wine as ink, to scrawl the address onto a slip of paper. The he had stashed the precious note in an old beer bottle for safe keeping. Then he had put the bottle ... he had put it ... he had put it *somewhere.* But where?

In the freezer! Dave raced across the kitchen and, stoically ignoring the bright light emanating from within, he wrenched the bottle from the ice. To dislodge the note he tapped the bottle on a cupboard, which unfortunately disturbed the delicate balance of the dirty dish pile, which came crashing down in a thunderous cavalcade of smell and sound. Plates smashed, bowls cluttered, insects scuttered. Even the mould seem to creep for cover. But Dave was oblivious to the chaos as he raced out the door, clutching the prized fragment of paper in a tight fist. Eight minutes to go!

He leapt down his front steps, sprinted across the magenta and turquoise lawn (it was embarrassingly out of date, he conceded, but he hadn't been able to update his *FashionTurf* since the mid 20s) and hurdled the low fence at the front of the property. "Elvis," he yelled at his watch, "Get me a hover cab." Elvis seemed to do as instructed, but three interminable minutes later Dave discovered that it had instead ordered him a home-delivered anchovy, jam and cheese pretzel with a side-serve of Japanese nori rolls. His second attempt at ordering a taxi resulted in Elvis instead downloading the complete collected works of 18th century poet Archibald Lampman.

Now with barely a minute to spare, Dave yelled aggressively at his own forearm.

"Elvis, change function!"

The dew is gleaming in the grass, the morning hours are seven, replied Elvis.

"I don't want a weather report, and I no longer want the time," yelled Dave in exasperation, sending his headache into new realms of pain. "I need you, Elvis, to CHANGE FUNCTION."

And I am fain to watch you pass, ye soft white clouds of heaven, continued Elvis, which Dave soon realised was giving neither time nor weather, but was instead reading him prose by the aforementioned Archibald Lampman. Dave growled.

"Elvis, you had better change function right now, or you will soon be keeping company with one very exasperated Iris Detection System."

This threat somehow had the desired effect, and the smart-watch screen blinked and became silent, awaiting further instructions. "Elvis, I want you to HAIL ME THE NEAREST HOVER-TAXI."

Elvis mercifully managed to interpret Dave's instructions correctly, emitted the requisite electromagnetic pulse, and soon an unmanned flying vehicle dropped down and landed gently on a nearby section of vacant pavement. Dave jumped in.

"Good evening Sir," said a pleasant automated voice as it prepared to ask the passenger's destination.

"Excuse me?" said Dave. "What did you just say?"

"I said 'good evening Sir'."

"Good *evening*, Sir?"

"Yes. Good evening Sir."

"That's what I thought you said."

Dave let himself out of the Hovertaxi and walked dejectedly toward his local bar.

Chapter Two

Dave walked slowly into the *Stranglers Bar*. The real name of the establishment was the *Angler's Hope*, but it had been nicknamed the *Strangler's Rope*. The bar's regulars had abbreviated the moniker even further, and now almost everyone knew it as the 'Stranglers Bar'.

"Just the usual for starters, thanks Billy," said Dave to his favourite barman as he slumped onto his regular bar stool.

Momentarily idle while waiting for his drink, Dave attempted to piece together the previous night. He remembered feeling anxious about the interview, and having a couple of beers to help settle his nerves. Naturally, he had then reasoned, it would have been wasteful not to finish the entire six-pack once he had opened it.

Then, feeling that a refreshing walk in the night air would help settle the last of his nerves, he had ventured out into the streets, not entirely coincidently in the direction of the Stranglers Bar. The last thing he remembered clearly was bumping into some old mates from the Australian Rules Football Club, and joining them for a few friendly rounds of drinks.

After that his memories became less refined, then progressively hazier, until all that remained was a distant impression of what might have happened. Dave had a feeling that it involved several jugs of beer, too many bets on the races, a few more jugs of beer, and judging from the stain on his jeans, at least two hot dogs with the works.

Sure, Dave admitted to himself, I might have gone just a little bit overboard with the nerve-settling drinks. But what self-respecting thirty-four-year-old bachelor would not have done the same?

A jug of generic-brand lager ascended from a well in the bar in front of Dave.

"How are you Dave?" asked Billy the barman.

Dave replied automatically. Their initial greetings were identical every night, for Billy was a virtual barman.

The hospitality industry had long ago realised that pouring a beer or a cocktail was easily automated, saving the hotelier thousands in wages. But many punters criticised the lack of atmosphere in such establishments, so the industry responded by creating a range of virtual waiters who would offer small talk as they poured drinks, and even interact with patrons. There were plenty of bartenders to choose from – from comely topless waitresses to sharply dressed college graduates to cartoonish apparitions – but Billy, with his down-to-earth chatter, was Dave's favourite.

Billy's intuitive technology had gradually learned Dave's favourite topics and patterns of conversation. The system was even clever enough to account for the blood alcohol readings that Dave's smart-watch transmitted to the virtual bar waiter system, although Billy occasionally required full recalibration after particularly drunken sessions.

"Good, mate. Yourself?" replied Dave,

"I am good thank you Dave. Have you had a good day?"

"Not too bad. Yours?"

"It was great thanks."

"Cheers, Billy."

"Cheers, Dave."

The pleasantries now dispensed, Billy evaporated into the ether where he hovered invisibly, awaiting Dave's next summons. Dave gulped down his first beer, and sat back to survey the room. It was a typical night at Stranglers. A dozen punters sat at the bar; most were engrossed in their own world, or talking glibly with their preferred virtual bartender.

The Babe-O-Matic flashed in one corner, popular as always. Half a dozen men - Dave knew most of their faces, and some of their names - crowded in front of the stage, as a carefully reconstructed virtual image last year's "Miss, Mrs or Ms Universe Pageant" winner, Honeydew Melons, danced and pranced provocatively around the dance floor. Dave had seen her show many times before. When were they going to download the software for his favourite last-century icon, Marilyn Monroe?

Two regulars, Bruce and Bevan, stood in a corner. Bruce was at the edge of an empty area of floor space, intently watching absolutely nothing. Bevan was bent awkwardly at the waist, and was also staring unerringly at nothing. He held his left arm outstretched in front of him, as his right arm jangled repeatedly in thin air behind him. A typical scene: another game of Virtual Snooker was underway.

Dave glanced across at the STOVE display – the Screenless Three-dimensional Optical Viewing & Entertainment system. The screenless bit was the clever part. Dave still marvelled at the way the characters from the STOVE walked about the room talking with each other, and even interacting with the patrons.

He had tried many times to learn how it worked, but had never had the concentration to fully understand. The technology had something to do with two bursts of gamma rays colliding with each other in mid air and obliterating each other's energy, apart from a tiny bit that escaped as a light ray. Some genius at the Hieshler Corporation – there was some dispute as to whether or not it was Harry Hieshler himself - had figured out how to twiddle the dials on the gamma ray emitters so that all the little bits of light could be manipulated to form three-dimensional pictures that moved.

Even the hopelessly outdated (four-month-old) STOVE at the Strangler's Bar was infinitely better than Dave's ultra-hi-fi, mega-Wi-Fi, hyper-hi-def, super-smart television that he had picked up from a weekend antique market.

Dave flicked through a few channel feeds on the STOVE and soon settled onto a news update of a nearby war. A life sized reporter appeared, and walked across to where Dave was sitting to discuss the finer points of the battle with him. But before he arrived, Dave lost interest and tried to change channels.

"Are you sure that you want to change chann...." said the news reader, before Dave interrupted with an abrupt "Yes".

"Are you certain that...."

"Yes."

"I'm sorry to...." Dave manually overrode the irritating channel-change confirmation system and flicked the STOVE to a horse racing broadcast.

Dave watched with just distracted interest as a miniature race course formed in front of him. Tiny thoroughbreds, with jockeys that were even tinier than in real life, raced around the course until the commentator's voice excitedly called the runners down the final straight. But before they crossed the finish line, Billy changed the STOVE feed again.

There was a gambling game on the next channel – some type of playing card game that a buxom dealer was tempting him to join - and another war report on the fourth. He continued flicking through a seemingly endless supply of war and gambling programs until he eventually found something different: a preview of that night's big match, the final of the World Super Football League.

"So Jimmy," said the show's commentator to the resident expert, *"do you think that we'll see the great man, Juan Carlos Manuel de la Espirito, make an appearance tonight?"*

"It's the question on efferrrybody's lips," replied Jimmy with a thick Glaswegian inflection. *"In my opinion, aye, we'll see the champ, orright. This is the final game, and we all know 'ow he loves finals. I think that we'll see him take the field no matter what the score line."*

The three dimensional projections of the two hosts ambled along the bar top toward Dave. When they were so close that he could almost touch them, the hosts spoke again.

"Let's all keep our fingers crossed that you're right, Jimmy. Let's have a look at some of his more special goals from last year's grand final."

The two figures faded and were replaced by a three dimensional simulation of a football pitch, on which a highlights package from previous games was played out in miniature. A few minutes later the preview ended, so Dave drained his beer jug and continued to surf the channel feeds.

"Anything interesting on the STOVE?" asked Billy as he returned routinely with Dave's second jug.

"Nothun 'cept war en' gamblin' en' rrracin'," said Dave, neatly imitating the Glaswegian accent of the football show host. "Thar's loots of war en' gamblin' en' rrracin' on the STOVE these days, in't thar?"

"Please repeat that Dave, I didn't understand you," requested Billy, his vocal recognition defeated by the brogue. Audio engineers had worked for decades to develop a system that could understand Scottish speech. Eventually someone produced not a solution, but instead an algorithmic proof showing that it was actually impossible for voice recognition to understand the accent. A later research paper concluded that it was incompatible with the fundamental laws of biophysics that such an inflection even evolved, and the whole project was summarily dropped. So despite the interactive voice technology being able to understand and converse in every existing and extinct known language, including Latin, Crimerian Gothic, Neanderthal and Ancient Gayak, it could not understand a Scotsman speaking English.

"There is lots of war and gambling and racing on the STOVE these days, isn't there?" Dave eventually repeated clearly for the benefit of his illusory friend.

"There certainly is," replied Billy. "They are always battling it out for the top ratings position."

Little did Dave know, but that ratings battle would soon inseparably entwine his life. Nor did he realise that another future-life-influencing figure was presently sitting at a party only a few blocks away. She was presently also having a battle, but against a different type of enemy: boredom.

Chapter Three

"I find it fascinating that the positron is a spin-reversed particle, yet its energy release following a collision is slightly less than that predicted by standard quantum electro-relativity formulae."

"Er, yes. That's fascinating, Siegfried. Would you like a drink?"

"A drink? No. No thank you, Alexandra. But don't you find the new research so exciting? It supports a theory of mine that the atomic nucleus represents the zero energy state, while the orbiting photons assume the positive energy characteristics previously assigned to the heavy particles."

"Well, yes. I find the research interesting, but only up to a point. Would you like to dance?"

"Up to a point? But Alexandra, this is the most important development in grand unified theory since Bohr."

Speaking of bores, thought Alexandra.

"Surely you understand the significance of the latest findings?" continued Alexandra's companion. "It explains why the positive energy of the atomic nucleus cannot be responsible for the gluon energy cycle. What could be more exciting than gluons?"

A thousand answers passed through Alexandra's mind, but she verbalised none of them. Instead she sipped her vodka and caffeine cocktail, and absently nodded her head as her partner waffled incessantly about nuclear physics. Sure, she found the subject interesting; it was, after all, one of her major university subjects this semester. However it was *not* her life, and nor was the development of a grand unified theory of physics the primary goal of her existence. Her major aspiration right now was just to convince her present companion to drop the subject of physics, and start to have some fun. This was a party, not a lecture. Exams were *over*.

"Well?"

Siegfried looked at Alexandra, waiting for a reply. She cut back to reality; she hadn't been listening.

"Yes, of course," she guessed.

"What do you mean?" scorned Siegfried. "How could the neutron spin direction possibly represent its gravity wave polarity?"

Alexandra shrugged. This was going to be a long night.

Chapter Four

Billy the virtual barman delivered a third jug of beer to Dave, and again initiated some light pre-programmed conversation.

"What have you been up to Dave?"

"Oh, nothing much," replied Dave. "Just taking it easy."

Billy's apparition dug into its database, compared the information with some biocompatibility data from his patron, and settled on a conversation topic. "How did the job interview go?"

"Ah ... I missed it actually. Slept in a little."

Dave was one person who could describe waking up twelve hours late as 'slept in a little' and not feel that he was understating. His sleeping feats were as legendary as was his quirky sense of humour. Once there was a well-worn urban myth about a bloke who went on a drinking binge in Mexico - he became inordinately drunk and had woken two days later with a painful scar on his belly, a beard on his chin, and lacking a kidney. That bloke was actually Dave.

"Don't worry," said Billy after input from his empathy circuits. "I am sure that you will get another offer soon."

Dave wondered whether another chance would arrive. Life had seemed so simple yesterday when he felt assured of a job, even though it was just for a chopstick manufacturer. But the fickle hand of fate had wrested that opportunity from him, so now all that remained was to have another beer and wonder what else life had in store for him.

Even his lucky shirt had let him down. He felt deeply betrayed by his shirt, as he had exercised considerable foresight and restraint to keep it for emergencies like this. He recalled dozens of previous dilemmas in which he had been tempted to wear the shirt, but he had deemed them not to be *true* emergencies - for example, the time that his mother had come to visit. Dave grimaced at the memory, and then quickly flushed the entire fiasco, including the regrettable *pawpaw incident,* from his mind, before taking a long pull on his beer to calm himself.

As Dave further dissected his interview failure, his feeling of disappointment ripened to one of self-condemnation. How could he have slept through the most important morning of his life? Two or three hours late might have been explainable under the circumstances, but twelve?

And Elvis had let him down, yet again. Wasn't this technology supposed to make life easier? All it seemed to do was make simple tasks more difficult, while at the same time rendering the easy old solutions as redundant. Like pens. He used to have hundreds of them that he had pilfered from various banks, post offices, government departments and anywhere else that they weren't tied down. But since the advent of technology - internet messaging, smart watches, LifeMovie replays etcetera - people had little need for this much-loved instrument and it had fallen out of use. Dave had no idea where the thousands of unused and now unloved pens had gone, but they had somehow disappeared from his unit.

Usually if he couldn't find something, he simply raked his way through the second top draw in the kitchen until he found it. However on this occasion even the magical drawer had deserted him. Why was a pen never around when he needed one?

Dave took another long gulp of beer. Using the in-seat remote control, he activated the bar's audio program. Despite the system recommending 84,762 songs that he might like based on his recent money-card transactions, Dave ignored them, for he felt that a good loud blast of some old-fashioned music might cheer him. Maybe even some historical rock, like Elvis Presley.

Dave had named his smart-watch after this 1960s rock star. Following the infamous court case of 2027 in which an order for Gong Bao Chicken in a crowded Chinese restaurant was mistakenly interpreted by a nearby smart-phone as a declaration of war that ultimately led to the annexing of Mongolia, each device had to have a unique name for its voice recognition software. The simple monikers were quickly reserved by the technologically savvy, forcing most people to invent convoluted names for their device such as Mesbreyseenaught62#bogarin, or Hipsnalballygoot$@smoot*bomb, meaning that the brevity and convenience of voice activation was lost.

Dave was, as usual, very slow to adopt to the new enforced name rules, but was rewarded for his tardiness when the simple moniker 'Elvis' came back onto the domain market just a nanosecond before Dave submitted his application. Even the name-rider bots, who scoured the registries for short, simple names to sell back to device owners at highly inflated prices, had, through sheer luck, been beaten by Dave on this occasion.

After his usual mismanagement of the screen controls, Dave eventually, after much cussing and cursing, somehow instructed the bar's audio system to play a list of Elvis Presley songs. Then he simply sat and let the old tunes wash over him. The nostalgia helped to fleetingly lift his mood. However, the thought of his missed job opportunity returned to annoy him, and soon began to wear him down. Dave was a forlorn sight as he mulled over his lager, his head drooping towards the bar and sinking closer to it with each beer. He became very introspective, trying to figure out where he had gone wrong, not only with today's interview fiasco, but also with his whole life.

Dave felt that he had always played within the rules - except perhaps during his childhood holidays with his boring cousin Adnor, when he had admittedly cheated while playing a computer game called *Monopoly*.

Never had he cried over spilt milk, although once he had shed a tear after dropping a half full bottle of bourbon. He had never played with a bull on thin ice, or anything else to that effect. Yet somehow life's cruel little hand of fate always dealt him a dud. Just like on the STOVE gambling channels, if he had a King, life had the Ace; if he had two pairs, life had three of a kind. Even on the odd occasions where Dave knew he had a Royal Flush, life had still somehow managed to split the pot. Life was a tough opponent, but Dave had always managed to laugh in the face of adversity, or at least snigger behind its back. But right now life had all the humour of a whoopee cushion in Windsor Castle.

Chapter Five

Alexandra again found herself listening to the music rather than her companion. The virtual lead singer of the night's simulated resident band was wrapping up.

"This is our last song for this evening. It's an old tune - almost seventy years old - but a very good one. We hope you like it. Thank you very much for being such a wonderful audience. Goodnight."

The voice soon finished its farewells and, in vestigial homage to the time when real people played music, it counted down a beat to start the song. A realistically synthesised soft-stringed guitar strummed in the background as the faux singer soothingly added the initial vocals.

"Love me tender. Love me sweet. Never let me go...."

Alexandra jumped up from her seat, and grabbed Siegfried by the hand.

"I can't possibly sit and listen to discourse on electrodynamic sub nuclear responses while the band is playing an Elvis song," she said.

"Who is Elvis?" asked Siegfried.

Alexandra sighed, and tugged Siegfried to his feet.

"But I haven't got to the solution yet," protested Siegfried as his date dragged him onto the dance floor.

"Let's just have one dance without thinking of physics," said Alexandra as she proffered her arms to her companion.

"I find dancing so primitively physical. Can't we virtual-dance later?"

Alexandra fired a steely glare at her companion. Acting under protest, Siegfried took his partner in a cold embrace and began stiffly stepping from side to side.

*

"All my dreams fulfilled. For my darling I love you...."

Alexandra's mind swam with fantasy as the sound system closed out the song.

"... and I always will."

Not wanting to break such a passionate moment, Alexandra gazed up into Siegfried's eyes, searching for a hint of romance.

"Thanks for the dance," he said. "Now about those photodynamics that we were discussing."

Alexandra felt like crying.

Ten minutes later, feigning nausea, she managed to extricate herself from Siegfried's interminable company. Quietly slipping out of the hall, she meandered slowly homewards. As usual, she chose not to patronise the hovering taxis; electromagnetic signals from her smart-watch had alerted them that she was on the move, so they buzzed about in the expectation that anyone with more than 10 metres to travel required a lift. Some nights they would follow her all the way home, their logic circuits unable to compute that someone might actually prefer a 30-minute walk to sitting in air-traffic for 45 minutes.

It had been another very tedious evening, Alexandra reflected as she ambled homewards, thankful for the light emanating from the genetically engineered glow-trees that lined the pathway. Siegfried had been just another failure to add to her growing chain of disastrous romances.

Her first dating debacle had been Charles. Alexandra's father had asked her to escort Charles, the son of a business associate, to opening night at the opera. The evening had been one of unadulterated banality. Charles had flashed his wide array of money-cards at every opportunity, and had added ludicrously large tips to every payment, including a four hundred and thirty-five-card tip for a cola that cost sixty-five cards *service compris*.

It was not the free evening to which Alexandra objected. Far from it. It was Charles's constant reference to money-cards - how many he owned, how many he had saved, and how many he spent - that really annoyed her. He talked about money-cards with a reverence normally reserved for more sacred subjects, such as death, love, or football. It appeared to Alexandra that he was attempting to impress her with his vital statistics - his card balance - but his self-inflating banter had induced the opposite effect. Even worse, she *hated* opera.

As Alexandra continued meandering home, her thoughts returned to Siegfried. She had jumped at the invitation to spend an evening with him, which she already regretted. Although he was tall, intelligent and handsome, his mind was a monorail headed directly for a station called 'Nuclear Physics'.

Turning at an intersection, Alexandra saw the dim lights of a local bar. Was the man of her dreams inside? This evening had already been disappointing enough - she would rather not know. Although it was early, she decided to go home instead, and curl up in bed with a mug of hot chocolate and download a trashy magazine. There was a new edition of *22nd Century Woman Magazine* that she was looking forward to watching.

Her gloomy disposition reminded her of another recent dating failure: a family friend named Brinley. Brinley was a pleasant, polite boy who was neat and well mannered in every respect. He was also considerate, courteous, cordial, cultured and courtly. Their evening had begun with tea and small talk, had continued with coffee and chitchat, and had rounded off with iced water and tête-à-tête. Apart from ten extra calories, Alexandra had left the evening with nothing more than she had arrived. No new stories, no laughs, and definitely no new boyfriend.

When was she going to find a guy who realised that sometimes a girl just wanted to have a good time? Someone down-to-earth, with a sense of humour. And finding a decent lover these days was so hard.

As Alexandra approached the bar, she heard the background murmur of conversations. She had ventured into the bar on a few previous occasions - a friendly place, but the decor was dated, the software systems were old, and it was not the type of establishment she generally favoured. With the mug of hot chocolate and magazine viewing still beckoning to her, she defiantly walked past the bar's entrance, heading for home.

Chapter Six

Dave's head was now practically resting on the bar, moving only intermittently for sips of beer. However deep inside his almost immobile head, things were beginning to stir. Dave's brain had never recruited its neurons with such intensity; their usual vocation was figuring out how to place an order for a home delivered pizza, or deciding whether to take the pink ball or go for the snooker. This life review exercise was a far tougher assignment, but his cerebral matter responded as best it could.

Neurons twirled around each other like worms in a bait bucket. Tiny electric impulses arced across infinitesimal gaps. Molecules of transmitter substances, most with names containing lots of syllables, bounced between nerves, while the beer molecules generally just made a complete nuisance of themselves.

Soon the transmitter chemicals began to pool and form ideas. He rejected most of them, particularly one very persistent one saying *clean up when you get a chance.* Eventually, however, a thought arrived that made sense. After memory his archive passed it through a compatibility check, Dave's consciousness assigned the thought its ultimate label: *The Reason.*

The Reason was now clear. The Reason stood out like a bacon bone in the murky pea soup of his mind. At last he had unmasked Fate's evil accomplice, and now knew the reason for every dud hand life had ever dealt him.

His lucky shirt. His bloody lucky shirt. His bloody mongrel lucky shirt.

For years he had trusted it. He had given that shirt every benefit of the doubt, despite nothing lucky ever happening when he wore it. He had been meticulous in caring for it, and had once even gone to the effort of replacing a button.

Dave had called upon that shirt in times of his greatest need, trusting it to carry him over the burning bridges of life. What had the shirt done in return? - It had pushed him off the edge. He had relied upon the shirt to throw him a lifebuoy when he was drowning in a sea of uncertainty, but it had just pushed his flailing body further under. This plethora of circumstantial evidence shattered his faith in his lucky shirt. He hated that shirt. It was an evil force. It had to go.

At that point, Dave felt a tap on his shoulder - the type of tap that can be life-changing. He looked up and saw before him the most beautiful woman upon whom he had ever laid his bloodshot eyes. Blond hair, shortish brown skirt, browner eyes. Vodka and caffeine cocktail in her left hand, right hand gently tapping his sleeve. Heavenly face, trim body, altogether one hell of a package. She spoke.

"That's a lovely shirt. Do you mind if I ask where you bought it?"

Chapter Seven

Luckily Dave awoke two minutes before Elvis's alarm was due to go off. He would not have felt the buzzer anyway. Even during sleep, one thought had preoccupied his mind; one delicious, all-enveloping thought had immersed his entire being: Alexandra.

He skipped into the kitchen and began busily tidying and cleaning, singing a short verse of his own recent composition entitled *Alexandra How I Love You* as he worked.

He paused to order a breakfast pizza at nine o'clock, giving longer than average consideration to its toppings. All five major food groups had to be adequately represented, as Alexandra had told him how important this was to maintain his tigerish good health. Salami would cover the protein, and double anchovy would do for the seafood. Fine, they were two of his favourites anyway. Fruit was a difficult family to include on a pizza, but he eventually selected pineapple, and then chose capsicum to represent the vegetables. He was stuck for a while on the 'breads and cereals' group, and was about to order a topping of sugarcorn-flakes when he realised that the pan-baked base already represented carbohydrates. Finally, to give the pizza a breakfasty feel, he topped it with a fried egg.

Five minutes later, as he munched away on the instant robot-created-drone-delivered pizza, Dave realised with excited delight that it was his old favourite.

"It's no wonder I've been so tigerishly healthy for so many years," he said to himself, before christening his creation *Alexandra's Choice* in honour of the most wonderful person he had ever met.

After breakfast, Dave returned to his cleaning duties. He danced around the kitchen like a dragonfly on drugs as he shoved everything into the ultraviolet desterilising autoclaving dishwasher, before discovering that either (a) it no longer worked, or (b) he couldn't remember how to turn it on, or, most likely, (c) both. Undaunted, Dave removed every dish and steadfastly washed them all by hand.

After that, Dave tried to use the ultrasonic degrader to clean the benches and floors. It's high energy microscopic vibrations were supposed to effortlessly disintegrate grease, grime and all other hard-to-remove stains, but Dave inadvertently used it upside-down so it achieved little except to remove the fingerprints from his left three middle fingers. Eventually he resorted to some hard scrubbing using an old dishcloth that he had discovered amidst the dish pile, which some rudimentary archaeology told him that he had left there about four months previously.

His vocal chords continued to emit a whole range of impromptu verse, including Dave's two personal favourites *Alexandra on My Mind* and *Alexandra You Are So Beautiful*. He paused only to finish the remaining four slices of *Alexandra's Choice* for lunch.

By mid afternoon the kitchen was spotless, so Dave started decontaminating the laundry. He even discovered the use of an old bottle marked 'detergent'. He sanitised and washed every piece of clothing that he owned, except one: his lucky shirt. His wonderful lucky shirt. His beautiful, wonderful lucky shirt.

Alexandra's lips had touched the shirt's collar during their parting embrace the previous evening. She had left a ruby-red lipstick impression of her dazzling pout, which Dave had vowed to keep as a souvenir of their first encounter to one day show their grandchildren. He would never wash, or wear, the shirt again.

The decision for Dave to retire the shirt from active service had been difficult. However, he adjudged that his recent explosion of good fortune must have drained all of the shirt's special power. Anyhow, he no longer required a lucky charm, for he had met the love of his life and he would never leave her.

As Dave soulfully eyed the lip impression, memories of the previous evening flooded over him. He recalled Alexandra arousing him from the bar by a tap on the shoulder - the first time her hands had touched him. She commented on his shirt - the first words that she had spoken to him. He was smooth, suave and casual in his reply. She was an angel.

She had seamlessly used her smart-watch to call up a recreated STOVE film clip of Elvis Presley; he had frequented this bar on hundreds of previous occasions but had never managed that feat, yet somehow Alexandra had mastered its intricacies on her first try. He remembered the closeness of her body as he gratuitously tutored her in the finer arts of cuing a Virtual Snooker ball. Later, her first ever laser darts shot had hit the bull's-eye. What a woman!

They laughed an hour away at the bar, during which she showed him how to hack into the software of Billy the Barman to access his "tip" function. This application had originally been designed for the American market, in which you could tip the virtual waiter a token money-card credit to refill your glass, rather than paying for a fresh drink. It had been disabled for the Australian market, where such practice was generally referred to as "stealing". Alexandra would only let him use the tip function once, just for fun; she was as honest as she was beautiful.

In return he showed her how to place a STOVE-TV bet on a cheetah race. His cat had jumped poorly from the gates, been bumped around the turn, and then blocked for a run in the finishing straight – just unlucky from start to finish. Fortunately Alexandra's choices had finished first and second, with the profit allowing them to shout themselves two glasses of ridiculously expensive Neptune Gold Beer.

Neptune Gold Beer was unrivalled as the finest beverage in the solar system. It was brewed on one of Neptune's moons, Galatea, in biospheres that were remnants of a decades-old carbon dioxide abatement project. To help prevent global warming, one scheme had used massive clear plastic balloons that were placed over the exhaust chimneys of factories to capture the escaping gas. When the balloons were fully inflated to the size of, roughly, a medium-sized city, their necks were tied with enormous knots and they were released into space.

But after a few years, the floating balloons started causing problems. Several inner-space aircraft struck them, causing nasty accidents. In one such incident, 40 senior citizens on a weekend trip to Mars (including sandwiches and tea on the moon, photo-opportunity fly-by around Mars, and a mah-jongg tournament on the return journey) were almost suffocated when their space craft punctured one of the giant balloons, encasing it in a thick film of plastic. The subsequently-deployed oxygen masks created such havoc that the mah-jongg competition had to be cancelled.

On another occasion, a cargo plane carrying weapons exploded after hitting a mega-balloon, ironically causing a fireball so big that it raised atmospheric carbon dioxide by more than the total abatement of all the balloons combined.

But the final straw for the mega-balloons came when one of them caused a telecommunications satellite to crash, thereby wiping out television reception for *an entire week* across three different US states. Once the police had cleared the streets and restored order, the government of the day quickly decreed that the balloons must be moved. Forthwith. If not sooner. Television must never be interrupted again.

A long piece of rope was tied around the neck of each balloon and they were gathered together like a gigantic bunch of kids' party decorations. They were then towed to Neptune, which was in the early stages of colonisation and therefore did not have the political or military presence to object to their presence, and released.

Although the temperature in the general neighbourhood around Neptune was well below freezing, the heavy concentration of carbon dioxide in the balloons meant that they soon warmed to a tropical 40 degrees. As luck would have it, some of the giant balloons had spent their earlier years collecting gas from the chimneys of a brewery, where seeds of hops, barely and malt had somehow found their way into the exhaust. The enterprising Galatean settlers later discovered, after the addition of several thousand tonnes of moon soil, that all three plants grew extremely well in these accidental biospheres. In fact they grew so quickly, and produced such fine ale, that Galatea's entire colony became dedicated to a gigantic beer brewery.

Neptune's standard brew was excellent ale, but Neptune Gold was *wondrous*. No-one disputed its claim as the finest-tasting liquid in the history of civilisation (except, perhaps, a select group of Venusian coffee snobs).

Dave was about to fold his lucky shirt away when a small mark below the lipstick kiss caught his eye. The stain was smudged, reddish-brown and smelled suspiciously of chilli sauce. Where had that come from? Ah, that's right, the hot dog.

Alexandra suggested that they order hot dogs. She laughed unashamedly as he serenaded her through the chilli dog microphone with an abridged rendition of *Hound Dog*. Dave thought that it was akin to a miracle that he had found someone who had not only heard of Elvis Presley, but loved his old-style music as well.

Not only that, but she shared his belief that although technology was cheap and sometimes even useful, it had sapped the world of all its character. A virtual-dance was *not* - despite the 'proof' provided by the manufacturers - as stimulating as an old-fashioned boogie. And they both knew that nobody represented that notion any more clearly than did the king, Elvis Presley. Alexandra was a real soul mate.

He recalled gazing deeply into her sweet brown eyes as they nibbled on either end of the chilli dog, their lips eventually touching as they swallowed the last bite. This was officially their first kiss, but it was not, Dave reminded himself with a wry smile, their most passionate.

Then the cool night air had invited them out for a stroll, which eventually terminated at a park bench where they had talked for hours. Alexandra knew a lot about all codes of football, and agreed with Dave that *Harry's Heroes* were a certainty to win the World Super Soccer League. She also shared Dave's opinion that Juan Carlos Manuel de la Espirito was, by far, the best player to *ever* kick a ball.

Alexandra had laughed at all his jokes and giggled at his funny stories - even the one about the kidney in Mexico, although he had to show her the scar to prove that it was true. Everything about her entranced Dave, even the simple things, like the way she combed her fingers through her fringe, or how she rhythmically slid her left foot in and out of her shoe. As the hours flowed by, the distance between them gradually lessened, and at midnight they had touched.

Dave remembered that touch, that defining moment. He had casually, almost accidentally brushed his hand against her knee. She had not flinched. It was Alexandra's *lack* of reaction that showed him that she now considered him more than just an acquaintance, more than a friend. They embraced spontaneously, and then kissed passionately. From that moment onward the night became a blur in Dave's mind, for as surely as a carton of Neptune Gold could intoxicate him, so had Alexandra.

In the early hours of the next morning came their inevitable parting. It was next to that park bench during their romantic goodbye that Alexandra's lips had touched his collar, leaving him a souvenir of their evening.

Parting was so painful that Alexandra could sever herself away only if Dave pledged to call her at six the next evening. As usual, Dave could not get Elvis to work well enough to record Alexandra's number, and his LifeMovie contact lenses were sitting in his bathroom at home, still awaiting synchronisation (he really must watch that instructional video). Alexandra had fruitlessly searched her handbag for the pen that she carried for emergencies, and although she was certain that one had been there earlier, it had inexplicably disappeared. Dave tapped his pockets in a token search. Why was a pen never around when he needed it?

Alexandra instead wrote her number on the back of an old hot dog wrapper with lipstick, and then sealed it with a kiss. Dave clutched the paper fiercely to his heart as he floated home. After stashing the wrapper into a beer bottle and hiding it in the freezer for safe keeping, he had drifted into a delirious reverie.

Dave looked at his lucky shirt again, and felt compelled to shake it by its imaginary hand at the end of the sleeve.

"Thanks very much, old mate," he said to it audibly. "I never should have doubted you. Playing that Elvis Presley track was a great move."

Upon hearing its name, Dave's smart watch blinked its way into life. That it heard its name at all was surprising, because some months earlier Dave had stuck a half-chewed piece of gum to its back face for later retrieval, but had subsequently forgotten about it, and the offending gum had been blocking Elvis's microphone pick up ever since. A simple trouble-shooting procedure would have detected the problem in an instant, but Dave had not yet learned how to do it.

"Where were you last night when I needed you Elvis?" asked Dave.

"*The Ye stray and gather, part and fold; the wind alone can tame you,*" started Elvis, inexplicably launching into the second stanza of *Among the Millet* by Archibald Lampman.

"Change function!" yelled Dave. "Clock mode."

As usual, Dave struggled to coax Elvis into the correct service. He inadvertently purchased a juice extractor, took his blood pressure, and hooked into a telecast of the Icelandic national curling championships, before finally arriving at the time screen. He soon saw that it was a quarter to six, meaning that in only 15 minutes he would again be talking to his sweetheart. Soon he would be hearing her honey-smooth voice replying *oh so coquettishly* to his casual remarks.

"Casual remarks? What remarks?" thought Dave, suddenly realising that he had not yet thought of anything clever to say. Audibly he began to rehearse and analyse a series of opening lines.

"Hi babe, you were great."

No, too forward.

"Hello Alexandra. That was a wonderful evening."

Way too formal.

"Hiya schnookums, howzabout I head around to your place."

Uh-uh, too colloquial.

The rehearsal did not progress well. Soon it was almost six o'clock, and Dave still did not have a catch phrase with which to open. One unimpressive comment could spoil everything. All of the dapper looks, the suave moves and amusing comments of the previous evening would go up in smoke if he said something stupid. His opening line had to be hip, sophisticated and humble. A tough combination.

Nervously, Dave tested a few more opening moves.

"Do you go there often?"

Hmm. He knew that she didn't.

"Alexandra my darling, where have you been all my life?"

Too clichéd.

"Was it good for you too?"

Arrgh, no! What if she said that it wasn't?

Dave became increasingly frantic. Soon he would be talking to his new love, and he didn't even have a line to throw her. It would be like fishing without bait on the hook. His overwrought mind hatched a nervous tingle, which raced up and down his spine before concentrating in his stomach. Then it spawned and multiplied, creating new and more powerful tingles that surged in waves to his fingers, lips and neck. As the dying minutes of the fifth hour ticked by, the nervous jitter stripped his brain of the power of logical thought. It then spread to his jaw muscles, which clenched so tightly no sound could escape bar a stutter. His legs became weak, and his breathing ragged. The tingle, born in his stomach, now controlled him completely.

With uncanny instinct, Dave fought back with the only antidote known to modern medicine: a shot of bourbon. And another. Then he took a few deep slow breaths, and a third, rather large nip to be sure. The medicine soon began attacking the insidious invader, although even a series of half a dozen more shots did not regain him complete control of his knotted mind. He looked at his smart-watch, which was miraculously still on "time" function. It was two minutes to six!

Dave stumbled his way through the kitchen, thankful that he had cleaned it up when he had the chance. He reached into the freezer, somehow extracted the prized lip-stick message from the beer bottle. Rather than rely on Elvis to make the call, Dave decided, in a rare lucid moment, to use his old-style house phone, towards which he staggered. Now confused, nervous *and* drunk, he again tried to rehearse some lines as he counted out the remaining seconds. Dave's became an emotional wreck as the final ten-second countdown began.

Ten. Nine. "I was great for ... uh.... "

Eight. Seven. " ... what's it, er, happening in the ... er.... "

Six. Five. " ... I mean where wasn't ... I meant.... "

Four. Three.

Blank patch.

Two. One.

Brain to Dave. "Why not try 'Hello Alexandra'?"

Dave to brain. "Bit boring."

Brain to Dave again. "Have you got a better suggestion?"

"Ah ... no."

Zero.

"Go for it."

Dave took a final deep breath, and picked up the phone. As his fingers vibrated nervously above the dial screen, he looked down at the hot dog wrapper for the number.

It was covered in ruby red lipstick, unfortunately not in any definable pattern. Every letter and number was smudged beyond recognition.

Chapter Eight

A small light flashed on Alexandra's smart-watch, and she felt the hum of a tiny vibration that signalled an incoming call.

"Whose calling, Einstein55?" she asked her watch.

Your friend Parice is calling via STOVE-chat, replied Einstein55. *Should I connect you*?

"Yes, thanks Einstein55 ... Hi Reesy!" Alexandra waved excitedly as her friend's image appeared in front of her.

"Hi Lexy," waved back Parice as Alexandra sat comfortably back in bed. "I've heard that you have some news...."

"He is just *gorgeous*," said Alexandra, barely even waiting for her friend to finish her question. "He's boyish yet ruggedly handsome. He's got dark hair that was, well, a bit messy, as though he hadn't brushed it for a week, but the tussled effect suited him."

"What's he like? Is he charming, or funny, or...."

"Funny. He's really funny - that's his best feature. He has great sense of humour. And guess what ... he likes Elvis!"

They both giggled. Alexandra gave a thumbs-up sign towards her friend's image before continuing her answer.

"Have a look for yourself."

With that, Alexandra tapped her smart-watch. "Einstein55, I want a LifeMovie replay from 9 pm yesterday." Within seconds, Alexandra's watch was replaying her evening with Dave, having been recorded from transparent optical sensors in her LifeMovie contact lenses and continuously downloaded to the tiny hard drive on her smart-watch. When she was satisfied that the footage adequately captured the essence of her new boyfriend, she used a few quick air swipes to cut a selection of footage and upload it to the STOVE feed. She lay back, giggling like a school girl, as the STOVE recreated, in her bedroom, fifty-four seconds of Dave serenading her with a hot dog microphone while singing *Hound Dog*.

Patrice's image clapped along, and she laughed enthusiastically once Dave's performance was over.

"Whatever happened to that handsome physicist?"

"Siegfried? Oh, no! Siegfried ... he's a looker, I grant you that, but to be honest if I wanted a lobotomy I'd go to a hospital, not on a date." She laughed to show that she meant no ill-will toward her original date, before continuing. "Dave's much more fun. He's from the old school of life. I like that a lot. But he's not money-hungry like Charles, and he's far more interesting than Brinley, and he can impersonate just about anybody. We even had a *real* dance. And he's a *great* kisser."

"When do I get to meet this prince?" asked Patrice.

"He's calling me tonight at six, so hopefully you can meet him tomorrow ... I can't wait either ... see you then."

Alexandra clicked off the STOVE feed and lay back on her bed, smiling. She had been chatting for hours, fielding calls from girlfriends as news of her budding romance spread along the gossip vine. But she didn't mind. She could talk about Dave for a decade and not get bored. Even after one late-night rendezvous she knew that she had found the man of her dreams.

Guiltily she glanced over at a pile of unopened virtual textbooks in the corner of her STOVE display. Her study would have to wait a couple of days. Sure, she'd have to do seven days work in five, but she would manage: Advanced Calculus from Monday until Wednesday, and then Multidimensional Matrix Integration on Thursday, before finishing with HyperPhotoFission Theory on Friday. It would be tough, but at least exams were still eight weeks away. Anyhow, she had allowed for a few contingencies in her timetable.

Alexandra turned away from her desk, actively deciding to prioritise her afternoon toward preparation for Dave's call. She noticed that Einstein55's battery was down to 2% - surprising, as she had already charged it twice this year. Although this residual charge would usually be sufficient for another week or so, she wanted to ensure that it didn't inadvertently switch off during her call, so she placed her smart-watch onto a charge plate.

Then, flopping contentedly onto her bed, she asked Einstein55 to open the latest edition her favourite magazine, *22nd Century Woman*, and scanned the contents page, which opened via the STOVE feed. She grabbed the edges of virtual magazine and then dragged the corners together until the image was small enough to hold in her hands.

The three-dimensional publication was filled with new, refreshing and informative articles such as *The Stars Reveal Their Beauty Secrets* and *Our Miracle New Diet - Lose 5kg In a Week*. However, it was another provocative subheading that caught her eye:

DO YOU REALLY LOVE YOUR MAN?
Our new quiz reveals the answer!

Alexandra jumped ahead to the appropriate section, finding the page crammed with multiple-choice questions. In the bottom corner was a small inverted box, which read 'How to score'. Using hand gestures to flip the magazine upside-down, Alexandra discovered that ten points would be awarded for all answers marked 'A', five points for all marked 'B' and no points for 'C'. Clearly a very objective and scientific marking scheme.

With great anticipation she read the first question.

Do you think that your man is?
A. Wonderful and gorgeous,
B. a decent sort of chap, or
C. A bit of a goose.

That was the hardest question in the quiz.

She continued through the test, and after finishing the first section had scored a total of 500 points from a possible 500, although admittedly she gave herself a default value of ten points for any questions that she felt were not applicable to her and Dave.

Alexandra's anticipation grew as she turned to the second part of the quiz. She was confident that she was in love with Dave, and felt that if a well-respected scientific romance publication like *22nd Century Woman* verified her feelings - well, that proved that they were true beyond doubting.

She read the single remaining question on the test, which was worth five hundred points: *Does everything that you see, feel, hear or smell give you pleasant memories of your partner?*

Hmm. A toughie.

Lying back and closing her eyes, Alexandra decided to test the theory. She would check one sensation at a time. If her thoughts always returned to Dave, well, it *was* love. For certain.

First, sight. Quickly she blinked open an eyelid: a blank white ceiling. Instantly the image of Dave's white shirt at the Stranglers Bar flashed into her mind, and memories of their meeting gushed back. She vividly recalled entering the Stranglers Bar – just to go to the ladies room, of course. As she passed by a young man wearing a crisp, clean, white shirt, she noticed him activating Elvis Presley's *Blue Suede Shoes* on the bar's sound system.

She had detoured around another group of patrons to ensure that she passed by him on her way back to the exit, and was delighted to hear another Elvis song playing – in this case *Heartbreak Hotel* – with the white-shirted man soulfully singing along. She recalled tapping him on the shoulder, that defining moment: it was the instant that they made the transition from complete strangers to potential friends.

She had greeted him gently but must have surprised him, because he had stuttered like an old laserdisc before managing to squeeze out 'Hello'. Alexandra smiled. Was there a more down-to-earth form of flattery than an obvious display of nerves? She thought not.

Continuing her test, she moved on to touch. Eyes still closed, she reached out her hand, groping for any nearby object. Her fingers clasped an object that she soon identified as Einstein55, sitting on its battery recharge plate. One image instantly flashed into her head: Dave. She fondly recalled him insisting that he teach her how to use her smart-watch to bet on a Cheetah race. She tried to explain that the system was so simple that she, like most people, had mastered it by the age of three. Nevertheless Dave generously let her pick the numbers, which subsequently finished first and second.

The win came as no surprise to Alexandra. Even a superficial analysis of recent form, track times and pay out dividends indicated that their bets had a 52 percent chance of success. Dave was thrilled, and spent most of the profit on two celebratory Neptune Gold beers that they had shared. He was a little over excitable, Alexandra concluded, but had a heart of gold.

This must be love, she thought. However, according to *'22nd Century Woman'* she still had two tests to go. Would she think of Dave in response to any sound, or any smell? Momentarily suspending her breathing, Alexandra listened carefully for any sound that might intrude her quiet bedroom. The climate control module in the ceiling whirred automatically to life, emitting a tiny click as it did. One click, one tiny click. Dave. Instantly, Dave.

How could she not think of him? The click sounded like a Virtual Snooker ball as it tapped another towards a pocket. Alexandra fondly recalled their snooker game. Dave had been a little tipsy - who isn't after Neptune Gold? - as he had grasped her hands, trying, but failing, to demonstrate the mechanics of a *good* cue stroke. Alexandra did not have the heart to tell him that she had been playing Virtual Snooker for years, and that a mathematical analysis of the game was part of a dissertation during her second year of physics study.

Alexandra's toughest job had been to play poorly enough so that Dave, thinking that he was gratuitously letting her win, wouldn't be offended. It had been a delicate balancing job: playing poorly, but still well enough to win, while at the same time appearing to be trying to win, while pretending not to notice that Dave was trying to play badly enough to lose, despite not having to try to lose at all. Dave had happily lost, and had subsequently acted unhappy, while Alexandra, who was happy to see Dave acting unhappy to lose, was acting happy to win, despite being happy anyway.

Alexandra, now thoroughly confused by her own analysis of the situation, decided that when all the logic was boiled out of the argument, the residual information showed that Dave was neither condescending nor overly competitive. He was a true gentleman. Not only that, but she had passed part three of the *'22nd Century Woman'* romance quiz. Another correct response would prove with finality that she was deeply in love with Dave. However, the last test was exacting. Smell.

Alexandra took a long, slow inspiration. Nothing. She chewed the air like a wine connoisseur, trying to extract subtleties of aroma from it. The tiniest hint of Chilli, which the auto-chef was preparing for dinner, hit her nose. Dave.

Dave Dave Dave Dave Dave Dave Dave Dave.

The scent of chilli immediately and overpoweringly evoked a picture in her mind's eye: Dave, using a chilli dog as a microphone, pretending to be Elvis Presley. The impersonation had delighted Alexandra. She had met very few people of her generation who had even *heard* of Elvis, but Dave not only knew of him but also loved his music and everything for which it stood. Alexandra was not sure if meeting a soul mate like Dave was fate or coincidence, but either way she knew that she was very lucky.

Dave even agreed with her that Elvis had faked his own death to escape the perils of public life. They were both confident that he was still alive, somewhere; there had been numerous recent sightings of him deep in the Amazon rainforest, in an igloo above the Arctic Circle, inside a small biosphere on a Martian cave, and buying tea in a supermarket in Putney, England.

After Dave's cameo caricature they had devoured either end of the chilli dog microphone, ending with a gentle kiss as their lips had touched. Then they cuddled, talked, kissed and laughed away the hours as they headed toward the consummation of a perfect evening.

Alexandra lay quietly, her full lips fastened into a broad smile, content in the knowledge that even the paragon of all romantic wisdom, '22nd Century Woman', had approved her new relationship. She lay until half past five, daydreaming away the rest of the previous night. At last she had found a man! A real, old-fashioned man, one who liked a dance floor, not a digital Bohr; football games, not fiscal gains. He was fun and spontaneous, not correct and routine. She sat by the telephone and waited in nervous anticipation.

Unfortunately for Alexandra, it was not only Dave's lack of nous that would prevent them from seeing each other. Presently, on the other side of the planet, two very rich and powerful men were brewing an argument so intense that its ugly tentacles were reaching around the planet — to Australia — and would soon entangle their fledgling relationship.

Chapter Nine

The United States of America
G.T.N. Headquarters
War Command Centre
Just after breakfast

Safari suits were back in fashion. In big bold letters on the front of the latest style magazine, the corroborating headline screamed: **SAFARI SUITS MAKE A COMEBACK.** Morgan was pleased. He had fastidiously refused to accept that short-sleeved suits with piped edging had ever not been trendy.

Fashion ideas are, by nature, very subjective. Most people accept that beauty lies in the eye of the beholder. Very few statements in such a fickle industry as fashion can be classified as fact, except one: safari suits had been out of fashion since the 1970's. Fact. Period. End of discussion, thank you.

Most people had happily accepted this unarguable truth for 60 years, except one man: President Morgan W. Morgan. For that whole period Morgan's entire wardrobe had consisted *in toto* of three safari suits. He wore his khaki green outfit to political gatherings, the chocolate brown on diplomatic occasions, while for business meetings he donned pastel blue. Now, finally, he felt vindicated. Safari suits were officially in vogue, which proved that for 60 years he *had* been fashionable. The rest of humanity had been too stupid to realise it.

His rotund form was deeply wedged in a large chair. A cheap mousy-grey toupee flopped over his narrow eyes, which in turn sat above his bulbous nose. A small bead of sweat hung, as it sometimes did, just off the nose's tip. As the sweat bead grew it reached a critical mass and dripped downwards, landing an instant later upon a section of a massive control panel.

The panel was Morgan's greatest pride, and the instrument of his most feared powers. Thousands of buttons, most of which emitted important-sounding beeps, crammed its surface. In the panel's centre, covered by complex layers of security systems, was Morgan's favourite button. It was, not surprisingly, large and red, and had one word inscribed on its surface. BOOM. How Morgan ached to push that button.

Mentally tuning in to work for the day, the president turned his attention to the display area that stretched above the control panel. It consisted of hundreds of STOVE units, each projecting a variety of sights, sounds and experiences. Morgan pressed the 'On' switch, and greedily rubbed his hands together as the displays collectively flickered into life. Every one of them portrayed destruction.

Live destruction. Real destruction.

People dying. People suffering.

The cleverest output device was undoubtedly the OVATION helmet - the Olfactory Visual Auditory Tactile Input and Output Neuro-transducer device - which not only projected sights and sounds directly to and from the brain, but smells and feelings as well.

Morgan placed the OVATION helmet on his head and relaxed as it electronically fed scenes from a far-off war zone into his mind's eye. It was, as he liked to joke, better than being there. Minutes passed as he experienced all the sensations of a battle zone. An orange and purple cloud spewed high into the night sky, and a shockwave shuddered through his body as a distant bomb exploded. The heat of far-off flames singed his skin as he watched nearby buildings burn and factories crumble. As the thundering echoes of the blast began to subside, they were replaced by a crescendo of crying and screaming. The sickening smell of burning human flesh filled his nostrils.

This was not virtual reality. It *was* reality. This was not some advanced executive video game - it was central station for war. And Morgan was in command.

A slow smile spread over his face. Not a bad little battle.

"This is good," he muttered, "but not good enough."

Ignoring a nearby laser probe, he looked across at a pupil scanner interface. Morgan found it hard to believe that some people still used the cumbersome, pencil-sized laser probes. Why were the poor people all so afraid of new technology?

Simply by moving his eyes across a monitor, Morgan scrolled through a few screens of information. With a blink, he stopped on a display headed 'Weapon Deployment'. He looked down various columns of choices and selected a plutonium-powered warhead missile – it gave off a pretty blue flame and a cute mushroom cloud after detonation. After a random process of elimination he chose a central European suburban ghetto as the missile's destination, then winked the system into 'execute' mode.

Suddenly, an automated voice emanated from the computer.

"Please confirm weapon choice and destination."

Morgan felt his temper beginning to rise. Hadn't he instructed his programmers to get rid of those annoying confirmation prompts? The OVATION system detected his increasingly aggressive thought patterns, and quickly intervened. Overruling the prompt, it duly executed the attack.

The president felt his blood pressure settle as he experienced his handiwork in action through the OVATION helmet. The cobalt-blue fireballs even bought a quivering smile to the edges of his lips. Another ghetto destroyed. An entire suburb decimated. And it was all done just by blinking an eyelid.

Plenty of peasants had probably survived. Morgan toyed with the idea of pressing the BOOM button. How he longed to push that button! However before he even began accessing the BOOM button's security levels, he reconsidered. This stoush still had a good week left in it, and his popularity rating was high enough at the moment. And hell, he needed someone to kill next year.

The voice of Sam Hopgood, Morgan's secretary, filled the air.

"Excuse me Mr President."

A short pause.

"Excuse me President Morgan."

As was his usual practice, Morgan chose to ignore his secretary a couple of times. He felt that it was vital to let his staff know that they should not interrupt him, even if it was important. Hopgood's voice, now quivering slightly, tried for a third time.

"Excuse me, Sir, President Morgan." After another short pause, Morgan replied.

"Speak."

"Good afternoon Sir. I have your appointment schedule."

"Go on."

"You have a meeting with the King of China at two, sir."

Big deal, thought Morgan, and grunted offhandedly to signify his feelings.

"And a discussion with the Minister for Energy Resources at two thirty."

Another grunt. Morgan did not waste his breath on inferiors like Hopgood.

"Then dinner with the President of England tonight, Sir."

"Arrgh!" Morgan grunted again, this time more forcefully. He *hated* the President of England - that handicapped, dwarf, greenie, aged, dark-skinned, middle class lesbian. He was sure she was elected because she was the only candidate, in fact probably the only person in the entire godforsaken country, who qualified under the politically correct antidiscrimination selection criteria for British government ministers.

"Tell her I'm busy," barked Morgan.

"Again, Sir?"

"Yes, again."

"Yes sir. Very good, Mr President."

"Is that all?"

"The Popularity Poll and Ratings Team are here for a review meeting."

"Send them in."

Morgan had been looking forward to this meeting, as he was sure the news would be favourable. Morgan's bespectacled secretary walked into the room with six suited people filing behind him. After a round of deferential nods toward their omnipotent boss, the discussion began.

"Our poll ratings this week have been particularly pleasing, Mister President." The nameless suits spoke in turn, while Hopgood displayed graphs and charts through a nearby STOVE.

"Overall our position has risen by 12.6% since the latest war began."

"We peaked at 42% of the east coast population during the carpet bombing this morning. May I add, Sir, that the florescent smoke looked wonderful on hologram."

Hopgood replayed the attack, complete with glowing, brightly-coloured smoke, on a nearby unit.

"Better than being there," said Morgan dryly.

Forced chortles from the suits.

More figures and charts were bandied about, with most of them showing that Morgan's popularity was on the rise. The latest war was clearly having the desired effect. After thinking for a minute, Morgan held up his hand for silence. After a typically annoying pause, he spoke.

"I am not unhappy with our progress."

The suits nodded in approval.

"We are performing adequately."

More nods.

Morgan's voice dropped, by both decibels and octaves, but gradually rose to a booming crescendo as he continued.

"This war has been good, and the latest battles have been even better. But this is only the beginning." His voice began to rise. "Because the war is not complete until my victory is absolute. So I want more fights orchestrated, and more hatred created! More blood and guts! More killing and suffering!"

He was now at fever pitch.

"Because I will not stop!" He paused briefly for effect. "Until the Enemy!" Another slight pause, then a booming tribal yell. "Is mine!"

He punched his fist into the air for emphasis. Although they had heard these exhortations many times before, the suits duly clapped, and the OVATION system activated some flashing lights. Hopgood shook everyone's hand and then replayed a few of the more colourful battles yet again.

Morgan cracked a rare smile. The despised enemy would soon be his.

Chapter Ten

President Harry Hieshler stepped from his nuclear-powered double-stretch Cadillac Convertible as it hovered delicately to an inch above the ground. He carefully avoided a dirty spot on the marble pavement so as not to sully his gold tipped boots, and summoned his ever-present assistant.

"Miss Dingwell!"

"Yes Sir."

"That dirty spot is embarrassing me. Get someone to clean it off at once."

"Yes Sir. I will notify the footpath cleaning crew immediately."

After allowing his auto-polarising sunglasses to adjust to the light, Hieshler checked himself in the mirror-like surface of his hovercar window. His black hair was firmly slicked back, his teeth gleamed lustrously white, and his dark skin looked smoother than an eight ball. The leopard skin lapels on his jacket looked superb next to the dark cashmere fabric.

"Perfect as usual," he complimented himself.

Hieshler was 55 years old but, after uncountable cosmetic procedures and at unfathomable personal expense, most people reckoned that he looked only fifty-four.

He continued his usual morning inspection of Hieshler Towers. Miss Dingwell followed a step behind, her Life-Movie contact lens cameras recording her boss's comments for later implementation.

"Marble step-treads: good. Gold handrails: hmm, I can see some fingerprints on the lower section. Have them repainted - carmine, I think."

The rapid assessment continued as he walked up the stairs and into the building.

"Carpets: clean, but the stars-and-stripes pattern is a bit unfashionable. Have them replaced by tomorrow."

"Any particular colour or pattern Sir?"

"A turquoise and magenta motif would be nice."

Miss Dingwell shuddered at the thought. However she quickly replaced her disapproving expression with a regulation smile. "Yes sir. Excellent choice Sir."

They passed through the foyer, and under the massive 'HH' monogram that dominated the entire western wall. The giant initials were fully eight stories high, and shone in a way that only twenty-four carat gold can. It was of paramount importance to Harry Hieshler that his initials remain completely unblemished, so he paused to scrutinise them carefully. He noted with pleasure that they gleamed with their usual dazzling lustre, and that he could not detect even one iota of dust. He continued his report to Miss Dingwell.

"Monogram: fair. I'll pass this today, but there had better be an improvement by tomorrow."

"Yes Sir. I'll let the monogram cleaning crew know of your displeasure, Sir."

The appraisal continued as Hieshler strode through the foyer, past the staff elevators, and into his Vertical Displacement Unit, the V.D.U. An instant later he was standing outside his office door, 231 stories above the foyer, where, after a DNA scanner verified his identity, the security system's virtual concierge greeted him with a programmed message in a thick, sensual, honeyed voice.

"Good Morning, Mister President. You look fantastic this morning - so fit, healthy and attractive. What can I...."

"Coffee, cream, with five," interrupted Hieshler, correctly predicting the question.

As Hieshler entered his office, a steaming mug of freshly brewed Venusian Mocha with five teaspoons of sugar appeared from a panel in his desk. Hieshler adored Venusian coffee. He had been delighted when the planet Venus's early settlers discovered that coffee grown in their biospheres made a wondrous brew. In fact Venusian coffee beans were so superior to any grown on Earth that the settlers reserved most of the planet's temperate regions for plantations. Venusian coffee was wondrously flavoursome but *extremely* expensive; each teaspoon took a team of Venusian labourers three years to produce. Hieshler bought it by the tonne.

He sipped his brew thoughtfully, feeling relaxed with himself. Why not? He had built this organisation from a snivelling electronic engineering company into the biggest broadcasting station in the United States of America - or, for that matter, in the known universe. Lounging on an antique Chesterfield sofa that he had reupholstered in polka-dotted suede, Hieshler reflected, as he often did, on his career. Reliving the hard slog that his climb to the top had required, he praised himself for the high standards he had set and the brilliant foresight he had shown. But as he began his usual self-aggrandising scan of the weekly ratings reports, something that was normally very insignificant shattered his indulgences.

It was a piece of paper - an old fashioned, twentieth-century type. White and A4 sized. To be fair to all innocent pieces of paper, it wasn't the paper itself that was the source of Hieshler's displeasure; it was a number that was printed on it. This was peculiar because a number of this magnitude almost never made an impact on such a massive organisation such as HHTV. But this number was vital, even though it was tiny. The trouble was that it wasn't tiny enough. If it was only half as big as it was, or totalled just one less than it did, the number would not have been a problem. But the number was too big, and nothing short of chaos could possibly follow.

The number was a two. It was sitting next to a highlighted line of type, which read *Overall Rating Position*. It was usually a one.

"DINGWELL!" bellowed Hieshler, uncharacteristically losing his cool.

She arrived almost instantaneously.

"Yes Sir. What can I...."

"Meeting. Floor 230. Top management only. Fifteen minutes."

"Yes Sir."

*

Less than one minute later, two of Hieshler's highest-ranking employees stepped into the VDU on the fourth floor. Jane Jones, the newest and blondest member of the upper management group, hesitated to allow the greyer Vera Versace to enter first. Vera, the company's vice president, thanked her junior colleague with a warm smile. After the DNA security system verified their identities it took them automatically to Floor 230; no actions, words, or even thoughts were necessary to instruct the V.D.U., because the security system knew that Hieshler had summoned both women to a meeting, and it would broker no deal to take them anywhere else.

"It's a long ride to the top, my dear," said Vera Versace.

"Literally or metaphorically?"

"Both, my dear. Both."

The elevator-like doors whirred shut, then, after a whir of moving pistons had shunted them rapidly up the building, reopened an instant later. The women stepped out into the foyer of Floor 230, the meeting room of the upper executive. They chatted idly as they sat in the bright pink angora-covered chairs, waiting for the rest of the management team to arrive.

"Thanks for coming down to go over those administration procedures with me," said Jane Jones. "It's been a nightmare trying to understand all nine thousand subsections."

"No trouble at all, my dear, I'm glad to help. I can see how difficult it must be for you. When I started in this company thirty years ago things were much simpler - in fact I was Hieshler's only employee."

"You were with Mr Hieshler right from the start?"

"Yes, I've been with him for the whole sordid journey. I became his secretary the day after he inherited this company, along with the rest of his fortune."

"He inherited this company? I thought that Mister Hieshler had built this company up from nothing."

"A shameless piece of propaganda, my dear, although he has told that 'hard slog to the top' story so many times that I think he almost believes it himself."

They heard a polite beep, which informed them that the V.D.U. was about to deliver another of their colleagues. The doors opened, and a middle-aged pot-bellied man stepped into the foyer: Arnie, the senior accounts executive.

"Good morning Ms Versace, morning Jane," he said as he nodded to each of the women cheerily.

"Good morning Arnie," they replied simultaneously.

"Any idea what this urgent meeting is all about?"

"None whatsoever, my dear. However I can only presume that Hieshler wants to raise profits so that he can gold plate his golf putter, or some other typically tasteless waste of money."

"I say that you're probably right, Vera. What was it last time? We had to cut two thousand jobs so that he could afford to encrust diamonds into the handle of his favourite garden trowel."

"I'm sorry?" said Jane Jones. "I thought that the solvency of the company depended upon those cuts."

The two older managers looked at each other and sighed whimsically.

"I'm not sure whether I find it refreshing or terrifying to see such an innocent young person like you promoted to the senior management," said Arnie, not unkindly. "But now that you're one of our top executives, I think that it is best that you know the truth about how and why this company really operates."

Jane raised her eyebrows, to which Vera replied with a nod. This, Vera assured her understudy without a word, was bona fide.

"The entire company," continued Arnie, "from here down to that goddamn monogram in the foyer, only exists so that conceited leech can cream off money to spend on his ridiculous indulgences."

Jane Jones looked at her colleagues with disbelief. Their pallid expressions told her that this was not a joke, nor a piece of jealous backstabbing.

"Is that why we've barely made a profit in the last decade, even though we've been the number one rated station on the planet?" she asked.

"Exactly, my dear. Exactly."

"If Mr. Hieshler wastes so much money, then how did HHTV grow so large?"

Vera and Arnie looked at each other again and collectively sighed.

"We've still got ten minutes until Hieshler arrives," said Vera. "So we may as well tell you the full story. You deserve to hear the whole truth, but please, for the sake of our stockholders and share prices, keep it quiet. This information must not go outside of this room. Ever."

Jane nodded solemnly in acceptance of the pact. Then for the next ten minutes she sat aghast as her two colleagues told her a company history; a history that was so different to the story that Hieshler indoctrinated into all his employees that it seemed unbelievable. Yet as the pieces fell into place, she could see its inherent truth.

Arnie began. "I first encountered Harry Hieshler about thirty years ago, when I was a junior filing clerk in an electronic engineering company. Hieshler's father Bill, the company owner, was unexpectedly trampled to death in a shopping mall during the January sales. The whole incident was most regrettable - he was a nice old bloke - and its consequences were dire. Unfortunately he bequeathed not only the company, but his entire multimillion dollar fortune, to his spoilt son Harry."

"Mr Hieshler," confirmed Jane.

"Correct," replied Arnie. "So at age 22, Harry Hieshler became managing director."

"At that time I was good friends with a young engineer named Simon. Simon had privately told me of his plans for a revolutionary concept that he called Screenless Vision Technology. It was the forerunner to STOVE vision, which although commonplace now, was a very advanced concept at the time."

"But didn't they already have three-dimensional television at the start of the century?" asked Jane. "I'm sure my parents have talked about watching it during their youth."

"They certainly did, Jane, but they weren't nearly as advanced or responsive as a STOVE unit. For starters, ordinary 3D-television needed a screen, and sometimes even for the wearer to don ungainly-looking glasses. Holographic TV was next, but it needed the viewer to be in line with the source. But the STOVE technology could reproduce a true 3D image anywhere. The public just loved it."

"Yes, I remember being very excited when my family bought our first STOVE unit on Christmas," recalled Jane.

"Not only that," added Arnie, but Simon had incorporated advancements in Virtual Reality implementation, Fuzzy Logic Data Harvesting and Human Thought Sensors, which allowed the STOVE units to be very interactive. You probably don't remember, Jane, but 30 years ago you simply watched what the television stations broadcast, when they wanted you to see it. Then the internet opened up view-on-demand. However any interaction was still based on clumsy concepts like clicking on icons, or pressing buttons on a television remote control. But now, as you know, you can interact with the broadcast itself. This combination of screenless-ness and true interactivity opened up new worlds of possibilities."

"Yes, although they've now been for nearly a decade, I can see that the STOVE concept must have been revolutionary at the time."

"Yes, it's very easy to become blasé, but I remember being astonished by the concept. Simon, hoping to similarly impress his new boss, showed Hieshler a prototype of his groundbreaking invention. I remember Simon telling me that Hieshler was very impressed; he immediately wanted to know all of the specifications and technological hurdles, and even took copies of the engineering files. Simon was buzzing with excitement that evening, for he was convinced that his decades of hard work were about to pay off."

Arnie paused, steeling himself for what was to follow.

"On the way home from that meeting, Simon was mysteriously run over by a black limousine; he never even made it to hospital. This 'accident' left Hieshler as the only other human with a working knowledge of Simon's idea."

He took a deep breath before continuing.

"I was immediately suspicious of Harry Hieshler. He struck me as a scheming and weasel-like young upstart. However, without any solid proof and valuing my job, I was powerless to act."

Arnie's eyes misted as he recalled a friendship long since gone - one whose premature end at the hands of Harry Hieshler he had been unable to avenge. Vera, her reassuring hand upon Arnie's shoulder, took up the story.

"Neither Arnie nor I could curtail the surge of greed that flowed from Hieshler's use of Simon's invention. My dear, it was simply awful. Rather than directing the technology toward the advancement of society, Hieshler developed the STOVE project for the wrong reasons, chiefly to assuage his own garishly expensive taste. Using money from his inheritance to buy government approval, he soon became the founding chairman of a new company: the Harry Hieshler Television station. As you know, my dear, HHTV was not a regular channel with documentaries and dramas, or heaven help us, anything cultural, but instead specialised in gambling."

"But they already had gambling at the turn of the century," verified Jane, who was born in the massive baby boom of early October, 2000 - one of many accidental products of too-fervent new year/millennium celebrations.

"Of course they had gambling, my dear, but not *STOVE* gambling. Even though it is now more commonplace than are government bureaucrats, this type of betting was an exciting novelty at the time. My dear, it was far more exhilarating than old-style wagering. Using the HHTV's new format, punters could gamble on a race as it occurred. They could watch the horses run around the track in front of them, and place a bet simply by touching the virtual image of the horse. They could join a poker game as if it was taking place in their living room, and look right into the faces of their opponents even though they were on the other side of the planet. A bored process worker could pull the lever on a virtual slot machine without leaving their desk."

"Almost everybody tried it. Even my grandmother, who had never bet on anything other than a call of bingo, quickly learned how to use the STOVE system. And as you know, my dear, history has since proved it to also be extremely addictive."

Arnie, now composed, rejoined the conversation.

"As Hieshler's gambling income grew, he became even greedier. Vera and I could only watch with disgust as his taste grew more garish with every dollar he earned. Soon millions were no longer enough. He wanted billions. So Hieshler employed the influence of every corrupt official, dodgy jockey and greedy corporate bookmaker that he could find. Over the next decade, he gradually took control of the gambling industry. Then with little opposition, he ordered his staff, including both of us, to expand his gambling empire. Much to our own chagrin, we succeeded."

"That's one thing I've often wondered. Why *does* HHTV offer so many different types of gambling? Surely just a few dozen channels would have sufficed, rather than thousands? Why do we race so many different creatures?"

"Well, my dear, the gambling public eventually began to tire of horses and greyhounds. We needed a strategy to keep their interest, as well as attract new punters. The development started with quadrupeds — camels, bulls and the like - but quickly grew beyond the farmyard. We introduced hundreds of different creatures, my dear, each bringing a different type of viewer to the 'sport' of animal racing. People in a hurry could gamble on ostrich sprints, while those who lived a more leisurely pace preferred the three-toed sloths' three-day marathons. We raced sharks to entice fishermen, and even newborn lambs to capture the child market. The African public took to the giraffes, the South Americans loved their armadillos, while the Australians went hopping mad for kangaroos. But it was the big cats - the lions, the pumas, and the blue riband sprinters, the cheetahs - that really captured the public's imagination."

"And their hard earned dollars," added Arnie.

"Gradually, my dear, with the incentive of small but frequent gambling credits and incentive schemes, many people became addicted. The racing telecasts grew so numerous that HHTV opened thousands of channels, and became the highest rating station in the world. The whole planet was soon losing inordinate amounts of money, which Hieshler obviously enjoyed spending."

"What do you think he spends all the money on?" asked Arnie, almost rhetorically.

"Himself?"

"Exactly, my dear," said Vera. "This is why we never make a profit."

"That, in a nutshell, is the history of Hieshler and HHTV," said Arnie. "Just remember, everything that you have just heard is confidential."

Just as Arnie and Vera sat back into their pink angora chairs, the VDU beeped. From its open doorway stepped two of the last three members of the management committee. Madonna Souwella, the senior personnel manager, stepped out first. She was followed by Mr Zachary Zzyzz, who, apart from being the last person checked at roll call every morning of his school life, was head of the 'Gambling Tastes: Future Trends' research department.

Good mornings were liberally exchanged, along with some good-natured banter about the purpose of the meeting. What did Hieshler want this time? A new warehouse in which to store his silk necktie collection, suggested one executive. Polished titanium toilet plumbing, ventured another. Or was it another payload of Martian mud to top-dress his petunia garden?

The answer, or at least the supplier of it, appeared a few seconds later. Hieshler appeared from his personal V.D.U., with Miss Dingwell in tow. He carved an almost palpable path of icy anger across the entrance as he cut directly to the meeting room. In short, he did not look happy. Unused to seeing their president in such a mood - he was normally too self-occupied to even notice that they were there - the members of the executive quickly sat themselves down around the large meeting table.

"Where is Maxwell?" asked Hieshler, noting the absence of the Chief General Manager.

"I'm sorry Sir," responded Madonna Souwella. "He just called to say that he is presently attending the birth of his first child. He sends his sincere apologies, and assures you that he will be here in ten minutes."

"Tell him not to bother," said Hieshler. "He's fired."

The last time any of the management could remember Hieshler being this angry was on the occasion that he had to wear the same lounge suit two days in a row. They shifted uneasily in their seats as Hieshler launched into his assault.

"We are in a CRISIS!"

The executive members shot questioning glances at each other, and surreptitiously shrugged back in reply.

"Do any of you know WHY?"

They shook their heads in unison.

"Then I suggest that you all read THIS!"

Hieshler flung the ratings page onto the table. The executives slowly transported the page through five sets of hands. Each pair of hands was steady as they received it, but trembling as they passed it forward. Hieshler waited for the committee to regain its collective composure, and then rekindled the meeting.

"We've lost the number one position in the ratings for the first time in over a decade. Our hated enemy, the Global Television Network, has taken our spot." He paused, and then repeated with different emphasis. "*Our* spot."

The management grimaced. They all knew that this day had been coming. Their own addictive racing format had been very successful for many years, but recently the programming of GTN, the Global Television Network, had skyrocketed in popularity. GTN's president, Morgan W. Morgan, had been orchestrating wars and blowing up defenceless countries, simply for a cheap ratings grab.

"This is all the work of that mongrel bastard Morgan. His war policy is obviously working. The people love it." He snorted to his assistant Miss Dingwell. "The charts."

Miss Dingwell responded by flicking a switch, which projected the latest ratings figures into the space above the meeting desk.

"As you can see," Hieshler continued, "GTN's ratings improved by 2.6% over the last week." The management squirmed.

"Even worse, they scored over 43% on the East Coast."

These statistics ripped at Hieshler's psyche like an industrial planer on a raw carrot. The market share that GTN was stealing from him was denying him of some of life's simple pleasures - pleasures that a man in his position so richly deserved. He hated GTN. He *hated* Morgan. So despite each member of the committee being thoroughly familiar with every detail of their opposition, Hieshler bombarded them with a typical ten-minute rant about his despised enemy.

"Morgan W. Morgan, our avowed enemy, is thought by many to be the most evil man on Earth." Hieshler began. "He is president of a heinous organisation known as the Global Television Network."

Jane Jones, despite being new to the management team, had heard this speech many times. She had hoped that her recent promotion would put an end to this dreary weekly ritual. Jane already knew Morgan's story, as did all of HHTV's staff and the majority of the public. In fact Morgan actively promoted most of the story himself - he was perversely proud of his tyrannical past.

"In the early decades of this century," continued Hieshler, "the current affairs programs, magazines, blogs and news web sites were desperate for sellable headlines, so they began to orchestrate scandals. Any public figure was fair game. The media collectively spied on royalty, misquoted sports stars, set up politicians, and created gossip and innuendo for their own satisfaction and ratings."

Everybody nodded on cue. Hieshler continued.

"In a measure to gain the upper hand in the sales war, tabloid tactics of such ilk proliferated rapidly. Journalists traded doctored films and photographs. Forged confessions were rife. The situation developed to the point where salacious stories, complete with fabricated footage and backed by wonky witnesses, were broadcast ... about real people."

Hieshler paused to scrutinise the staff for signs of inattention. However the executives had seen what became of employees, or more correctly ex-employees, who did not listen vigilantly. They did their best to feign interest.

Hieshler continued. "The public initially enjoyed the scandal, and at very little cost. Sure, a few reputations may have been dented a little, but nobody died. After a few decades, the public grew tired of reading and hearing about scandal. Who cared if the King was homosexual? So was the President. Did it really matter that a Hollywood actress murdered her grandparents? Something like that happened every week. The public wanted more. And that fat bastard Morgan had given it to them."

Hieshler paused briefly for effect.

"War."

After another brief pause to further emphasise the gravity of the preceding word, Hieshler launched into what his staff privately referred to as 'chapter two'.

"Morgan's career in war reporting had begun completely by chance. Showing no great skill or foresight, he had simply been at the right place at the right time. He had been privy to some leaked information concerning an imminent American attack on a small, defenceless, but obviously hostile country. This country, by pure coincidence, also happened to contain the last major oil deposits on Earth. Morgan, who was only a lowly television journalist, had milked the information for all it was worth. Travelling to the war zone, his crew filmed the entire battle, and his report was transmitted live around the world and quickly went viral on multiple platforms. Morgan, by fluke of fate, had a ratings winner on his hands."

"Through dint of not-so-delicate incentives..." mumbled Zachary Zzyzz under his breath.

"Through dint of not-so-delicate incentives," continued Hieshler, "Morgan obtained more information leaks. Soon, that scavenging mongrel was broadcasting live from every known battle, and reaping huge financial rewards. This worked just dandily, until one day, unfortunately for Morgan, the world found peace. War ceased."

Hieshler stopped and wiped his brow. He looked at his managers in turn, ensuring that he had their undivided attention. The next line was his favourite part of the whole speech.

"Morgan watched his fortune disappear more quickly than does a Mormon doorknocker when you release the Dobermans."

Hieshler grinned at the executive party, who convincingly chortled in return. Appeased, Hieshler continued into less favoured territory of the story: Morgan's recovery.

"Morgan was down. But like all miscreants and conmen, he used devious and devilish means to force his way back. Using a donation of random unmarked hundred dollar bills tightly stashed in a two-tonne truck, he persuaded the equally slimy Minister of Defence that perhaps a few of those pesky central European countries were becoming a bit hostile. After considering his options for a few days, the minister could count about ten million reasons why he agreed with Morgan, and obliged by quelling the hostility of those minor European countries with a few nuclear weapons. Morgan had an exclusive. Unfortunately for modern society, he was back in business. It boomed, literally and metaphorically."

The staff, now mentally numb, had trained themselves to nod on cue at this particular point. Hieshler, pleased that his speech was making its usual startling impact, pressed forward.

"He continued operating in this fashion for many years as his greed for power drove him further. As Morgan's 'business' expanded through underhand means, he realised that he had enough money, contacts and hardware to organise the whole show for himself, from creating the first diplomatic tensions to triggering the final explosions. The filthy blight on humanity that we call the *Global Television Network* became incorporated, with Morgan as the sole shareholder.

It appealed instantly to the crass and macabre instincts of the viewing public. But the real winners were the leech-like politicians, who suddenly found themselves on a never-ending upward spiral of wartime popularity. They ensured that all impediments to Morgan's war-for-rating policy were surreptitiously removed.

Naturally there were cries of resentment from all fair-minded people. However, Morgan and his political cronies quickly dismissed their opinions, sweeping them away under a giant metaphorical carpet with *Ratings, Money* and *Power* embroidered in its surface. And that, people, is how the despicable and loathsome entity that is GTN came into existence. It is our duty both to the public and to ourselves to rid the world of this evil menace."

The staff stirred. At last, he was finished. The standard sermon was over.

"And that menace, ladies and gentlemen...."

"Huh?" The executive collectively shook their heads. This was not part of the usual lecture.

"That menace, today, for the first time...." Hieshler's voice grew tighter and louder with each subsequent word "... is the most *watched station ON THE PLANET!*"

Then he was silent.

The members of the executive felt completely stunned. They were used to an air of relative indifference from their president, provided his salary was maintained at its ludicrously high level. However, this situation was different: Hieshler's bottom line was shrinking for the first time in decades. This meant trouble of the deepest variety.

The president glared at the shell-shocked faces around him.

"Well, what the *Hell* are we going to do about it?"

He sat back in his chair and waited for his employees to present him with an answer.

The room remained completely silent.

Five seconds passed. Then another five. Nobody moved.

The ten seconds of silence were repeated, and still nobody had even blinked. It was so quiet that Madonna Souwella could hear her pulse thumping above the stillness. Hieshler's patience was clearly wearing thin, but he sat motionlessly. After 30 seconds or so had elapsed, Vera Versace shifted uneasily in her chair. All eyes swung towards her movement, grateful for a break in the void. Yet still nobody spoke.

After another ten-second pause, Arnie could bear it no longer. He sat forward and cleared his throat. Heads turned and eyes widened. Finally someone would speak. However the pressure of the moment choked the words in his throat, so he pretended to adjust his neck tie and sat back deeply into his chair. The tension jumped another notch.

Fists gripped more tightly, feet tapped more quickly, and jaws clenched firmly closed with panic. Everybody developed an instant migraine. Soon a whole minute had elapsed, yet nobody had uttered a syllable.

Just as it seemed the tension could build no higher, Jane Jones moved almost imperceptibly forward in her seat. She quickly received her colleague's full attention as they collectively prayed for a break. She opened her mouth.

Nothing came out.

The other executives leaned further towards her, mentally compelling her to speak. Again she opened her mouth, and this time a small sound emanated from deep within her emotionally strangulated set of vocal cords.

"Perrapps."

"Pardon me?" said Zachary Zzyzz, now feeling braver with the breaking of the verbal drought.

"Perrappsits agoodedea." Jane stopped again as Hieshler's expression made it clear that he did not have a clue what she was attempting to say. As perspiration beaded on her forehead, Jane Jones took three long, slow breaths and began again.

"I ... I ... I'm sorry," she blushed. "I just wanted to ... ah ... suggest that ... um ... perhaps it might be a good idea if we gave the viewers ... er ... more free gambling credits."

She sat back as one with the entire executive party, all extremely relieved that at least someone had vocalised something. Hieshler too sat back, and appeared to be lost in thought for a second. Then he stared icily at the young executive, and addressed her personally.

"So you think that I should give my viewers more of *my* money to tempt them to gamble, is that right?"

"Well, ah ... yes sir," she replied hesitantly.

"That is the stupidest idea that I have ever heard. You'll never work for HHTV again. Get out."

Then Hieshler looked casually around the boardroom table.

"Now, does anyone else have a *sensible* suggestion?"

Chapter 11

It was half time during the major semi-final of the World Soccer Super League. To be more precise, it was half time of the last match of the fifteen game semi-final series. The winner of this match would progress to the Grand Final Series, in which they would play the best of twenty-one matches to decide the overall Global Club Champions. Multiple finals were always good to screw extra money out of the fans.

A major upset was on the cards. The *Premier League Strikers*, an all-star composite side featuring the best players from the English competition, were leading the mighty *Harry's Heroes*. Despite the Strikers impressively downing the Brazilian national team in the quarter finals, everyone, even the Strikers' captain expected them to be consummately thrashed by the might of the world's most powerful team, Harry's Heroes.

The reason that the Premier League Strikers expected to be flogged by Harry's Heroes is that *everybody* expected to be flogged by Harry's Heroes. The club's chairman, president, benefactor and patron had seen to that. These four jobs, and in fact the entire administration committee, selection panel and pay officer had only ever been the domain of one man - one implausibly, improbably, disgustingly wealthy man. This overlord was none other than the president of HHTV, Harry Hieshler.

Hieshler had formed the team one boring Wednesday morning about a decade previously. Work had been a little quiet, so to pass the time before morning tea he decided to form a team to win the World Soccer Super League. A few calls later he had successfully amalgamated four of his favourite smaller teams: Liverpool, A.C. Milan, Bayern Munich and Glasgow Rangers. He moved the new superclub to his base in the USA, and named it in his own honour. They hadn't lost a series since.

However, that was now looking a distinct possibility.

Adolph McConichie, the coach of Harry's Heroes, was finishing his half-time address to his players. They were down by two goals, and he *desperately* did not want them to miss the finals series. Mr. Hieshler would *not* be happy. Coach McConichie foamed at the mouth as he literally spat instructions at his besieged charges.

"You, Okabala, what the hell are you doing out there? Hanna, if you give away another free kick then I'm pulling you off. Merkalisich you were hopeless. H-O-P-L…" He paused to think. "Hopeless."

Taking a deep breath, he continued his stinging attack on the team in general.

"More aggression. We need more aggression. Think like a rabid dog - Okabala, that shouldn't be too hard for you. Attack the ball. Firm passes. Pass to feet. That first half effort was pathetic. What a bunch of jokes. Hapless idiots. If we don't win, I'm docking you fifty thousand each. No, make it a hundred. I've had enough of this rubbish. Lloyd, stay on your man. Wear him like a shadow. A wet dishrag has more get-up-and-go than you have today. Koutifedes, if you stuff up another free kick then consider yourself dropped. Why did you kick it backwards? You idiot. You bunch of imbeciles. Lift your game. If I don't see…"

The siren to resume the second half interrupted his monologue.

The players stirred. Merkalisich yawned, stretched and gingerly rose to his feet. Lloyd gently elbowed Hanna, who had drifted off into a gentle sleep. Okabala jumped nervously, as he had been daydreaming and the sudden movement of his teammates had startled him. Most of the team's members were eventually on their feet and making idle chatter as they headed back to the centre of the pitch. Nobody had listened to a word that Coach McConichie had said. They didn't have to. They all knew that they would win anyway.

God was on their side.

Meanwhile, in a private cubicle in the Heroes' dressing room, Juan Carlos Manuel de la Espirito was luxuriating in a hot tub, oblivious to the plight of his teammates outside. He lay relaxing, hoping that the steam from the tub wasn't damaging the mink carpet or the da Vinci originals on the walls. As he sipped on a goblet of Neptune Gold - he was glad that the space race had bestowed such tangible benefits on humanity - he felt his chunky gold chain beginning to irritate the back of his neck.

He summoned one of the semi naked women who shared his hot tub. "Chiquita. Come here," he ordered, his accent a rich mix of his Latino-Hispanic-Afro-Caribbean heritage. "Would you remove this golden chain from arrrrround my neck"

"What shall I do with it?" asked Chiquita, as the other women dejectedly pouted at not being chosen for the task.

"You may keep this leeeetle trinket as a sign of my affections."

Chiquita burst into tears of joyful exuberance as the pouts of the other women turned to hisses of jealousy. A catfight was about to follow when Juan Carlos Manuel de la Espirito interjected.

"Do not worry, my little pussycats. I shall geeeeeeeve you all a matching one," he lied.

The hisses quickly transformed into broad smiles as Juan, the ultimate politician, quickly restored the hot tub politics to its status quo. Yet another hassle of the rich and powerful.

He drained the remaining Neptune Gold from his goblet, and rolled over so the women could massage his back. There was a flurry of activity as they jockeyed for position, and soon three gorgeous ladies had settled on either side, and twelve hands lovingly caressed every inch of his tanned, muscular body. He was just beginning to unwind when a loud call from outside his dressing cubicle rudely interrupted him.

"Hey God, are you in there?"

Juan pretended not to hear. The voice waited a while, and then repeated its message. Again Juan ignored it, hoping that the voice's owner would lose patience and leave him in peace. The tactic normally worked, as all of the media had realised long ago that he *never,* gave interviews.

However the voice persisted, and was accompanied by a frenzied rapping on the door.

"Hey God, I know you're in there. Open up."

Juan lost patience. "Who is it?" he asked, clearly irritated at having been disturbed.

"It's Coach McConichie, God. We need you."

Juan, or 'God' as everybody including his grandmother knew him, sighed. The nickname was a legacy of his earliest footballing days, where his incredibly handsome looks, superb athleticism and chiselled body had earned him the title of 'The Gorgeous God of Football'. The name had subsequently been shortened to plain old 'God', which had stuck.

God threw his head back in exasperation, and curtly signalled to one of his harem to unlock the door. Despite the arrogant rudeness of his gesture, the women again rushed to perform the task. They, for reasons known only to themselves - and sports groupies throughout the history of the world - continued to worship the powerful superstar, despite the fact that he treated them like dirt. Nevertheless, Coach McConichie soon gained entry through the hallowed portals of God's private dressing room.

"What is the meaning of this interruption?" snarled God, as the women cooed at his wonderfully sexily rolled 'R's.

"I'm sorry to disturb you, God," said the coach, his head contritely bowed. "We need you again."

"What!" bellowed God. "This is the fifth such interruption this season."

"Ah, yes. I know that God, sir," replied the coach meekly. "But we are down by three goals with only ten minutes to play."

God sighed again. When were they going to get some decent backup on the team?

"Mister Hieshler would be extremely unhappy if we lost," added the coach. "He does not like to finish second. What is more, we'd miss the finals."

This last fact seemed to strike a chord with God. A loss was bad, but not being in the finals was unthinkable. He hated the notion of missing the parades and victory parties.

"All right," God conceded. "I will soon make myself ready to win this victory for my fans."

The women's pouts returned, echoing their disappointment that their hero would now have to depart. They stared through Coach McConichie as though he had just killed their mothers. God dressed very quickly - he had plenty of help - and after slicking back his hair and turning back his sleeves to better reveal his tanned, muscular arms, he acted out a perfunctory warm up routine.

"Right God, do your thing," yelled coach McConichie as his star player pranced onto the field.

The stadium announcer screamed in excited delight.

"Ladies and Gentlemen! We are all in for a magnificent treat tonight. Please give a fantastic welcome to the greatest football player of all time, the biggest sports star in the history of everywhere, the magnificent Juan Carlos Manuel de la Espirito!"

The stadium erupted in a frightening explosion of cheering, applause and adulation. It continued for fully five minutes as even the referee joined the homage. Eventually the explosion of exaltation dimmed to a roar. As it did a distant rumble of another type could be heard in the background. First just a mumbling reverberation, it gradually established a steady rhythm. Background clapping began and quickly synchronised, amplifying the beat. As more people joined in, the rumble grew into a chant that continued to mushroom. A few seconds later it became an unmistakable, deafening tribal yell.

"We want God - We want God."

"We want God - We want God."

The stadium was alive with energy and awe. Those present knew they were privileged beyond belief. They were about to witness God in action.

The referee blew his whistle to signal the restart of play. Three goals to nil, six minutes left on the clock - only one tenth of an hour separated Harry's Heroes from the most unexpected catastrophe since Pompeii. Heroes kicked off and immediately passed the ball to God. He toyed with it for an instant, evaluating his options as four defenders encircled him. As one of them made a thrust for the ball, God tweaked it with his foot, flicking it to the left. The defender adjusted his line, and in the split second it took him to rebalance God had tapped the ball between his legs. As the flanking defenders closed in, a lightning fast backward heel-flick sent them spinning in circles.

God broke free from the ring of defence and sprinted down field, controlling the football as if it was glued to his boot. Without breaking stride he wove through four more defenders and cracked at the ball, sending it hurtling through the air like a bullet. The goal keeper made a desperate lunge and thrust his hand in the ball's path. An instant later the ball crashed into the back of the goal net, breaking two of the goalkeeper's finger bones on the way. Score: Three-one.

The crowd burst into a massive explosion of applause, even outdoing the welcome of a minute earlier. God back flipped his way down the sideline, and then treated the crowd to a short solo exhibition of bodybuilding muscle poses.

Meanwhile his teammates hugged, kissed and licked each other in celebration. They piled on top of each other in a clearly over-exuberant yet somehow appropriate expression of their joy. Outside the stadium, street parties erupted in celebrations that were tempered only by the knowledge that more was to come. It was fully ten minutes until the stadium had calmed enough for the referee to recommence the match.

Soon after the kick-off, God again had the football under his spell. He seared through the defenders as if they were sacks of potatoes, even nonchalantly patting one of them on the buttocks as he passed by. As he approached the goal square, he unleashed a kick so powerful that the sound of boot on ball could be heard in three separate postcodes. It fizzed through the back of the goal net, leaving torn and frayed threads around the perimeter of a gaping hole. Three-two.

Another on-field celebration ensued, this time with so much emotion on display that an uninitiated observer would have questioned the sexuality of the players. But celebrate they did, along with most of the population of the planet.

A couple of minutes later the Premier League Strikers were on the attack. They were not giving up without a fight. Their captain struck for the goal: a fine, powerful shot - straight, hard and fast. However with God on the opposition it they might as well have been power-kicking a party balloon. God sizzled across the goal face and leapt high into the air, somersaulted mid flight and then caught the ball between his knees. Before hitting the ground he released it, spooning it upwards. Using his powerful legs like shock-springs he catapulted into a back flip, delicately heading the ball forward as he did. Defenders rushed in, but he double back flipped across the turf and again headed the ball goal-wards. Twice more he repeated the back flips, both times finishing the movement with a clever juggle of the ball and a delicate lob. He was soon in his attacking half, and wasted no time in thumping a volley towards the goals. The keeper just managed to dive out of the way as the equaliser scorched into the net.

A few minutes later the game was over. God had scored six goals in as many minutes to lead his side to an amazing victory. As the referee blew his whistle, all one hundred thousand fans streamed towards the pitch, heading for one man. But by the time the first of them had breached the pitch's security fence, God was already luxuriating in his hot-tub, enjoying his second Neptune Gold. For although they were virtually his sole reason for existing, God did not care much for his fans. And he *never* gave interviews.

Chapter 12

Hieshler was irritated. The meeting had festered like a purulent wound for the whole afternoon, yet still no-one had suggested a workable proposal for HHTV to regain the number one ratings spot from GTN. What was the point in hiring management who didn't contribute? He was about to terminate the employment of his entire executive staff when Sally Dingwell, his trustworthy assistant, averted a crisis.

"Perhaps, Sir," she said hesitantly, "we could run some type of competition?"

The executive members looked at their boss's face for a reaction before committing themselves to an opinion. Slowly, almost imperceptibly, Hieshler nodded his head. Sensing a positive vibe, the committee's collective migraine dropped a notch as they extrapolated Miss Dingwell's suggestion through a general brainstorming session.

"A competition. Yes, a terrific idea. Just thinking down that line myself actually."

"Good brain work, my dear. Anything to pull the punters back."

"A simple and workable solution, as we've already got the infrastructure in place. The viewers could use the STOVE system to activate a competition icon, which would pop up at random times. They'd have to watch to enter."

"And when *they* watch, *we* win."

The executive paused, and turned towards Hieshler for comment.

"Everybody listen carefully, because I have important announcement to make," said Hieshler. "What I think we should do is run a competition. I feel that this is the simplest short term solution to our problem." He straightened his coat lapels, signifying a sense of self-acclaim for conjuring up such a clever solution.

"Excellent thinking, Sir," was the consensus of the committee's replies.

"You there," said Hieshler, pointing to Zachary Zzyzz. "I want Engineering to reconfigure the program drivers. I want every STOVE in the world to flash a competition icon at random intervals throughout the gambling telecasts."

"Very good idea, Mister President," said Zzyzz compliantly.

"Of course, the more frequently that the public watch my station, the more opportunities they have to enter. Naturally the more they watch, the more they are tempted to have a flutter on my races."

"Wonderful reasoning, Mister President," chorused the committee.

Hieshler slowly rubbed his hands together, basking in the superior air with which he surrounded himself. Arnie and Vera glanced knowingly at each other. They could see the greedy gleam in Hieshler's eyes, but on this occasion it was even more fervid than usual. They sensed that he would not be satisfied unless people tuned to HHTV in such overwhelming numbers that it almost paralysed life on earth.

Even to Madonna and Zachary, Hieshler's vision of Nirvana was transparent. He fantasised about workers absenting factories, shoppers deserting malls and fans emptying sports stadiums. He dreamed of whole populations heading home to glue themselves to their STOVES, waiting in desperation for their chance to grab the HHTV competition icon. Hieshler would not care if global disaster ensued - he would see it as a sign of victory. Humanity was of no concern to Hieshler when a pair of baby-platypus-leather shoes was at stake.

At this point Hieshler departed the meeting to attend a manicure appointment, denoting to the committee that it was their job to hammer out the finer details of the proposal. They quickly decided on a method by which contestants could record their telephone number on the STOVE as they entered.

They all acknowledged that the competition's logistics were made far easier by the recent collapse of the Earth's telecommunications and IT industry. With their boss temporarily gone, they relaxed for a few minutes, and became sidetracked by a conversation on the recent capitulation of one of history's largest industries.

The number of telecommunications providers had been rapidly proliferating for the previous 30 years. The expansion had begun innocently enough at the turn of the century, when most businesses had half a dozen or so different contact numbers: a telephone or two, a fax, mobile phone, as well as their email and web site addresses.

Within a decade, the rise of the internet caused the communications options to grow exponentially. Soon people had multiple emails, Skype contacts, Facebook pages, Instagram accounts, Twitter feeds, LinkedIn profiles, various blogs, info-lines, automated information services, YouTube channels and more.

Companies and corporations, eager to grab any advantage over their competition, continued to jump at any new product or service that entered the market. First they added dedicated videophone, virtual-phone and even gimmicky aromaphone services. In-head-phones, in which the entire apparatus was concealed inside a tiny chip and surgically implanted inside the ear canal, quickly became popular. Options later appeared for contact via microwave, x-ray and gamma wave transmission, each service naturally requiring another contact for each voice, text, information or video link.

Yet still the number of options expanded. Competitors to Google flooded the market: u-GrobaGgle, iFantingL and e-Baglzlt became huge, as did the rival Chinese search engines *Mee-Hing-Go-Net* and *Go-Hing-Mee-Net*.

Even the two largest Indian providers - namely the *Really Good Internet Company* and the newer *Even Better Really Good Internet Company* – established a strong global presence.

By the early 2020s, even the smallest business required hundreds of different numbers and addresses, just to remain competitive. Traditional company letterheads were replaced by entire introductory pages that listed hundreds of contact options.

Eventually people began to realise that the only industries making any profits were the information and communications trades. All of the others – from doctors to grave diggers, masseurs to managers, typists to tea-leaf readers – all went bankrupt trying to keep up payments of their various internet and telecommunications bills.

Then, in 2028, the world hit back. As more and more people realised the folly of the situation, the bottom abruptly fell out of the information technology market. Within a year virtually all telecommunication options became defunct - except, ironically, for the telephone, which regained widespread support; it was what most people had always preferred to use anyway.

So since the great IT collapse of 2028, each company was again blessed to require only a few select contact points, while householders could manage with just a couple. The planet breathed a collective sigh of relief and went back to gainful work, while the ex-presidents of the telecommunications companies became management consultants, somehow doubling their already-ludicrously-high salaries in the process.

So it was not a problem for the HHTV management committee to organise for contestants to simply enter their telephone numbers into the STOVE competition icon. Over coffee, the discussion returned to more pressing issues, and after some further polite debate they agreed on the rest of the plan.

The idea was that when HHTV had regained the number one rating, Hieshler would, amidst a festival of great pomp and celebration, select a winning entry. He would then ceremoniously dial the winning entry's number, and declare the person who answered as the beneficiary of the most sensational gift since the Garden of Eden.

The scheme was workable, understandable, and likely to be effective. However, one vital issue remained unsolved: the carrot. What could they offer as a prize? This prize had to be more than just appealing. It had to be so extraordinary, so desirable, and so rare that it would beget an insatiable desire for it from the Earth's entire population. The public must crave this treasure so ravenously that everything else in life became secondary to activating the elusive competition icon. As Hieshler returned to the table, his fingernails buffed to a mirror-like sheen, the discussion turned to this perplexing question.

"Money. What about money? Ridiculous amounts of money," suggested Madonna Souwella.

"How much?" asked Arnie the accountant, nervously.

"It would take at least ten billion, I guess."

Hieshler stopped admiring his nails, and grunted with disapproval. He did not want his staff giving away any of his hard-earned fortune.

"Or maybe just a round billion," corrected Madonna.

"Don't be ridiculous," chided Hieshler, aggressively re-entering proceedings. "A billion dollars wouldn't tempt a ten year old. The super-sixteen dividend from my last tiger race yesterday was almost a billion."

"I am sorry sir, of course. It was a silly idea."

Money clearly wasn't the answer for once. Huge cash prizes were commonplace, and would only serve to devalue the size of the racing dividends. Another form of inducement was obviously required.

"How about an all-expenses-paid cruise around the solar system?" proffered Vera.

Hieshler glared at her. "That might have worked in the twenties. Didn't you hear what happened to that senior citizens trip to Mars?"

"Of course, Mr. Hieshler. I don't know what I was thinking when I vocalised such an inane idea." She mopped her brow, gave a polite cough, and sat back into her chair. Unperturbed, Zachary Zzyzz offered a proposal.

"A swimming pool filled with diamonds?"

"The English tabloids did the diamond pool a decade ago."

"A gold mine?"

"Labour costs."

The session continued in a similar vein. The executives made many suggestions, only to be rebuffed by Hieshler. However they absorbed his comments with forced humility, as they were well acquainted with his condescending style. None of them would have risen so far up the company hierarchy had they not capitulated to Hieshler many times before.

"How about a royal title?"

"Unfashionable. Monarchies are being disbanded. Only last week the Queen of Canada was dethroned."

"Why not make the prize a small country, say Bolivia or Madagascar? We're not doing much with them right now."

Heads nodded, eyebrows lifted, lips pouted thoughtfully. Madonna's suggestion seemed to be generally well received. Except by her boss.

"Morgan would bomb it. What would I do then? Do you expect me to give away a piece of dirt with more holes than a cheese grater? Perhaps I could include a hundred thousand corpses into the bargain?"

"Of course not Sir. I'm very sorry Sir. That's very true."

The executives twisted their imaginations through vigorous angles, hoping that a workable suggestion for the major prize would tumble out. But Hieshler dismissed every suggestion before it could develop, or run off at a useful tangent.

As the rejections piled higher, Hieshler's frustration increased. He had his eye on a new mink carpet for his downstairs bathroom - the cashmere was looking *so* tired - which would have to wait until HHTV had regained the top spot. He wanted it *now*. Just as the meeting's collective imagination had almost evaporated, Miss Dingwell chimed in with her second comment of the morning.

"How about a date with a famous person?"

The management committee looked at each other, struggling to contain their obvious disapproval.

"I don't think that prize is sensational enough, Sally," said Madonna Souwella. "We are talking about prizes with values in the billions, and you are suggesting a mere night out with a famous person?"

Arnie continued the explanation.

"The answer cannot be as simple as that, Sally. We are looking for a prize that is so special, so desirable, and so unattainable, that the entire population of the Earth will almost go insane with the desperation of trying to win it."

Miss Dingwell hadn't anticipated the interrogation. Arnie smiled to show that he felt no enmity towards her, and then finished with a question.

"Do you really think that there is any person in the solar system, or beyond, that would drive people to act completely insanely - to give up their jobs, lives, and families - simply for the chance to go on a date with them?"

Without warning, Hieshler answered for her. "Yes, there is," he said. "He's just scored six goals to put my team into the finals."

Chapter 13

"NOOOOOOOOOOOOoooooooooooo."

Dave wailed in disbelief and anger.

"NOOOOOOOOOOOOOooooooooooooo."

He repeated his cry, this time in frustration and depression.

He stared down at the horrible lipstick smudge on the hot dog wrapper. This was too terrible to be true: he had lost his only means of contact with the one person in life whom he had ever truly loved. Sure, he had just met her the previous evening, and admittedly he had been intoxicated throughout most of their encounter. Nevertheless Dave felt a deep sense of everlasting love at first sight for Alexandra. Now it seemed he might never see her again.

The lipstick smudge sniggered back at him, looking more like a ruby red Rorschach inkblot than a telephone number. Dave desperately tried to identify a letter or, more importantly, a numeral, but without success. He held the envelope up towards the ceiling light, hoping the translucency of the paper would reveal the hidden message. Again, he saw nothing but a blotch.

His mind whirred. What could he do? He sat on the floor, trying to calm himself, and evaluated his options. Half an hour later, he tried to list them.

So far, there weren't any.

Despite not yet having any ideas at all, Dave decided that when he formulated a strategy that he would call it Plan H. He felt that the letter 'A' was generally overworked in this situation. Furthermore, he realised that he would need a backup idea, which he pre-named as Plan G. Just to be certain of eventual success, he added a framework for five more reserve tactics that he listed as 'F', 'E', 'D', 'C', and 'B'.

He hoped things wouldn't get as far as his final desperate measure that, not surprisingly, he labelled Plan A.

Having established what he felt was an efficient and workable naming structure for his plans, Dave now needed some actual ideas. He headed to his office - the Stranglers Bar - to think.

Twelve generic lagers later, after discarding many incredibly bad options, he finally produced a possible solution. Not a very good one, he admitted to himself, but solid enough to register as Plan H. Maybe a stronger light would help.

Dave staggered home, and then, after mastering the key to his door (which he had assumed was locked but wasn't, meaning that his repeated efforts to unlock the door simply locked it) he searched around his small apartment for a few hours, looking for a light, a torch, a lamp, a lantern, or even a very big candle. When it eventually dawned on him that he didn't have a stronger light, he became anxious. Plan H was failing before it had begun. Where could he get a more dazzling light? He decided to have another can of beer to help him think - which, surprisingly, worked. As he headed through the kitchen, he was struck by a place where he might find a brighter light source: the refrigerator. Its interior light always seemed fierce through his bloodshot early morning eyes.

Dave flung open the appliance's door. A pathetic, feeble beam emanated from within. The red LED on his old stereo was more powerful. The glow was barely bright enough to illuminate the smudge, and no chance at all of shining through it. How bizarre, thought Dave. It had seemed so powerful yesterday morning.

Plan H was a failure - a qualified failure - but hundreds of rejected job applications had endeared Dave with good resistance to disappointment. He ploughed ahead, despite having no idea in which direction he was heading.

Plan G soon came to mind. Thinking that a person more detached from the smudge's significance might be better able to decipher it, he decided to take the envelope to the nearest available human being: his neighbour, Old Mr Smiggins.

Dave was not looking forward to the visit. He considered, like most of his fellow apartment-dwellers, that Old Mr Smiggins was a perverted, sex-starved old bastard. On this occasion, however, a greater goal was at stake, which overrode any personal antipathy Dave felt towards his adjoining tenant. Old Mr Smiggins looked surprised as he answered his door.

"Good evening Old Mr Smiggins," greeted Dave, unsure as always whether 'Old' was an adjective or a name.

"Er ... yes young Brian, what can I do for you?" replied Old Mr Smiggins.

"I'm not Brian, I'm Dave."

"You're not tryin' to save?" questioned Old Mr Smiggins, cupping his hands around his ears. "Save who?"

"I'm not trying to save anyone," corrected Dave.

"Why are you," asked Old Mr Smiggins "hot frying two date honeybuns?"

Dave quickly realised that he was wasting his time.

"My - name - is - Dave," he said, enunciating each syllable separately and clearly.

"Your game is babes?" said Old Mr Smiggins. "Why didn't you just say so? Come in and let the Smig-miester give you a bit of advice."

Dave at this point tried to usher himself away, but Old Mr Smiggins, sensing that he had a rare visitor to talk at, led him quickly inside.

"What do you want to know about babes, young ... er ... what was your name again?"

"I'm Dave. I live next door."

"Ah, Paul, that's right," said Old Mr Smiggins. "What's the trouble you're having with women? Cause if there's two things that the Smig-miester knows, it's women, and how to catch 'em."

Dave was about to remind Old Mr Smiggins that he had been a bachelor for all of his eighty-something years, and that paying a few thousand dollars for a lap-dance at the local bordello did not, in his opinion, constitute a very skilful 'catch'. However he realised that this would simply inflame, and probably prolong, the conversation. Instead, with some sense of relief as he realised that the conversation had accidentally got straight to the point of his visit, Dave asked Old Mr Smiggins a question.

"Could you do me a small favour?"

"Flavour?" said Old Mr Smiggins, surprisingly closely.

"FAAAY - vour," repeated Dave.

"Strawberry."

"No no no," pleaded Dave. "FAAAAAY - vour, not FLLLLAY - vour."

"Hang on a minute Paul," said Old Mr Smiggins. "I can't quite hear you. I'm eighty-six years old, you know."

Old Mr Smiggins rose slowly from his chair, and shuffled off in the direction of his bedroom. Momentarily idle, Dave picked up a nearby magazine - its tattered, dog-eared cover bore the title *Stonemasonry & Woodwork*. Absently flicking through a few glossy pages, Dave came across a 3D hologram of a large-breasted woman, who obediently blew kisses at him as he tilted the magazine. A perfunctory examination of the rest of the publication revealed that it was really a copy of *HoloHeaven Angels*, a raunchy holographic magazine, incognito in a false cover. As Dave returned the magazine to its place, he wondered what was really inside the box of antique *Walt Disney* videodiscs on the shelf.

After five minutes of scuffling about, Old Mr Smiggins emerged wearing a pair of spectacles.

"Ah, that's better," he said. "Now I can hear you much more clearly."

Dave seized upon this partial opportunity, and thrust the hot dog wrapper into Old Mr Smiggins' trembling hands.

"Can you read this?" asked Dave, now feeling embarrassed that Plan G was asking a deaf, senile, blind old pervert to help him decipher a smudge.

"Why sure," replied Old Mr Smiggins. "It's frogs dancing on top of a mushroom."

"No, no, no," said Dave, acting as restrained as he could manage under the circumstances. "A number. Can you see a number?"

"Ah. I see what you mean."

"What?" asked Dave, suddenly feeling animated with hope.

"Yes, I see the number clearly now."

"What?" pleaded Dave, now quite impatient with anticipation. "What is it?"

"Three," said Old Mr Smiggins with authority.

"A three!" yelled Dave, for the first time feeling that he was getting through to Old Mr Smiggins. Soon, he might be able to get through to Alexandra. How many telephone numbers could there be that started with a three?

"Yes, definitely three," repeated Old Mr Smiggins. "Three frogs dancing on a mushroom."

Dave felt like he had been head butted by a buffalo.

"Thank you Old Mr Smiggins," said Dave, taking back the sacred hot dog wrapper as he let himself out the door.

"Strange lad," said the old man to himself after Dave had departed. "That young Paul should find himself a good woman."

Dave persisted in his belief that he would soon be talking to Alexandra. After just a few further minutes thought, Plan F wobbled its way into his mind. It was a simple strategy. Dave went back to the Stranglers Bar to see if Billy the barman's database had recorded Alexandra's surname. Or where she lived. Or who her friends were. Her hair colour? No. It hadn't.

Dave also quizzed Bruce, Bevan and the other regulars as well. Alexandra? Who is Alexandra? Oh, that blond woman that was canoodling up to you last night - nah, haven't seen her before, but did ya get with her? D'ya want a beer, mate? He coerced a few of the less inept patrons to rewind their Life-Movie recordings on their smart-watches. A couple of them caught fleeting glances of Alexandra, including a 30-second clip from Bruce's vision in which he appeared to be focusing entirely on her breasts, but none of the footage produced any useful information.

Unfortunately Dave's money-card, along with the profit from the Cheetah race, had been used for all the purchases, so Alexandra couldn't be tracked by the normal means of hacking into her money-card account.

Dave also contacted a mate whose housemate's brother's friend's auntie's partner worked in IT at the Hovertaxi company, but unbelievably it seemed that Alexandra had not even taken a cab home that night. How, Dave wondered, had she got home?

In short, every lead at the Stranglers Bar lead to a dead end. Dave left the bar after an uncharacteristically short stay. Knowing that he had to start work on his next strategy, he had diligently limited himself to only six beers. Plan F: over and out.

Immediately after dreaming up his next idea, Dave's confidence soared. This plan was so good that it even justified his wowser act of leaving the pub early. Dave could sense that he would not require Plan D, because 'E' was virtually guaranteed to succeed. He would go fishing - for Alexandra. The bait?

From a local charity shop he purchased a white satin body suit with widely flared bottoms. After padding his slender frame with a few cushions, he used an old burnt cork to replicate a mean-looking pair of handlebar sideburns on his face. Then armed with a portable music player pumping out *Elvis's Greatest Hits Vol. 216*, he danced onto the streets. If Alexandra was out there, this bait was sure to attract her.

Two hours later he limped home, having sprained his ankle from attempting to walk in high platform shoes. He had also been mobbed by three octogenarian women screaming "the king lives", and sweated out half his body weight due to the tight-fitting costume. It was, he conceded in hindsight, not such a good plan after all.

With the failure of his valued Plan E still harrowing hard into his psyche, Dave decided that some detective work would be a more realistic approach. Following the motto of all good detectives to *Be Prepared* - or was that the Boy Scouts? - Dave went to the local antique market to buy himself a pen. Never again would he rely on complex LifeMovie lenses or his smart watch that had a single digit IQ. If he saw Alexandra again, there *was* going to be a pen there when he needed it.

He purchased a quaint looking ballpoint that was adorned by a blue and silver swirl, and crowned with a lime green tip. He didn't trust his pockets — they were forever losing things like keys and moneycards that he had carefully stowed in them — so instead he taped it securely to his left shin for safe keeping.

Dave walked back to the park bench where he and Alexandra had spent the latter part of their evening, and commenced his investigations. Convention forced him to designate his inquest as Plan D. Meticulously he searched the seat and its environment for clues. He found nothing but pigeon droppings, which unsurprisingly provided no additional information as to Alexandra's whereabouts, and the trail of chilli sauce from their hot dog withered after a few drops. Dave was so desperate to find Alexandra that he crouched on all fours and tried to follow her scent, but only ended up being stung on the chin by a wasp.

The entire visit to the park bench served only to heighten Dave's sense of loss, and made him even more disbelieving that the world he was just starting to understand had so cruelly turned against him. However he had no choice but to push onwards into Plan C.

Plan C consisted of an old bed sheet and a can of emerald green paint. He painstakingly brushed the message "Alex, I love you. Please call me. From Dave" onto the sheet, and followed it with his ten digit phone number. He positioned the banner in a prominent place at the top of the local shopping mall (which was strangely quiet that day) and went home and waited. After two solicitations from gay men called Alex, four crank calls from schoolchildren, a fine from the local council and a message from a woman wanting to know whether he was the Dave whom she had met in Peru last summer, he decided to remove the sign. Alexandra had told him that she hated shopping anyhow. Plan C: Never a chance.

Dave had almost run out of ideas. He feared that he might not even make it to the dreaded Plan A. In desperation he returned to the Stranglers Bar, and took up a position in the seat in which he had first met Alexandra, simply hoping that she would reappear. He waited for seven days.

She didn't.

He decided to give it one last week. Sitting morosely at the bar, Dave waited, hoped, prayed and, well, had a couple of drinks to help pass the time. He even went to the extreme of un-retiring his lucky shirt. However, after three hundred and forty something beers, twenty-two pizzas, one cigarette, seven hot dogs, and very little sleep, Dave gave up.

It was time for his last throw of the dice. He shuddered at the thought. The dreaded Plan A. He trudged dejectedly home, let himself in, and called his watch Elvis into service.

"Elvis, wake up," instructed Dave.

With the chewing gum over its auditory receiver now thinned by weeks of wear-and-tear, Elvis was better able to comprehend Dave's instructions, and awoke immediately.

"Download the telephone directory for the local area within a 20 kilometre radius of my current position." Again Elvis responded correctly, and within seconds Dave had opened the listing to page one. Without ceremony, he dialled the first number.

"Hello, is this Mr Aaron Aaaba?"

He paused to allow the reply.

"Is Alexandra there?" he asked.

"No?"

"Thank you anyway," he said, and hung up.

He dialled again.

"Hello, Mrs. Aabadoo".

"Is Alexandra there?"

"Terribly sorry, thank you, goodbye."

Seconds later.

"Mister Aacadaca...."

*

Dozens of greasy pizza boxes lay in rotting piles. A huge mound of festering dishes lay in, above and around the sink. The room stunk of decomposing anchovy, while dozens of cockroaches feasted gleefully on an assortment of discarded pizza crusts. As Dave gulped down the last mouthful of cereal from an old flower vase, he washed it down with a mouthful of generic lager.

He wearily picked up the telephone receiver, and dialled.

"Hello, Mr Zzyzz?"

"Would Alexandra be there?"

"But ... but ... but...." Dave's voice trailed off dejectedly.

"But she *must* be," pleaded Dave.

"Are you sure?"

"Are you sure that you're sure?"

"No need to swear...."

Dave heard a click, then silence. A long silence, a horrible silence.

Slowly the realisation spread over Dave, injuring him more fiercely than would a speeding hovertrain. *He would never see Alexandra again.* The tiredness, hunger and desperation of the previous fortnight overtook him. He collapsed in a ragged heap, as his fragile shell succumbed to the weeks of unrelenting and unresolved frustration. Voracious anger almost overcame him, but his weakened mind didn't have the strength to raise its own temper. Instead, his mind fell into a more physically sedate emotional flavour: melancholic depression. As Dave drifted off to sleep - or, more correctly, he passed out - one thought rebounded mercilessly around inside his head:

I am a complete and total nincompoop....

I am a complete and total nincompoop....

I am a complete and total nincompoop....

No matter how much you liked Dave, or how unlucky that you felt he was, it was very difficult to disagree with him.

Chapter 14

Most of the time the room was completely silent. Apart from a regular breathing sound, the room was even quieter than that deathly second that follows a bad joke. The room was also very dark - so dark that it was brighter if you closed your eyes. Ideal conditions for sleeping.

Then, suddenly, at 5.30 am in the morning, nothing happened. Or at least that is the way it would have appeared to a casual observer. Yet despite this apparent lack of change, two incidents put a small but a definite dent in both the quietness and darkness of the room. First, a lamp in the ceiling activated, releasing just one photon of light. This tiny piece of light whizzed across the room, briefly lit up a molecule on the adjacent wall, then transmorphed itself into an infrared ray and disappeared. Second, an array of speakers emitted a tiny sound - just one vibration of one frequency. The noise was so weak that it only travelled a few microns before it collided with an oxygen molecule, lost its oomph and vanished.

A millisecond later, another sound and another beam of light flashed across the room. However, these were only very slightly louder and brighter than the first pair, so their overall effect on the room status was essentially identical: no change. However this process gradually intensified, and eventually a dull grey glow dawned over the room, revealing a body lying in a vast, presidential-sized bed. A hint of a whispering melody began, and slowly amplified into a dancing symphony. The breathing sounds showed signs of stirring.

Meanwhile in the kitchen, an automatic chef activated itself. A robot laser-sliced three rashers of bacon, and then laid them neatly on a hot irradiated pan. After that it expertly cracked and cooked two genetically modified eggs, which had been altered so that whoever consumed them would have smoother skin around their eyes. Simultaneously the breakfast robot conveyed a few slices of freshly-kneaded bread dough to an infrared griller, from which they emerged a second later as hot buttered pieces of toast. A huge pot of sweetened Venusian coffee boiled away under a shortwave heater.

The system then piped the wonderful kitchen aromas into the bedroom. The country-bake smells hit the nostrils of the sleeping figure; it stirred, yawned, and then slowly opened its eyelids. This was, without any doubt at all, the gentlest, most user-friendly wake-up system ever devised.

Hieshler sat up, yawned again, and stretched casually. He enjoyed mornings. His engineers had installed, at enormous non-tax-deductible expense, an Ante-Meridiem Soporific Deactivator Unit. Most people knew primitive models from the late twentieth century as 'alarm clocks', but they had the nasty habit of making sudden loud noises. Hieshler infinitely preferred his Ante-Meridiem Soporific Deactivator Unit, which artificially brightened the room in the most gradual manner possible - one photon at a time - and gently amplified relaxing morning music, before waking him with a plate of bacon and eggs and a pot of Venusian coffee.

What is more, he was looking forward to the rest of this particular morning even more than usual. He had an important meeting on his agenda, which he was sure represented the start of the end for GTN, and the beginning of unlimited riches and luxuries for himself. He had a meeting with God.

*

The alarm rang out like a fire siren.

Morgan woke with a jolt. He shot bolt upright, his shoulders hunched, eyes wide and jaw clenched. In a reflex action, his hand tightened into a fist and smashed down hard onto the alarm. The device splintered into pieces and fell to the floor, where it emitted a few more feeble rings before whimpering a premature death.

"Grrrr," growled Morgan while shaking his bruised hand. "I *hate* mornings."

It was not that Morgan necessarily hated being awake. In fact he perversely savoured the invigorating sense of power as he walked through his office doorway every - yes, every - morning. Nor did he particularly love sleep; he couldn't dictate to staff, create fireballs or strengthen his global power base while he was slumbering. He just despised the exact moment of transition between peaceful slumber and stark wakefulness.

This moment had always been a particular source of irritation to Morgan because, despite being the most powerful man in history, he still had to endure waking up, just like every other pathetic creature on the face of the Earth. Even lowly animals appeared to cope with that transitional moment without noticeable stress. A filthy Grizzly Bear, with its sickening advantage of hibernation, seemed better off. Morgan had tried to employ someone to wake up for him in the morning - not to wake him up, but to wake up for him - but the experiment had been a complete failure. He had, as one would expect, eventually woken up, and had logically been forced to sack the proxy waker-upper on the spot.

Nevertheless, Morgan still despised mornings. He was going to hate this one more than most. The headline of the news feeds on his kitchen STOVE would see to that.

He lumbered out of bed, rubbing his arthritic hip as he did. His joints always ached in the morning, but Morgan was too bull-headed to admit that hips and knees were not designed to carry nearly two hundred kilograms of body mass. What did it matter anyway? He did not have a spare hour for the corrective surgery. Nor did he have time for physiotherapy, exercises, weight loss programs, or any of their ilk. His company would fall apart within minutes if he were not there to supervise.

After limping across to a cupboard in the corner of his modest bedroom, he reached in and took out one of a hundred identical alarm units. Then he positioned the new device on his bedside table, and kicked the ruined one under the bed with all the others. Then, with his daily wake-up ritual completed, he readied himself for work. After wolfing down a breakfast consisting of two takeaway hamburgers, a pre-packaged chicken Kiev, a bowl of chocolate sauce and a bacon-and-peanut butter roll, he washed it all down with a large bottle of quadruple-caffeine-sextuple-sugar cola.

After hastily dressing in a sky blue safari suit, Morgan hurried through his morning ablutions. He was already late. Then he trotted out to his small hovercar, squeezed in, slammed the door, and sped off. Then he sat in air traffic for two hours on the way to work, blasting the horn and shouting his usual expletives for the entire journey.

Upon arrival he rushed up towards his office, still under the autosuggestion that he was late for work, despite the facts that (a) he wasn't, (b) he was actually early, and (c) he owned the company and could damn well arrive anytime he wished. Nevertheless Morgan knew that if he rushed then he would have more time to peruse the news feeds on his office STOVE, which, along with wanton use of his power, was his favourite pastime.

Ignoring his staff as they greeted him good morning, Morgan closed his office door and sat in his familiar leather armchair in front of the control panel. He nuzzled back into its seat until he had wedged himself so tightly that he could hardly move. This was a habit that he had developed many years previously when dieting. He felt that if he jammed himself firmly enough between the armrests, then he could not move until he had lost at least a couple of pounds. This tactic had caused him a couple of embarrassing moments, particularly once when an extra tortilla had trapped him for twenty-two hours without a toilet break. He persisted with this ridiculous habit in the belief that it kept his weight below the *grossly obese* stage. It didn't.

As the STOVE clicked into life, Morgan wondered, with his usual sarcastic disdain, what disasters had befallen the poor unfortunate souls of a certain central European ghetto in recent times. He could write tomorrow's headlines now if he wished. After all, he was the one who created almost every major story. Where would the news content industry be without his beloved war programming policy? Their unofficial support was most gratifying.

He poured a deep scotch, and ordered his STOVE feed past the advertising supplements – a privilege for which he paid dearly - to the first news item. That was as far as he got. The virtual newsreader, although using a professionally restrained voice, seemed to be screaming at him louder than a lime green neck tie.

HARRY HIESHLER IS GIVING AWAY A DATE WITH GOD!

His next words were almost as damaging.

Tune in to HHTV to win.

Morgan bellowed with rage. Then he bellowed again, repeatedly vowing to beat Hieshler if it was the last thing he did. As he smashed his fists wantonly onto the control panel, he unfortunately hit an 'Execute' button on the control panel, taking out four southern Asian islands as he did.

*

God was in his usual position: in his private cubicle of Hieshler's Heroes dressing room, laying in a hot tub, a Neptune Gold beer in his hand and several semi-naked women jostling for the chance to massage his shoulders. Lounging in another corner of the tub, but still within talking distance, was Harry Hieshler. He, too, was enjoying a cool drink and plenty of special attention. God bestowed a very high level of hospitality to his guests.

Or, we should say, to his guest - non-plural - because Harry Hieshler was the only person whom God had ever truly invited into his hot tub. Sure, he had *permitted* hoards of admirers, all female and stunningly attractive, into this sacred area. However, Hieshler was the first person that he had actually *invited*. This was a coincidence, because God's invitation was the only one that Hieshler had ever bothered accepting to anywhere.

Hieshler and God shared a common characteristic that somehow drew them towards each other - not forcefully, like a pin to a magnet, but slowly, almost imperceptibly, like a tide towards the high water mark. This characteristic was *not* that they were both wealthy to the ironic point where more money was useless to them - although neither of them realised this fact. It was *not* that they were both universally famous, their likenesses brandishing magazines and billboards from Antartican alleyways to Martian mega cities. The characteristic that drew them together was that they held all other people in complete and overwhelming contempt. Except, perhaps, for each other.

Not that they were friends. They were both too rich to have real friends. However, God intimately tolerated Hieshler, and Hieshler non-despised God with a similarly familiar type of bond. This arrangement held so long as Hieshler kept up payments of God's ridiculously high match fees, and God scored a few quick goals whenever the Heroes, Hieshler's favourite toy, were in trouble. So Hieshler and God lolled in the hot tub, each dismissive of all other carbon based life forms, not hating each other out of personal necessity. This common thread, despite its almost infinite fragility, held them together like riveted steel.

Hieshler idly pointed to a nearby STOVE, and replayed the headline announcement for the eighth time. A slow smile spread over his face, which increased to a maniacal cackle as he watched the rest of the story. He adored the notion of the billions of dollars presently pouring into the HHTV coffers, and fantasised about the luxuries he would soon purchase. The solid gold toilet seats were now a realistic aim, as was the team of people that he planned to employ to sit on them 24 hours a day to keep them warm.

God looked across and smiled at Hieshler. God, too, broke into a rising cacophony of laughter as the thought of his universal popularity overflowed his bulging ego account.

*

In the nearby offices of GTN, Morgan W. Morgan was also laughing, which was very unusual for him. It was not a joyous laugh, but more of a maniacal cackle. The reason for his display of emotion was that he had just devised a crafty plan for revenge. He hollered for his assistant.

"Hopgood, get yourself in here NOW."

"Yes Sir, right away sir," came the hurriedly mumbled reply from the office next door.

While Morgan waited, his mind wandered over the details of his plan. As he did, his thoughts drew him back to the early years of GTN. Memories of his rise through the power-ranks of society, from lowly television journalist to head of the largest company on Earth, filled his thoughts. He had run the whole show the right way, the only way: his way. He had overseen every detail, right from the very beginning. Nothing had been left to chance.

Even when GTN had outgrown its first premises, Morgan had controlled every facet of the construction of the new office towers. What did architects and engineers know that he didn't? He had designed every detail, from the building's complex communications systems to the uniform grey colouring of the walls and furniture. Every room was a masterstroke of control, from the one-way mirrors that windowed the staff offices to the self-destruct security coding on the 'BOOM' button.

Ah, the 'BOOM' button. A smile crept onto the corners of Morgan's lips for the second time within a minute (a new record). He adored that button for the fingertip control over the planet that it afforded him. What was more, only he knew the security codes. If anyone else attempted to use the button then the entire building - from the penthouse offices to the dungeon-like basement - would be blown to smithereens within minutes. The self-destruct mechanism was virtually impenetrable. The power was his, all his, and only his. He had always been in control ... and, he vowed, he always would be. A pretty-boy lightweight like Harry Hieshler was not going to interfere with his plans for world domination.

A polite knock on the door roused Morgan back to reality.

"Who is it?"

"Hopgood, Sir, your assistant. You called for me."

"Enter."

Hopgood timidly entered the room and nodded deferentially toward his master.

"I want you to do three things," commanded Morgan. "First, rent an unobtrusive downtown apartment. Second, have a telephone installed in it - nothing fancy, just an old-fashioned telephone – and a simple STOVE unit. Do it all under an anonymous name. Do you understand me so far, Hopgood?"

Morgan had dispensed with his customary pauses, which had thrown Hopgood out of kilter. Assuming from Hopgood's look that he had missed at least one vital detail, Morgan taciturnly repeated the message.

"Rent a small downtown apartment. Install a telephone and STOVE in it. Do both these tasks under an anonymous name. And then," said Morgan as he passed a slip of paper across the desk, "see that my entire staff gets this memo."

No matter how hard Morgan tried to look vengeful and determined, he just could not keep the third smile of the morning off his face.

Chapter 15

Alexandra sat at her desk, staring at a university physics lecture through her STOVE display - not listening, not understanding, just staring. Her mind, still shrouded by a cloud of melancholy, would not soak up information like it normally did. Instead of reviewing notes for her paper on 'Nuclear HyperPhotoFission and its Application to the Health Sciences', she sat lamenting, examining her memories of the past month, wondering for the millionth time why Dave had not called. It had been a devastating few weeks.

During the days after meeting Dave, she had experienced a series of psychological states. At about ten past six on that first evening, she entered what she now defined as the *He's Probably Just Got the Wrong Time* phase. The next morning this developed into the more serious *Just Got the Wrong Day* condition, which then deteriorated to the pathologically optimistic *Wrong Week* state of mind. Existing concurrently with these conditions was a phenomenon that Alexandra now called the *'Oh, There's the Telephone Ringing - It's Probably Dave'* effect.

It never was.

Dave didn't call.

After three weeks of soul searching and self-evaluation, Alexandra became more proactive. She decided to call Dave, and ask him why he hadn't kept his promise to contact her. The answer might hurt, but she realised that knowing a painful truth was preferable to an infinity of uncertainty.

Her mother kindly tried to counsel her against this move, gently suggesting that calling a gentleman was unladylike. But hell, Alexandra thought, a girl could call a guy if she wanted to - these were the thirties, not the twenties.

Besides, this minor matter of etiquette was the least of the obstacles in her way. A far greater obstruction lay between her and an answer. How could she find Dave's contact number? Her first obvious step was to watch a Life-Movie replay from that evening. Although it hurt her emotionally to see Dave's image again, the replay unfortunately didn't provide any precise contact details.

Unperturbed, Alexandra called the Stranglers Bar. Did anyone there know how she could contact Dave? No.

Sure, he was a regular. In fact, he was here every day and night for the last two weeks, but we don't know anything about him apart from his first name.

But hadn't he frequented the bar almost every night for years?

Er … yes … but we still didn't know anything about him, except that he drinks a lot of beer, eats a lot of pizza, and plays an average game of Virtual Snooker.

Could she leave him a message?

Sure.

Alexandra briefly regained a positive outlook. She temporarily re-entered the *'Oh, There's the Telephone Ringing - It's Probably Dave'* phase. However as the hours of anticipation became days, and the days turned into longer, more angst-ridden days, her hopes withered. Tiring of waiting, she called back to the Stranglers Bar, only to be told that nobody had seen Dave for at least a week - an unusually long time for him to be absent. They thought that he had run off with *her*.

The Stranglers Bar was a dead lead, so Alexandra tried a different tactic. She instructed Einstein55 into a telephone number identification application. Using every fact that she could recall about her beloved, she gradually narrowed the list of possible numbers.

Vat is da search name? asked Einstein55 in the old genius's soft German-tinged accent.

'Dave,' replied Alexandra, "surname unknown."

I haf found 4 802 561 matching data files, replied Einstein55 unhelpfully.

Alexandra did not know Dave's exact address, but assumed that he lived within a short hovertaxi fare of the Stranglers Bar. Entering a postcode and a search radius, her smart-watch responded positively.

I now haf 6 366 matching data files."

Amazing, thought Alexandra. Who would have dreamed that 6 366 men named Dave lived near the Stranglers Bar? However, she clearly still had to reduce the list. Firmly calling instructions and deftly gliding her fingers across Einstein55's touch-screen face, she called up files from the local social security office. Merging these files with her existing data, she found four hundred and thirty-two remaining 'Daves' who not only lived near the Stranglers Bar, but were long-term unemployed as well. *Her* Dave had to be one of those.

Alexandra concentrated on memories of their meeting. What else did she know about him? He had a good sense of humour, but that knowledge was not much help when dealing with a database. His eyes were deep and dreamy, but you couldn't tell that to a computer, regardless of how intelligent it was. Dave's boyish good looks and impish charm were there for all to see: wonderful information if you were dating him, but useless for an electronic file matching facility.

Mexico! Dave had told her about his trip to Mexico. It was many years previously, but the Horizontal Displacement Company's records surely must contain some mention of it. With her fingers tapping her watch face like a woodpecker on speed, Alexandra called up files of all personal Australia-Mexico transitions in the last decade. After Einstein55 had compared these with her existing possibilities, she received a heartening reply. Eight matching files!

She toyed with the idea of calling each 'Dave' in turn, but dismissed that option as ungainly and embarrassing. There had to be one more tidbit of information that she could use to narrow the list. What else did she know about him, besides the fact that he drank a lot of beer, played an average game of Virtual Snooker and ate a lot of pizza? She sat thinking as the minutes ticked past. She just could not think of any other information to use. Then, slowly, a wry grin spread across her face.

"Of course," she exclaimed. The answer was so obvious that she hadn't seen it. Pizza.

With a final burst of inspiration, she collated the number of times each of the eight 'Daves' had called for Dial-A-Pizza in the last year. Her smart-watch displayed the results of the search individually.

Dave #1.....5 calls
Dave #2.....0 calls
Dave #3.....3 calls

Dave #4.....3 calls
Dave #5.....0 calls
Dave #6.....0 calls
Dave #7.....3 calls
Dave #8... 278 calls

She had found her man!

Chapter 16

The Global Television Network was a very big organisation. It was so huge that the words 'very' and 'big' did not even come close to justifying themselves being used to describe it. Even a dozen or so 'verys' in a row would be hopelessly inadequate, even if combined with other words like 'enormous', 'giant' or 'immense'. Simply, no word existed in the English language that conveyed the notion of size to the extent required.

One word, GHjh!as#bid, from the ancient language of Gayak, came close. However, very few people understood Ancient Gayak, so saying that the Global Television Network was a GHjh!as#bid organisation was unlikely to provide much useful enlightenment on the subject for most people. So 'very big', despite its obvious limitations, was usually used as the simplest alternative.

GTN was not simply a television station. It was a macrocosm. The company had hundreds of different branches, divisions and sub-organisations that were spread across thousands of interwoven industries: producers and directors started wars and orchestrated battles wars; factory workers laboured to produce everything from paper clips to nuclear weapons; scientists researched and developed, while the Military Generals yelled at soldiers and dined in expensive restaurants. GTN's employee list included almost every occupation, profession or trade from war pilots to lawyers to tea ladies. It had its own hospitals, schools and universities. In total, the corporation had over one hundred million employees.

Every one of them was watching television. The Harry Hieshler Television Station to be precise.

The memo had come from the top, from Morgan himself. Every employee was to stop work immediately, and start watching the rival station on television. Had the fat old bastard finally cracked? The sudden impact of Morgan's directive was felt all around the globe. Factories jerked to a halt, gross national products dropped by 30%, peace returned to the Middle East, and some sandwiches were left only half made in a hospital canteen. Millions of workers, acting on order from their highest command post, downed their tools and took up comfortable positions in front of the nearest STOVE-TV set.

They only had one further pair of instructions from Morgan. First, enter Hieshler's competition as often as you can. And second, use a special *Hotline Telephone Number* on the entry.

Any worker who won would contractually forfeit the prize to Morgan. The workers accepted this consequence without too much protestation, as they were being paid to sit in front of a STOVE-TV all day, plus the overtime for all HHTV watching after hours. Also, Morgan had pledged that he would sack the whole global staff if he were not victorious. They knew that he meant it. He was that type of bloke.

As a hundred million extra pairs of eyes sat glued to their STOVE-TVs, two hundred million extra hands grasped not tools of work or productivity but at thin-air projections, ready to activate the 'Win a date with God' competition icon when it appeared. Slowly but unerringly, Hieshler's competition, coupled with Morgan's greed, reduced civilisation to its knees.

Morgan knew that his chosen tactic was risky. He was putting all his golden eggs - his fortune, his life and his power - into one very fragile basket. If this plan failed, he would be ruined. Meanwhile, Harry Hieshler couldn't believe his luck. His wildest fantasies were all coming true.

Chapter 17

Morgan was thinking so hard that he accidentally forgot to go home for the weekend. The first stage of his revenge plan had progressed well so far, considering the circumstances,. GTN now had, through its 'dedicated' employees, registered over a trillion entries into the 'Date with God' competition. This total represented more than half of all global entries, which was not as high as Morgan had hoped, but still enough to give him a decent chance of winning.

The competition had only two days left to run. Then the world would hold its breath as the HHTV computer randomly selected a telephone number from its vast array of entries. Hieshler would then call the chosen number, and the winner would be the person who answered. Even though he was agnostic, Morgan prayed that it would be his hotline number, from any one of his trillion entries, which the HHTV computer selected as the winner. The survival of his vast power base depended on it. As did the coveted number one rating, which HHTV currently held by a considerable but not uncatchable margin of 99 percent.

Morgan was not stupid. A complete prick maybe, but he wasn't stupid. Intuitively, he felt that Hieshler would attempt to prevent him, or anyone within his organisation, from entering the competition. To help confirm or deny this suspicion, he had studied the competition icon with unparalleled obsession. His engineering department recorded an image of the virtual icon, and upon scrutinising it, they discovered a minuscule dot, about the size of a real estate salesperson's brain, in the bottom left corner. The fact that they even noticed it was an impressive achievement, as it had flashed into virtual existence for only a nanosecond.

They magnified the tiny dot to the size of a football field, and re-examined it. In the centre of it was another dot, which, even when magnified to this extent, was smaller than the original. This sub-dot was again re-magnified, revealing a string of unusual looking molecules. They had been arranged to spell out a tiny hidden message, which read:

'Directors, employees and extended families of the Global Television Network are ineligible to enter this competition. By direction Harry Hieshler.'

It was the finest fine print in history. As usual with fine print, its message represented a problem. Sure, Morgan had a fair chance that Hieshler would dial his hotline telephone number in two days time. However, if he answered, Hieshler would instantly invalidate his entry. He would be disqualified in a very ugly, public brawl that would leave him with enough egg on his face to bake a frittata. What could he do?

That night he worried so much that he did not sleep at all. At least, Morgan thought as the morning sun dawned, he had saved the price of another alarm device.

His uneasiness was, to be fair to Morgan, perfectly natural. His entire multi-zillion-dollar corporation had existed for the last four weeks purely for the purpose of trying to win a date with a good-looking football player. Now, through a combination of luck and planning, Morgan had the infrastructure in place to overcome the first part of this problem ... he hoped.

He thought back to his youth and recalled sitting for hours by the telephone, maddeningly trying to win a radio station phone-in competition. He had even forced his little brother to monitor the radio in his absence so that he did not miss a vital prompt to call. Now, he laughed, he was forcing about one hundred million people to do the same thing.

Morgan allowed himself a fantasy. He imagined what he would do when he won: he would arrange for the winner to secretly record the meeting with God, and then telecast it as an interview. God *never* gave interviews. It would be the most watched program in history.

He pictured GTN soaring up the ratings, returning him to his position as the most influential person on the planet. The thought of the power made his veins throb warmly. He indulgently imagined Hieshler lying dishevelled in a gutter, weeping, and crying out "Why didn't I leave that Morgan alone? I could see he was strong. Why me, why me, why me?"

Hieshler would be shot with his own weapon: Juan Carlos Manuel de la Espirito. That egotistical football player would unwittingly propel GTN to the top of the ratings tree, with Morgan riding pick-a-back for the journey.

Morgan suddenly snapped back to reality. Two major obstacles lay in his path. His employees were actively pursuing the first obstacle of winning the competition. However the second obstacle - who would answer the hotline telephone, collect the prize, and conduct that history-making interview - he had not yet finalised. Whom could he entrust with such a vital, pivotal role?

Morgan analysed the problem slowly and methodically. First, this person could not be employed by, or connected with, either GTN or HHTV. When the employees' families were also considered, this excluded in excess of one billion people. No worries, thought Morgan. What about my friends? My many close, personal mates. They are a loyal and trustworthy bunch. Morgan tried to list his friends. Two hours later, he had six names.

He gave the list to Hopgood to research. His sheepish assistant returned soon thereafter, reporting that from the register that Morgan had supplied, two were dead after a bomb blast in a central European ghetto, two refused to talk with him, one had moved to Southern Madagascar, and the last had instantly developed - as his mother had subsequently explained - a severe case of acute laryngitis and had been unable to continue the conversation. So much for friends, Morgan thought. Where were they when he needed them? Although, he had to concede, he had not talked to any of them for over 20 years.

Morgan continued in his quest for a solution to his problem. Family members were out. Employees were out. Friends were out. That left, in Morgan's reckoning, only one subgroup of human beings. Complete strangers.

But which one? There were over ten billion of them from which to choose. How could he narrow the list down? Morgan made a mental list of attributes that he felt would be an advantage.

Anonymity. The person had to be completely unknown, particularly to Harry Hieshler and his executives. Therefore, Morgan assumed, a *foreigner* would be best.

Trustworthy. Hmm, this was tricky. How could he ensure that a completely random stranger was trustworthy? How could he be confident that the stranger would not try to blackmail him, or solicit counteroffers from Hieshler? Anyone but a complete idiot would see the opportunity.

This thought eventually led Morgan to his third and ultimately highest priority attribute. *A complete idiot.* He could only rely on a complete idiot to not see the opportunity for what it was worth. The chosen person had to be stupid. Not mean spirited or selfish, just hopelessly stupid.

Morgan called in Hopgood. After quickly dispensing with his pauses, he launched into his order.

"Hopgood, listen up."

"Yes sir. What can I do for you, Sir?"

"I want you to do some research on our private database. So immediately get down to the main databank...."

"Yes sir."

Hopgood turned on his heel, and began quickly marching from the room.

"Not yet, you idiot," thundered Morgan.

"Sorry Sir," said Hopgood, even more meekly than usual. "I just thought..."

"I don't pay you to think," said Morgan. "I pay you to listen."

"Er, pardon me Sir, I think I missed that last bit."

Through clenched teeth, Morgan hissed as an outlet for his growing, gurgling pool of exasperation.

"Get down to the main data bank," he repeated.

"Yes, Sir. I heard that bit, Sir," said Hopgood, not realizing how close he was to losing not just his job but his remaining life span as well. "I just didn't catch what you said after 'I don't pay you to think'. I thought that...."

Morgan's exasperation overflowed into barely-controlled rage.

"You'll be on permanent cleaning duty in the bottom storerooms of the dungeon if you get this wrong. So unless you want rats and spiders as your only company for the rest of your working life, you had better listen up."

Hopgood listened intently; he had heard stories about 'The Dungeon' in the bowels of the building and knew this was a threat that his boss would deliver.

"For the third and final time," Morgan yelled, "get down to the main data bank. I want you to scan every name on Earth for a suitable candidate for an extremely important task."

"Of course, Sir," said Hopgood nervously but politely, trying to restore some composure to the conversation. "What type of candidate are you looking for?"

Hopgood's tone worked. Morgan settled a smidgen.

"I want you to find me a person with three particular characteristics. First, they must not work for, or be related to anybody who works for, GTN or HHTV." Hopgood looked startled, but Morgan continued: "Second, they must not live in the USA. They must be foreign born and raised, and the more remote the country, the better. Try Iceland or Moldavia or Australia, or some other similar backwater. "

Hopgood's inquisitiveness was growing, but was about to become outright confusion.

"And third."

Morgan paused for emphasis.

"He or she must be a complete and total nincompoop."

"Pardon Sir?"

"You heard me, Hopgood. A *nincompoop*. A complete and total idiot."

Chapter 18

The world of human endeavour is a very competitive place. People will go to ridiculous lengths, simply to achieve a PB - a personal best. Athletes subsist on a lifestyle of nothing but running, exercising and working out, simply to gain a PB. Businessmen live on diet of nothing but worrying, working and stressing out, simply for a profit PB. Somebody once made 177 737 jumps on a Pogo stick, simply for a PB.

Dave had just set a PB, but without any effort at all. In fact, he did not even know that he had achieved it. He had just slept for 37 hours straight, breaking his Mexican record by more than four hours. He was still napping strongly, and would have easily gone on to break the coveted 40 hour barrier, had it not been for the overly competitive greed of two particular television network presidents.

As Dave slumbered, two shadowy figures loitered outside his apartment. They wore black jeans, black polo neck sweaters, and covered their faces with balaclavas that were not surprisingly coloured black. Both carried carbon fibre batons, and wore laser stun-pistols on their belts. They whispered to each other.

"Geez, Duke. Are you sure we've got the right place?"

"Of course I'm sure, Biff. What do you think I am, some sort of dunderhead?"

"Well, you did take us to Austria first, instead of Australia."

"It looked the same on the memo."

"What sort of dunderhead would miss a turnoff by thirty thousand kilometres?"

"Are you calling me a dunderhead?" said Duke, his voice gradually escalating above a whisper.

"Well, you did keep insisting to that little old Austrian lady that she was a 34 year-old male named Dave."

"I thought she was in disguise."

"Even after you pulled at her nose, to check if it was real?"

"Are you calling me a dunderhead?" said Duke loudly, falling back onto his main line of defence.

"Well ... yes"

"That's it! I've had enough of your insults. Another comment like that and I'll ... I'll ... I'll ...."

"What's all this racket going on out here?"

Biff and Duke turned to see Old Mr Smiggins standing in his doorway, waving his fist at them.

"Keep it down, will you," he scowled. "I've got company in here, and you're ruining the ambience."

Biff and Duke looked meekly at the floor, mutually embarrassed to be admonished by a walking advertisement for incontinence pads.

"What are you doing here anyway?" asked Old Mr Smiggins testily.

"Er ... delivering pizza," said Biff, hoping that their balaclavas would not raise suspicion.

It was their lucky day. Old Mr Smiggins couldn't distinguish between a balaclava and a baseball cap. Not only that, the old man actually managed to hear Biff's reply quite clearly.

"That boy eats too much pizza."

Biff and Duke sighed with relief.

"And get that ugly hover-jet out of my driveway," said Old Mr Smiggins.

"We will Sir," said Duke as he kicked down Dave's front door. "Just as soon as we've made this delivery."

"Well make it snappy, I'm entertaining a lady," said old Mr Smiggins, as he closed his door and went back to his x-rated STOVE-TV movie.

Biff and Duke entered Dave's apartment, and were promptly overcome by nausea. The stench was *unbelievable*. Dave's cleaning effort of a happier time was no longer even a memory: no function of the human mind was powerful enough to override the obvious assumption that this room had *ever* been anything but filthy. If possible, the room was now even more fetid than before Dave had cleaned it. Many physicists would argue that this broke at least three laws of thermodynamics, but Biff and Duke would not have argued, even if they could have opened their mouths for long enough to speak.

During the weeks in which Dave had tried to contact Alexandra by ringing his way through the telephone directory, he had spawned a mess so complete that every major type of bacteria in the known universe had found something to eat in it. If germs have dinner parties, then this one was an open-invitation smorgasbord.

"Let's make this quick," choked Biff, when he eventually found some air.

"Aaaaarrrgurgurg gurgurg-arallahaharrrrr," replied Duke agreeably. They stepped over piles of filthy laundry and grimy kitchenware as they hurried towards Dave's bedroom, ignoring the constantly ringing telephone, trying not to inhale as they went.

Dave's mental clock had just chalked up 37 hours and 29 minutes of continuous slumber (and to think that Dave's high school teacher had nominated him as 'Most unlikely to achieve anything of great significance' in his high school yearbook). The two thugs entered his room, and stood over his bed. Without even arguing about who was going to perform the task, Biff cracked the back of Dave's head with a baton. Dave lapsed further into unconsciousness, which is the state in which he remained as Duke dragged him by the ankles, past the persistently ringing telephone, out the door, and into the waiting hoverjet.

Chapter 19

Alexandra clapped with joy as Einstein55 read out the last piece of data: 278 pizzas in one year! That one *had* to be her Dave. Within seconds, she had traced his number, and then headed straight for her old fashioned telephone. Despite an overwhelming sense of nervousness, she did not hesitate before dialling.

The transmission process caused a tiny pause, just a fraction of a second, as a distant audiovisual satellite relay station established the connection. That tiny grab of time was the longest second of Alexandra's life.

Dialling the number had given Alexandra's mind something on which to concentrate: a positive distraction. But now, as she waited through that interminable split second, her thoughts raced off at various tangents as they replayed, dissected and analysed the history of her relationship with Dave. Was he in love with her? Had she been just another conquest for his primeval urges? Why hadn't he called? Alexandra fought determinedly against her own index finger, which was hovering tantalisingly close to the *Terminate Call* button. She gulped, as a month of doubts and suspicions collected their ugly heads in her mind.

It is the easiest way out: just push that button. Push that button, and then you can continue the rest your life, unhurt and un-rejected. He doesn't love you. He would have called if he loved you. Forget him. Push that damn button.

As that single second ticked excruciatingly by, her index finger moved within a hair's breadth of the *terminate* button. No! She pulled the finger away. Ignorance was a greater burden than disapproval. The pain of rejection would be temporary and passing, but the nadir of not knowing would last forever.

She heard a tiny, almost inaudible click as the connection was made. *Why hadn't he called?* Every possible answer was caustic to her self esteem. *Just hang up* it screamed with all the intensity it could summon. No!

Alexandra breathed deeply as the call connected. "Just be yourself," she urged. A long, slow tone pulsed into her ear. Then there was a slight pause, before the tone repeated itself. Alexandra depressed the 'Terminate Call' button.

Dave's telephone was engaged. She would try again later.

*

Alexandra lay in bed, moist eyed, re-watching ancient copies of *22nd Century Woman*. She had been doing little else for weeks. However, the magazine's innumerable love stories and sex-charged articles failed to trigger even a shred of romanticism in her thoughts. The part of her mind that excited her passions had withered, and even *22nd Century Woman* had so far failed to resuscitate it.

She had endeavoured to call Dave. Not once, but hundreds, no, thousands of times she had tried to call. Every time she was unsuccessful. The man of her dreams had disappeared from her life.

Following her initial nerve-wracked attempt to call, Alexandra repeated her effort - accompanied by a similar serving of self-doubt - about an hour later. However, Dave's telephone was busy again. Over the rest of the afternoon, she made many impromptu attempts to contact Dave, but curiously his line was busy every time. As Alexandra's frustration increased, so did the frequency of her calls, and by the day's end she was ringing every fifteen minutes. However, each call was as unsuccessful as was its predecessor.

Immediately upon waking the next day, before breakfast, after breakfast, and before settling down to study for the morning, she again dialled Dave's number. These efforts represented four calls in ten minutes, but on each occasion the infernal beeping of the engaged signal repelled her. Shortly afterwards she repeated her attempts, but the monotone sentry again refused her entry into Dave's life. As the hours ticked by, her frustration escalated. No, the phone company representative told her, nothing was wrong with Dave's phone. No, the receiver had not been left off the hook; the phone was simply in constant use. So Alexandra kept trying, and the engaged signals kept coming.

Alexandra's wish to contact Dave gradually progressed - or, more correctly, deteriorated - from a desire, to a need, and then finally became a fully-fledged obsession. For a week she used every opportunity, every spare moment, to try again. It did not matter whether she dialled quickly or slowly, or whether she called during the morning, at noon, or at night, the result was always the same.

For once, Alexandra began to lose her composure. Her frustration escalated to the point where even listening to an entire playlist of Elvis Presley love songs while eating a bowl of chocolate ice cream did not ease her pain. Her ears throbbed, her fingers developed RSI, and her mind mercilessly replayed the engaged tone as she slept. The telephone assumed control over her every thought.

Then, a week later, just as she was capitulating to despair, a breakthrough. A ring! For the first time in seven days, she did not hear the engaged signal. Instead she heard the dull standardised tones of a telephone ring. To Alexandra it was not dull; it was the most wonderful sound she had ever experienced. To her, the gentle harmony of the tones, the lilting of the beat, and the sweetness of the melody all combined to create a musical piece unparalleled in its beauty. She waited in joyous anticipation for Dave to answer.

He didn't.

Despite that initial affection for the ringing sound, she rapidly grew to regard it with unbridled hatred. During the following week, that sound dominated her life. Every time she called Dave, the line remained unanswered. The situation was unexplainable, unfathomable and worse than unbearable.

At least when the busy signal had plagued her, she could hang up in an instant. The unanswered ringing was far more malicious. It kept her waiting, hanging, hoping, for minutes on end. The unanswered ringing was an evil torture of the most insidious kind.

The whole situation simply did not make sense to Alexandra. How could a person possibly be on the telephone an entire week, and then suddenly refuse to answer it at all? Where was Dave? What was going on? She could think of only one way to find out. She took a few deep breaths, wiped her tears, and, following Einstein55's directions, she walked determinedly toward Dave's place.

Alexandra was just beginning to climb the steps to Dave's apartment when she was stopped, physically stopped, by two forces. One force was a smell, which was so powerful it could have stopped a charging elephant. The other force came from an arm, which gently halted her progress up the stairs. The arm came from a body that was wearing a police uniform and a gas mask, which appeared from Dave's apartment as she approached his front door.

"Hine horry, oo ant go in der," the policeman from under the mask.

"Pardon?"

"I'm sorry, you can't go in there," said the constable after lifting his mask just far enough away from his face so that his lips could move properly.

"What's wrong?" asked Alexandra nervously, stepping backwards a few paces to lessen the pungency of the odour.

"There's been trouble in this apartment."

"Trouble? What sort of trouble?"

"We suspect foul play."

"Foul play?"

"We're not sure of too many details just yet, young lady. It appears that the young man may have been kidnapped. Whoever it was has also trashed the apartment, at least a few months ago judging by the disgusting state we found it in."

"But that's impossible," protested Alexandra. "He was on the telephone only two weeks ago. I've been trying to call him."

Alexandra attempted to explain her situation. She revealed how she and Dave had met, how she had tried to call, and how she could not make contact as his telephone had been in continuous use for two weeks. She felt exceedingly foolish as she tried to explain how Dave had suddenly stopped using his phone and disappeared.

"I'm sorry, ma'am, but that is simply impossible," replied the policeman after he had listened to her tale. "There is no way that someone could have survived living in such filthy conditions'"

"But, but..."

"Thank you for concern," the policeman interjected, "but I think you'd best leave this to the experts. Good day."

He signified the visit was over by talking some officious sounding instructions into his smart watch. Ignoring the vile smell, Alexandra tried to climb the last few stairs to see for herself, but the constable would not allow it. The more she pleaded with him, the more authoritarian he became. Eventually, under threat of arrest, she was forced to submit. She trudged off, completely dejected. She had played her last card, and lost. She knew, both emotionally and logically, that she would never see Dave again.

Chapter 20

Old Mr Smiggins howled a blood-curdling scream. Then he stood tall, puffed out his chest, crowed loudly, and continued performing his strange dance. He romped around the perimeter of the room, chanting a mantra with each step, and flailing his head in random directions. Periodically he would stop, repeat the scream-and-crow routine, and then continue his dance in ever decreasing circles. Fearsome war paint made from chocolate sauce striped his cheeks, and crazy hatred glowed in his eyes. He carried an antique telephone directory in his hands.

Dave lay on his side in the centre of the room, feeling decidedly awful. His head throbbed with its most serious headache for at least a week - or perhaps even longer. Yes, Dave decided on reflection, this was the worst headache he had accommodated since the fateful morning of the missed interview, now almost a month ago. However, despite being completely sober the previous evening, Dave was not at all surprised that he had a headache. He surmised that it had something to do with the rapidly growing pile of telephone books that was balancing on the side of his head. The thick, heavy directories - which hadn't been used by anyone since the turn of the century but were still nonetheless reliably printed every year - now numbered about two dozen, with a crazed Old Mr Smiggins adding to their number each time he circled the room.

Old Mr Smiggins became even more bizarre. He leapt around Dave in even tighter circles, chanting at a faster and faster rate. Every time he added another book to the pile, Dave's headache spiralled into new paroxysms of pain.

"Please, please, please stop," begged Dave. "My headache is killing me."

Old Mr Smiggins obviously did not hear the plea, because he simply kept dancing, chanting, and tossing telephone directories onto Dave's head. Just as Dave thought that he could take it no longer, he spied out of the corner of his unsquashed eye something that gave him an overwhelming feeling of relief. In the doorway, sitting patiently on its back legs, was a large adult African bull elephant.

Just as I suspected, thought Dave.

The elephant peered at Dave through a glinting eye. Raising its trunk, the elephant pointed it directly at Dave's face, and unleashed a torrent of water. The liquid hit Dave in all the wrong places. Most of it went up his nose, the rest in his mouth. A splash even managed to find its way into his left ear, despite the weight of dozens of telephone directories pressing down upon it. Dave coughed, spluttered and choked as he fought for breath. He felt, quite rightly, that things could not really get any stranger. Wrong. Old Mr Smiggins suddenly produced, from nowhere, a wet fish. He tossed it to the elephant, which gratefully accepted it and gobbled it down through its trunk.

Yuk, thought Dave. *Imagine eating a fish through your nose.* An instant later, the elephant sneezed. The fish flew through the air and swatted Dave directly on the left cheek. He tried to move his head but the weight of the books had pinned it to the floor. Then the fish began to kick and flip around, slapping Dave across the cheek each time it did. In the background, over the roar of his headache, he could hear Old Mr Smiggins yelling at him. The words, distant at first, became progressively clearer.

"Bakers cup ... fade luck ... chafe butt ... fake tough ... waves up ... wake up ... wake up ... wake up...."

With a final blast of water from the elephant, and another slap in the face from the wet kipper, Dave did exactly that: he woke up.

"Just a dream..." murmured Dave as he drifted back to consciousness, "... it had me fooled until I saw the elephant."

Dave opened his eyes just in time to cop another face full of water, not from an elephant's trunk but from a glass. The wet kipper transformed into a clammy palm, which was gently slapping Dave rhythmically on each cheek. Old Mr Smiggins' facial features faded and were replaced by those of a younger man. Unfortunately, the headache stayed at the same level.

"Oooaaaahhhh," wailed Dave. "My head."

"Would you like some painkillers?" asked the young man sheepishly. "I'll get you some painkillers."

As the man hurried off, Dave's eyes slowly focused on an unfamiliar room: it was sparsely decorated, with flat, featureless grey walls, but was clearly very technologically advanced.

How did I get here? he wondered. What am I doing here? When did I arrive? Where am I? Why am I here? Dave realised with a sense of pride that he had just analysed the situation in the exact manner espoused for essay writing by his junior high school English teacher: the how-what-when-where-why system. His analysis did not, despite its rhetorical correctness, provide him with any answers. His head contained only vague memories of telephone books, a yearning for Alexandra, and four types of serious pain, none of them pleasant.

He yawned, adjusted his scrotum, and then, to fully complete his wake-up routine, he scratched his head. It was then that he discovered why he had a headache. On the back of his skull was a massive bruise, swollen to the size of a Virtual Snooker ball: Biff and Duke's calling card.

"Here, take this."

The young man had returned to the room, and was holding a large green pill on his outstretched palm. Dave remembered his childhood, when his mother had constantly drilled him about the dangers of taking drugs from strangers. However he was in no position to argue with this particular stranger, so he swallowed the tablet. Instantly, the pain began to subside. He also accepted an ice pack from the young man, which almost immediately made his head ache again. He tossed the pack aside, accidentally spilling the ice onto the floor.

"What a waste," said Dave. "All that ice and we haven't even got any beer to cool."

"Would you like one?" asked the man.

"Er, ah, yes. Why not?" said Dave, hesitating only to give himself time to disregard his father's innumerable childhood warnings about not accepting drinks from strangers.

"What brand would you prefer?" questioned the man as he headed out of the room.

"I only drink Neptune Gold," replied Dave with a grin, knowing that no one could afford to buy that brand of beer to keep at home. The young man returned seconds later, carrying an *entire carton* of Neptune Gold. Dave's jaw dropped at the sight. Even the gold-trimmed diamond-encrusted titanium-fibre packaging would have cost more than Dave would earn in his lifetime.

"I bought a few extras, just in case you were thirsty."

Dave was too flabbergasted to reply.

"By the way, my name is Hopgood," said the young man as he passed over a beer.

"My - name - is - Dave," he said between gulps. "Would you mind telling me," he added as he gleefully opened his second beer, "what is going on?"

*

"Sir, the Australian man has awakened."

"Good," barked Morgan. "Bring him in."

Hopgood returned soon afterwards with Dave, who was clutching the remaining half-carton of beer preciously to his chest, following dutifully behind him. Dave looked with amazement at the vast array of technological gadgetry that filled the office.

"So you like beer?" questioned Morgan by way of introduction.

Dave loved beer more than he could begin to describe. Temporarily at loss for a powerful enough reply, he simply nodded.

"Then you like football as well," said Morgan, automatically associating beer drinking with football watching.

"Uh-huh."

"If you could meet any person in the entire world this evening, who would it be?" asked Morgan, expecting the obvious response.

Dave didn't stop to think.

"Alexandra."

"Who the hell is *Alexandra*?"

"She is this lovely girl that I met at the pub the other night. I reckon she is just wonderful, but her number was...."

"Enough!" interrupted Morgan. "If I wanted to hear about this 'Alexandra' then I would have asked. So tell me, who else would you like to meet, besides her?"

Again, Dave's answer was automatic.

"Elvis Presley."

"Elvis Presley?" scorned Morgan. "Who the hell is Elvis Presley?"

"The King of Rock'n'Roll. The greatest of all entertainers. An all time legend," said Dave, doing a fine impersonation of Elvis's southern-twanged accent.

"Didn't he die back in the 1970s?" asked Morgan, vaguely recalling the name from his youth.

"That is what some people will tell you," said Dave, still impeccably in character, "but I know I'm still alive. There's a new book out which proves that I faked my own death, and I...."

"Spare me the detail," interrupted Morgan. "Even if he was still alive, I'm sure that Mr Elvis has other plans this evening. So I'm going to ask the question again. If you could meet any person in the world this evening, *except* Alexandra and Elvis Presley, who would it be?"

"In that case," considered Dave, reverting to his own voice, "it would undoubtedly be Juan Manuel de la Espirito. But..." Dave said gently as his voiced trailed away, "...I know that's not possible either."

"Well," drawled Morgan as he sighed with relief. "This should all come as a very pleasant surprise."

Morgan went on to explain all that he wanted Dave to know about the 'Date with God' competition. After a lecture lasting about three bottles, during which he had whooped and hollered with unabashed joy, Dave had a rudimentary understanding of the situation. Morgan had, for some vaguely explained reason, arranged for him to *probably* win the 'Date with God' competition. If he won, Morgan would give him a special cap, which would secretly record his meeting with the legend. Morgan gravely warned Dave that God's security would check his eyes to confiscate his Life-Movie contact lenses, at which Dave simply shrugged. They were still sitting in his bathroom cabinet anyway. (He would synchronise them properly as soon as he had a chance.)

Morgan also suggested some questions - some very probing, private questions – for Dave to ask the great footballer during their time together. However, Morgan had stressed that Dave was not to let either God, or that evil HHTV president Harry Hieshler, discover that he was recording their meeting. Simple. Morgan finished his instructions.

"That is all," Morgan said as he stood to leave, "unless you have any further queries?"

"Just one," said Dave after a long pause. "Are you aware that safari suits are out of fashion?"

*

It was 12.30 pm - smack in the middle of the lunchtime traffic period, which stretched from 10 am until 3 pm. The lunchtime peak was of course preceded by the morning peak from 5 am until 10 am, and followed by the afternoon peak from 3 pm until 9 pm.

Usually at this (or any other) hour, the streets and airlanes were jammed. Progress was typically very slow, despite the modern four-wide-by-three-high lane configuration. Usually the only way to travel anywhere with reasonable speed was to find an ambulance, and speed along in its wake as the traffic moved out of its way. However, the traffic was not slow today. Dave and Morgan sat in the back of the hover-limousine, zooming along without even having to change levels.

Morgan knew the reason why the streets were so empty, and he didn't like it. Hieshler's successes grated him like nothing else. His anxiety showed in obvious ways: his shoulders hunched so tightly that his collarbones almost dislocated, and his gnashing teeth ensured that his dentist would one day retire to the Bahamas as a result of this trip alone. Dave sat next to him, steadily emptying the carton of Neptune Gold, oblivious to the fact that over ten billion people were presently jostling for position in front of their STOVE-TV sets or tuning into the broadcast on their smart watches. Hieshler would draw the winner of the 'Date with God' competition in just under half an hour.

They quickly arrived at their destination: a small, unobtrusive apartment in a well-to-do part of town. Morgan led Dave into the room, which was furnished very simply. Included among the basic fittings was a simple STOVE-TV unit, a red turn-of-the-century telephone and two armchairs.

"Hopgood has finally done something right," mused Morgan, "so sacking him will be even more fulfilling if I lose."

Dave immediately and erroneously claimed the larger of the two armchairs, and settled in to make some more progress through the carton. He had set himself a mission of drinking the carton's entire contents before dinner, and knew that finishing another six-pack before three o'clock was vital to maintaining an even pace. Morgan placed the special cap carefully on top of the STOVE-TV. His engineers had embedded a minuscule video camera and microphone into the very fibre of the cap so they were essentially undetectable. He hoped that the cap would soon be recording the most sought after interview in the history of journalism.

Morgan paced nervously around the room, aware that his entire fortune rested on the outcome of the next few minutes. Begrudgingly overriding his aversion to watching HHTV, his nervous apprehension compelled him to watch the STOVE-TV feed of the prize drawing. He tipped Dave out of the large armchair, sat, and barked out a set of instructions.

"STOVE-TV on."

A test pattern flickered into life. The difficult part for Morgan's ego would be instructing the STOVE to change to his rival's station. The letters did not flow from his lips very smoothly.

"Switch to channel ... hay ... ah ... hay ... er ... hay ... haitch...."

A voice emanating from the STOVE-TV unit interrupted Morgan's command.

"Channel A.R.A.R.A.H not recognised. Please confirm channel selection."

The STOVE-TV receiver had misinterpreted his stuttering. Morgan tried to repeat his message.

"Channel hay ... hay ... haitch ... hay ... haitch ... tee...."

"Channel A.A.H.A.H.T. not recognised. Please reconfirm channel selection."

Morgan tried again, fighting his instincts as if they were diseases.

"Channel haitch haitch ... tee...." Morgan took a deep breath, unable to bring himself to utter the last syllable.

"Vee!" chimed Dave, helping Morgan even though he already did not like him. The STOVE switched to HHTV#1, just in time for a close-up of the immaculately groomed face of its president to appear in front of Morgan and Dave. The sight of Hieshler's face was almost more than Morgan's ego could tolerate. Every sinew in his rotund form cried at him to leave, or change feed, or do anything other than confront Hieshler's vain, conceited face directly in front of him. He took some ineffectual swinging punches at the virtual face, but nonetheless he stayed in his seat, torn between two conflicting forces. The only thing worse than watching Hieshler's face would have been not knowing what was happening to his empire. Hieshler's face spoke.

"Laaaaadieees and gentlemen."

He sounded more like a circus ringmaster than a program host.

"Good afternoon and welcome to HHTV. Today we're broadcasting live from our headquarters, Hieshler Towers. What a wonderful occasion it is. In just a few minutes time, we'll be drawing the winner of our latest and greatest competition."

The assembled crowd, each carrying or wearing a phone of some sort, hummed excitedly. Every member of the gathered throng knew exactly what the prize was, and buzzed with a frenzy of anticipation.

"Yes, that's right, good people. One lucky viewer of HHTV is about to win an evening with...."

Nobody heard Hieshler finish his sentence. The buzz of the crowd erupted into wild cheering, drowning his amplified voice. The women screamed, the men yahooed, and the children yelled and sang as even the unspoken name of their hero generated uncontainable anticipation. Their nervous tension now unleashed, the crowd became increasingly excited, and the festive mood grew more frenzied as the moment drew near. The size of the already massive congregation swelled by the minute, as the cries for God began to amplify through the streets.

Hieshler allowed the crowd to continue their clamouring. He was in no hurry, and was enjoying his moment of triumph. After about five minutes the din had slightly diminished, so he yelled over the noise as he continued his introductions.

"That's right, wonderful viewers. The magnificent Juan Carlos Manuel de la Espirito will accompany one lucky person for not just one minute, not just one hour, but for an entire evening!"

Attending paramedics quickly moved in to collect and revive those who had fainted at the thought. Fireworks exploded overhead, and a trumpet fanfare heralded Hieshler's next announcement. The winner was about to be selected.

As the word steadily filtered back through the assembly that the drawing was imminent, a hushed buzz steadily replaced the pandemonium. Then, as Hieshler moved to the HHTV computer to officially select the winner, silence replaced that hum - silence on a global scale. Almost every human being on the planet became quiet. All eyes were focused and unblinking and all ears were strained and taut as the planet's populace waited in suspense.

"Now the moment you've all been waiting for."

Hieshler pressed a ceremonial button, starting a computer application. Scrolling at light speed through the billions of entries, the curser stopped on a random entry: the lucky winning number.

"The computer has just drawn a phone number from our trillions of entries. That lucky number is...."

The moment arrived. Hieshler announced the first digit of the winning number as he ceremoniously dialled it on a giant keypad.

"Six."

Suddenly, for 90 percent of contestants, it was all over. If their telephone number did not begin with a six, they hadn't won - it was as simple as that. They had wasted months in front of the STOVE-TV screen. They had abandoned friendships, lost jobs and broken marriages, yet for 90% of the entrants it was already all for nothing. Cries of despair echoed across the globe, and more people simultaneously contemplated suicide than on a lemming summer vacation.

Morgan smiled crookedly. He was still in the running.

Hieshler called the remaining digits slowly, pausing between each announcement, milking the occasion for all it was worth.

"Eight."

Ninety percent of the remaining 10% of entries were suddenly eliminated. Most of these people were soon too depressed or too numb to make much noise. However, those lucky few million people whose telephone number began with the digits 'six-eight' wouldn't have moved if a firecracker had exploded in their underwear. They were too focused on Hieshler's voice to have noticed.

"One."

This figure eliminated another nine-tenths of the survivors. Meanwhile, Morgan's smile stayed put. Three digits correct, seven to go.

As Hieshler called each new digit, many people despaired, while fewer and fewer cheered with ever increasing exuberance. After he called the second last digit, ninety people were eliminated. Those people simultaneously contracted a very rare depressive illness which doctors would later label '*Almost with God* Syndrome' in psychiatric textbooks.

A mere ten people now remained standing on the precipice of the opportunity of a lifetime. Morgan was still hunching his shoulders, still sweating and still grinding his teeth, but he also wore an unmistakable hint of a victory smile. One more digit - just one! He now had *at worst* a one-in-ten chance that he would win that prize. One further correct number and he would again be the most powerful person on the planet, able to destroy whatever he wanted, whenever he wanted to. One more digit!

Dave began leaping about the room in an unrestrained display of glee. He was whooping with such gaiety that he didn't notice that he was spilling his beer, which he usually equated with homicide on his list of evils. Although drunk with both alcohol and emotion, Dave was lucid enough to know that he was one correct number away from meeting one of his, and everybody else's, heroes.

Hieshler paused as his finger hovered agonisingly over the telephone touch pad.

"And the final number is...."

Dave looked at Morgan. Morgan looked at Dave. They both looked at Hieshler's virtual face in front of them. They both looked at the telephone. Then they looked at each other again, and then at the telephone again.

It rang. "I think that's for you, Dave."

Chapter 21

Wanting to avoid being linked in any way to Dave's win, Morgan vacated the building immediately. This proved to be a wise decision as the paparazzi arrived within minutes. The small downtown apartment was soon the focus of the worlds' media, and the star of the moment was definitely Dave. Lights blared in his eyes and microphones were shoved towards his face as reporters of all nationalities clamoured for a story.

"What's your name, Sir?" asked a journalist.

Dave gave his name, hoping that all the questions remained as easy.

"How many entries did you make?"

This was not so simple. Dave hesitated, unsure on how to reply. Morgan had not coached him on any of this.

"Several," he finally settled on.

"Several?"

"Er ... probably a few more than several."

"A few more? Than several?"

"Well, I suppose I might have made a couple less than a few more than several," replied Dave, not sure whether he was clarifying his answer or making it more confusing.

The reporters eventually desisted with that line of questioning, so Dave could cease covering his original lie. But the assembled media mass still needed a story focus, so the inquisition continued.

"Do you work?"

"No."

"Have you ever worked?"

"No."

"Are you married?"

"No."

"A girlfriend?"

After a painful pause, Dave answered truthfully.

"No."

"Are you homosexual?"

"No."

"Any ambitions in life?"

"Not really."

"Family?"

"Just parents."

"Are they famous?"

"No."

As the interview continued in this fashion, the reporters became impatient. Most of them had deadlines to meet for the 24-hour news cycle that were only minutes away, and so far didn't have even a hint of an angle for their respective stories. Then, just as their impatience was developing into aggressive panic, an opportunity arose. Spying the empty bottles of Neptune Gold, a tall journalist with a British accent asked a pivotal question.

"Do you like beer?"

"Yes."

A breakthrough! A positive answer. The reporters' minds collectively whirred, attempting to expand that answer into an entire story. It took only one follow-up question to give them a headline.

"So what do you think that you will do on your evening with God?"

"Well," considered Dave, "I suppose we'll just have a few quiet beers."

That was it. Good enough. Every program that hit the news feeds that afternoon carried the same headline:

"Dave to have a Few Quiet Beers with God"

After some more intrusive photographs, rude questions, and further general interrogation about his personal life, Dave was mercifully left alone to prepare for his big moment. As he showered, his first for quite a while, he noticed some flesh-coloured tape around his left ankle. Where had that come from? As he began to tear it off, he removed not only a few dozen ankle hairs, but the mystery as well. A small, lime green tip was the first thing he noticed, followed by a hint of blue and silver; it was the pen that he had taped on his shin many weeks ago when he had first set out to look for Alexandra. The memory quickly became more painful than the ripping of the tape, so Dave, deciding that one type of agony was enough, left the pen in place.

After scrubbing himself scrupulously clean, he washed his lucky shirt in the bathroom sink. Then he hung his lucky charm on a towel rail, and sat on the bidet as he waited for it to dry. This was the first occasion that he had been alone with his thoughts for a long time. Although clouded by his abandoned attempt to drink a carton of Neptune Gold in a day, his mind was still functioning with reasonable coherency. Excited as he was by the prospect of meeting God, he wished, not for the first time, that Alexandra were with him to share the emotion.

Chapter 22

Alexandra was pleased with her progress. The psychiatric therapy software she had downloaded had been very helpful: she had just survived a full hour without thinking about Dave. Apart from the obvious paradoxical moments where she had congratulated herself for not thinking about Dave, she had not given him even a moment's reflection.

After the police fiasco, Alexandra had decided that her relationship with Dave was over - officially - although she was aware that she had no choice in the matter. She decided that the best thing to do was to wash Dave completely out of her life: she would not try to find him; she refused to fret about what might have been; no longer would she even *think* about him. So far, her progress had been satisfactory.

Suddenly it became inexplicably difficult for her to maintain control of her thoughts. She sat on a bus, hovering along the uppermost transit layer of the freeway, trying desperately to not think of Dave. But somehow, his presence seemed to be all around her. Everywhere she looked, she saw his face, and every direction she turned she heard his name. Was this a new psychiatric condition?

Alexandra didn't take long to discover why she was having this relapse: Dave's face *was* everywhere she looked - magazine shows, news feeds, billboards. His virtual image was actually standing in front of her courtesy of the bus's STOVE-TV projection. Dave's name *was* being talked about by almost everyone. Dave, *the* Dave, the winner of the competition, was *her* Dave. HER Dave. She had found him!

After weeks of effort, just as all seemed lost, fate had intervened. Perhaps Dave's theory about his lucky shirt was right after all. Her earlier vow to forget about her beloved was quickly washed away by a flood of eagerness and excitement.

Anticipation had opened the door to Alexandra's mind, allowing self-doubt to again stroll unchallenged through the portals. What if Dave didn't want to see her? After all, he was about to spend the evening with the greatest sports star in the history of the galaxy. Perhaps Dave had other things on his mind? Maybe he had never liked her at all?

Alexandra, in her usual positive fashion, decided that there were only two possible ways to solve her dilemma. First, she checked the horoscope section in the most recent edition of *"22nd Century Woman."* Although she was pleased to discover that she was again likely to lose weight this week, she did not see any inferences to Dave. Alexandra quickly moved to her second option. Half an hour later she was standing on a queue for an USA-bound Horizontal Displacement Unit.

Eventually she reached the front of the line, and without hesitation stepped onto the slowly moving conveyor belt. Thankfully, the lane to her right was empty so she stepped across onto the next conveyor, which was moving at twice the speed of the original. After checking behind her she stepped right again onto an even faster belt, and was now travelling at running speed.

Alexandra, like most people on the H.D.U., usually took her time to step laterally from one conveyor belt to the next. Each belt moved 10 or 15 km/h faster than its neighbour, so it took only 80 or so steps to the right until you arrived at the inside lane, which rotated at a spritely 1000 km/hour. But Alexandra was in such a hurry to get to the USA that she bounded like a wounded giraffe from one conveyor to the next, falling often, and apologising profusely as she dodged the upcoming traffic from behind.

By midnight she was approaching the USA, but stayed in the fast lane until the last second before bounding unceremoniously across the slower lanes, just managing to step off onto the platform at the very farthest end of the station.

Thankful for the abolition of customs and immigration procedures a decade previously, she immediately used Einstein55 to summon a hover-taxi. She jumped in, and with minimal use of pleasantries she instructed it to head for Hieshler Towers. She even opted to pay three speeding fines in advance to shorten the trip.

Chapter 23

Dave was definitely the centre of attention. As he sat nonchalantly on a velvet throne and gulped the last tad of beer from his goblet, he motioned to one of the gorgeous waitresses for a refill. Despite pouring carefully, she lost her balance and accidentally spilt some beer on Dave. Horrified at her mistake, she began apologising profusely.

"Not to worry, love," replied Dave casually. "It's free."

Ordinarily the waitress would not have lost her balance while pouring beer. On this occasion she was unsteady because she was unaccustomed to serving drinks while standing on the roof of a moving vehicle. Dave's throne was atop a very impressive limousine, which was slowly hovering its way through the throng of people, heading toward Hieshler Towers.

Dave waved casually to the crowd as the limousine floated slowly forward. People had come in their thousands to join in the festivities that accompanied this very rare public appearance by God. From his high vantage point, Dave could see Hieshler Towers in the distance. Harry Hieshler himself was standing atop the marble and gold staircase, waiting to receive him for the prize giving ceremony.

*

Morgan was not enjoying his afternoon at all. Things were not going smoothly. Deciding that he would like to attend Hieshler's 'execution' as he was now mentally referring to it, Morgan had made a considerable effort to disguise his appearance. He did not want Hieshler to know that he was attending, as his mere presence may have aroused suspicion that he was the mastermind behind Dave's victory.

Morgan detested his disguise. He had opted for a full length navy blue double-breasted suit, which was heavy and tiresomely hot. Long sleeves and trousers just didn't allow a comfortable freedom of movement like a Safari Suit did. Morgan had also removed his toupee, rendering his balding crown liable to sunburn. To complete his disguise, he had used a burnt cork to create an artificial beard and moustache, which was now smudging as he sweated in the heat.

As Morgan pushed through the swelling crowd, he spied Dave sitting atop the limousine in the distance. As he nudged closer, he began to sense that something was wrong. Then, as Dave came clearly into focus, Morgan realised his worst fears. The big man screamed in emotional pain, stamped his feet on the ground, and tore imaginary hair from his scalp. Then he screamed again, and found a few strands of real hair to tear out. Then he *really* threw a tantrum.

Dave had forgotten to wear the cap.

Morgan crashed back to reality. He barged back through the flowing tide of humanity, waddling as fast as his overweight frame would carry him towards the downtown apartment. He had to get that cap back on Dave's head, or his whole empire was doomed.

*

Alexandra milled patiently along with the crowd. Everything still seemed unbelievable, although certain parts of the mystery - such as why Dave had not answered his telephone for weeks - were perhaps a little clearer. However, she still couldn't fathom how his apartment could possibly have become so filthy, especially as Dave had told her that he was generally a neat and tidy person.

Nevertheless she was still very excited to be seeing Dave again, and was finding it difficult to be patient in the slowly moving congregation. She felt as if she was trying to drive somewhere urgently, but every car in front of her was driven by a little old lady wearing a lawn-bowling hat.

Suddenly a fat, bald, unshaven man in a navy suit pushed past her, heading in the other direction. Apart from registering that he was very rude, Alexandra thought little more of him. If she had known that he was the man who had almost ruined her life, it is doubtful he would have survived the explosion of Alexandra's anger - anger that only dialling to an unanswered telephone for a week can foster.

However she simply ignored him, and continued patiently threading her way through the crowd. Soon, she too had Hieshler Towers in her sights.

*

Morgan burst through the apartment door. He saw the cap innocently sitting on top of the television, exactly where he had left it. Without so much as pausing for breath he crashed across the room, grabbed the cap, bounced himself off the far wall and rebounded out the way he had come in. Then he trotted double-time back to town and was soon bulldozing his way through the crowd near Hieshler Towers, this time with a triple helping of his usual rudeness and impatience.

*

Alexandra was emotionally and physically exhausted. After milling patiently for hours, the surging of the crowd had come to a halt. Her progress had stopped. At first she had gently attempted to push her way through, but with no measurable effect. Petite body frames like hers were simply not built for barging. Then she had tried dozens of excuses and persuasions to be permitted ahead, but had not succeeded with that method either. Even telling the truth had been a waste of time. For the last half an hour she had not moved a centimetre, and she was beginning to despair. It seemed that the closer she got to Dave, the harder it was to reach him.

Then fate intervened again.

Something was causing a commotion in the crowd behind her. She turned to see a fat, balding, unshaven man propelling his way through the pack like a jackhammer through jelly. Alexandra was about to intercept him and unleash a piece of her irritated mind onto him when she was struck by a more profitable idea.

She recalled being stuck in innumerable air-traffic jams. The only way of getting through the really big stoppages was to tuck into the wake of an ambulance and follow it closely as the traffic parted to allow it through. The crowd was not exactly parting for the fat man, but he *was* making good progress. So with only a tiny hint of guilt, Alexandra slid into the man's wake, and followed him closely as he forged a tunnel towards the stage.

Chapter 24

Dave's limousine stopped at the foot of the staircase of Hieshler Towers. Four lackeys appeared and lowered him, still sitting resplendently on his throne, to the ground. They moved with such precision that they did not spill a drop of his precious amber fluid. Then they helped Dave to his feet, where his favourite fantasy model, Honeydew Melons, greeted him with a kiss. She then took him by the arm, and gracefully led him up the stairway toward a raised platform where Hieshler was waiting.

Dave's head swam with more indecision than the night at Stranglers when he had won the virtual-snooker championship after betting on his opponent. He was definitely enjoying himself, but something did not seem right. Sure, he was having fun ... but free Neptune Gold, a kiss from Honeydew Melons, a meeting with God ... he should be *dying* from happiness. Yes, Dave decided, if ever anyone was in danger of dying from happiness, this should have been it. Yet he was simply just having a *great* time - nothing more, nothing less. Something was missing.

Dave and his voluptuous escort soon reached the top of the stairs. From there they ascended further onto a makeshift platform, where Hieshler was droning through a rambling speech.

"... and the wonderful world of big cat racing ... "

"Blah blah blah," mumbled Dave to himself.

Dave's mind was having difficulty coping with so much input. His thoughts became blurred as he gazed out across the massive crowd, which stretched into the distance as far as his bloodshot eyes could see. He found himself absently focusing on various parts of the crowd, trying to discern what was happening below.

A baby was crying because its mother was inadvertently holding it upside-down.

" ... I am dedicated to the spirit of this great nation ..." Hieshler continued.

"Blah blah blah."

A tall lady had just discovered that her pantyhose had caught her skirt when she had dressed that morning.

"... and I have strong community values ..." said Hieshler.

"Blah blah blah."

A balding fat unshaven man was pushing his way up the stairs.

"... *indebted to all of my loyal viewers ...*"

"Blah blah blah."

The fat balding man was getting closer. He was madly waving a cap about, and was yelling in Dave's direction.

"... *please give a huge welcome to our special guest, GOD!*"

"Blah blah ... what?!"

A massive explosion of human sound blew away all of Dave's distracted thoughts. Millions of people, not just those present but on all surfaces of the globe, broke into spontaneous screams of adulation. Almost all of humanity vented the fullest capacity of their lungs in a cheer, a whistle, or an excited yowl, while others beat on drums or blasted horns. It was the most frenzied, exuberant, over-the-top cheer ever bestowed upon one person.

The noise quickly transformed into the most thunderous, awe-inspiring chant imaginable. The beat was so forceful that meteorologists measured it at 6.2 on the Richter scale. Its message could not possibly be mistaken.

"WE WANT GOD - WE WANT GOD"
"WE WANT GOD - WE WANT GOD"
"WE WANT GOD - WE WANT GOD"

The deafening cry continued for minutes, as those present beseeched their hero to appear. The chant's intensity surged periodically, but each time it began to wane the crowd responded by amplifying the beat even louder than previously.

Dave was awestruck. Just as he thought that the congregation could not possibly roar any more powerfully, the volume would jump another notch. The beat was so forceful that it cracked windows in nearby buildings, knocked kitchenware off distant shelves, and shook the very foundations of Hieshler Towers.

Finally, after five minutes of thunderous chanting, God appeared on stage.

The volume doubled.

As the world literally shook, Dave stood directly on its metaphorical centre. He watched in awe as God sauntered and strutted around the stage, waving to his adoring public. As the superstar was flexing his biceps, Dave became aware that the fat man had crashed his way up to the platform. It was Morgan.

Damn.

He had the cap.

Damn!

Dave had forgotten to wear the cap. Morgan had asked him to follow one simple instruction - to wear the special cap that would record the interview – and, like most other undertakings in his life, he had failed. Even though Dave felt that Morgan was an arrogant, power-obsessed pig of a man, he felt that he owed him as much. After all, he had just gifted him an entire evening with one of his heroes, not to mention 19 bottles of Neptune Gold. The least he could have done was remember to wear the cap.

Dave had to make amends. If he could just sneak far enough across to the edge of the stage....

Surreptitiously he edged towards the corner of the platform where Morgan was gesticulating wildly. But just when Dave was almost near enough to grab the cap, his mission was interrupted. Hieshler grabbed him by the hand, shaking it vigorously. Photo time.

Bugger, thought Morgan, before repeating this sentiment vocally three times with ever increasing volume.

"I've got to get this cap on that idiots head," he growled, "or my life is ruined."

While Hieshler posed with God, each magnanimously shaking one of Dave's hands for the cameras, Morgan clamoured awkwardly onto the stage. With all the stealth that his large frame could muster, he stole across the platform behind the assembled reporters. Leaning across from the edge of the media pack, he reached over towards Dave. Stretching so far that he almost overbalanced, he managed to pull the cap onto Dave's head, and attempted to tug it downwards to ensure it was firmly in place.

Dave's mind whirred. The crowd was chanting deafeningly for God. God was shaking one of his hands, while Hieshler was shaking the other, and Morgan was pulling the cap down onto his head. The stress was overwhelming. This barrage of activity was too much for an uncomplicated man like him to handle. He began to wish that he were back in his apartment, sharing a simple beer with Alexandra as they sang their way through Elvis's entire catalogue.

Suddenly, he heard a sweet voice calling his name above the roar.

No, it couldn't be.

As he turned to look in the direction of the voice, Dave realised his most wonderful hopes.

It was *her*.

It *was* her.

Their eyes met. Wow! They felt an explosion of love, unparalleled since Adam first set eyes on Eve. Bilateral, equilateral, unequivocal, love. As Alexandra's whole body smiled back at Dave, he realised that he was a contented man: he had found, and bestowed through a fleeting glance, love. He had never been happier.

Suddenly, from nowhere, a blinding flash of whiteness scorched across the stage. It was more powerful than lightening, and mightier than a thunderclap. Then, almost instantly, soothing calm returned. Nobody was injured, not even scratched.

Except Morgan, Hieshler and God, whose smouldering corpses lay twisted on the stage.

And Dave, who had disappeared without a trace.

PART TWO

Chapter 25

... Blackness

... Nothingness

... An eternity of emptiness....

Then, suddenly, there was an infinitely massive explosion.

From nowhere materialised a mysterious object that defied definition or description. It was not flat, but nor could it be held. It was neither black nor transparent, yet it was not any particular colour. Yet despite its apparent insignificance, this object was extremely important. It was a proton, a subatomic particle – one of the building blocks from which all other matter is constructed. This particular proton would ultimately form a vital element in our story.

This proton whizzed off into the empty infinity, eventually ending up in a newly formed star. Another proton, which was travelling inconceivably quickly through the same infinitely large space, had an impossibly unlikely collision with it. Yet instead of obliterating each other, the two particles simply stuck together, and, with the help of some passing light rays, they formed a helium atom.

Roughly ten billion years later (give or take a few billion years) the star became incredibly hot, forcing the atom into an otherwise impossible collision with two other helium atoms, forcing them together to become carbon. Then the star exploded, sending that tiny carbon atom flying across space. Very soon after that, less than a few million years later, it landed in some water on a distant planet.

Then the tiny piece of carbon joined lots of other similar atoms. The conglomeration formed bizarre shapes that resembled microscopic worms. Then, something truly amazing occurred: the worms began to divide and join up with other pieces of carbon, essentially reproducing themselves. *They were alive.* Billions of chains of carbon-based worms proliferated, and although they were still really, really, really tiny, the worm chains were so important that they had a big name: *deoxyribonucleic acid* - DNA.

One evening, about 4,000,000,023 years later, a sudden incident interrupted the pleasant, humming universe of the DNA strand that contained our original proton. A tadpole-like ship arrived and deposited a throng of spiralling DNA worms amongst the original inhabitants. The new worms began a flirting process, and before long, each had latched onto a partner, passable as a wormy embrace. A new life had been conceived.

A few days later, this DNA dance had grown so massive that it was visible to an unassisted human eye. It looked like a tiny, throbbing piece of raw liver. Nurtured in a warm, soupy environment and nestled in the soft spongy walls of its cave-like home, this piece of tissue, which we shall name Scooter, grew steadily.

Directing Scooter's growth patterns from inside, the DNA steadily transmorphed him as the months passed. They changed him into a grotesque beanlike shape, and made him sprout four limb-like tentacles. Meanwhile, one end of Scooter developed a bulb in which six hollow cavities formed, each of which developed incredibly complex sensory systems. After a couple of months, a tiny, teeny little tentacle sprouted between two of Scooter's larger tentacles. It grew only a minuscule distance before it halted its growth altogether. Scooter, it was now confirmed, was a boy.

Then Scooter slept. This strange, throbbing, alien-like creature did very little except wallow in his soupy cave, like a marshmallow in a warm cup of chocolate milk, and grow.

After nine months of this bizarre growth cycle, a terrifying incident shattered Scooter's peaceful existence. The soft walls of the cave that housed him began to collapse. Scooter instinctively fought back, programmed to resist the invasion to ensure his survival. Further and further the cave walls closed in, as Scooter flung his limbs in a hapless attempt to ward off his impending doom.

Then, just as the pressure was about to crush Scooter to a premature death, the powerful walls relented. They softened, and gently expanded to their original positions. Scooter lay still, regaining energy after his harrowing experience.

But Scooter's pulse rate had barely slowed when the next contraction began. The evil walls of the cave had a mind of their own. Attack followed retreat; aggression followed submission. The compression cycle continued unerringly, becoming more ferocious each time. The rest periods became shorter, the squeezing attacks more prolonged. Scooter was tiring.

After scores of unremitting attacks, the cavern closed down on Scooter. With a final monumental wave of pressure, the evil walls crushed him so that he could not move, or breathe, or even think to defend himself. He could not possibly survive.

Suddenly a split appeared in one wall of the cavern. It was narrow at first, but the pressure soon forced it wider. Scooter, although utterly exhausted, somehow sensed that the hole was his only chance of escape. As the walls bore down upon him, his head managed to force its way out through the slit. As the cavern collapsed, it spurted Scooter out like a dried lump of toothpaste from the tube, into the great unknown void of the universe outside.

Scooter was no longer a growing lump of tissue. He was a baby. A human newborn baby, shirt size 0000. Not only that, but Scooter now had a real name.

Dave.

*

Dave woke with a start. He felt cold, wet, and clammy, and did not like it. He wanted to feel warm and dry, and most of all he wanted a drink. Patiently, he waited ... waited ... waited, for many seconds. Why was no-one helping him? Dave took a deep breath, and then unleashed a scream at the top of his infant lungs. Soon a familiar pair of hands lifted him into the air, and a comforting sound filled his ears.

"What's the matter, boy?" said a voice. "What is the matter with my baby boy?"

As his mother lifted him from the cot, a notion synthesised itself in Dave's mind.

I want a drink, he thought. It was the first conscious decision of his young life. This was an appropriate first thought for Dave, as he would experience this notion on another 248,226 times, usually when thirsting for a beer, during the remainder of his existence.

Over the next few months, Dave quickly built upon his repertoire of thoughts. They came to include such classics as "I'm hungry", "I'm tired", and "Would somebody please turn down that opera music".

With these and many other ideas, the infant Dave began to develop the peculiarly human characteristic of *self-awareness*. He realised that he was different from, for example, his pillow, or his fish-and-seahorse mobile. Even his fluffy bear could not do some things that he could do. In short, he came to know that he was alive.

As this knowledge developed in his young mind, an unnerving realisation dawned on him. At first, it was a hazy notion, vague in every sense. Then, as Dave became more aware of his own existence, the thought grew stronger. Although its implications terrified him, eventually the thought was so clear that he could no longer deny its inherent truth. It was on his second birthday that he finally admitted the horrifying fact to himself.

I am not a baby at all. I am thirty-four years old. I am not living my life. I am watching it.

My life is flashing before my eyes.

Chapter 26

The first period of Dave's existence - when he was a proton (which, incidentally, ended up in his left earlobe) then a carbon molecule, and then a spiral of DNA - had passed through his awareness at a leisurely rate. As his foetus Scooter evolved, the pace had gradually accelerated. Now that he was an infant, the scenes from his life were positively flicking past, like a Life Movie replay stuck on fast-forward. Although Dave was still vaguely aware of each instant as it flashed through his mind, the scenes and emotions of his life began to meld into a boiling pot of fears and desires.

In a dreamlike trance, he experienced impossible combinations of feelings. He felt the happiness of a childhood Christmas, alongside the grief of losing his pet puppy, Rudolph. The welcome familiarity of the Stranglers Bar coexisted with the cold vulnerability of a job application rejection. As these feelings wove like tendrils through the fabric of his mind, Dave sensed that he was floating.

His emotional pudding thickened as scenes from his life continued to flit past at an ever faster rate. The humdrum of his apathy overwhelmed the thin satisfaction of his rare achievements, but his humorous spirit shone amongst occasional anxiety and fear. While Dave continued to ride upon this metaphysical roller coaster of his own creation, the dreamy weightlessness became a sensation that he was drifting downwards, until Dave reached the final scene stored in his memory. He experienced the agony of an excruciating physical pain, juxtaposed with an unfathomable wallop of Alexandra's love.

Dave's mind vaulted to the present. The feeling of drifting was still with him, although he now felt like he was falling. Not gently wafting like an autumn leaf in the breeze, but definitely falling. He sensed that he should wake immediately, as it might only be another instant before he splattered onto the iron-hard ground. Still, it was so pleasant, and so comfortable, to be falling; falling through harmless empty space. It was just like flying.

Wake up.

I'm falling ... flying ... just another minute.

Wake up. You have to wake up.

Just a few more seconds ... of flying ... flying....

Slowly, painfully, Dave forced open his ten-tonne eyelids, and received an instant surprise. The reason that he felt like he was falling was very simple. He was.

Or, more correctly, he was hurtling through space in a direction that he decided must be downwards. This, it was clear, was not an ordinary dream.

The void through which he was falling was not black like he had expected. The space was white - a pure, perfect white – that filled his world like air fills the sky. And although he could see nothing through its opaqueness, it felt less dense than a vacuum.

Dave sensed that his speed was increasing. He felt as though a giant magnet was attracting him, gently at first, but the nearer he got to it, the stronger it pulled. After a while, he further realised that not only was his speed increasing, but his rate of acceleration was as well. Despite failing physics, chemistry and all mathematics-based subjects at every level of his education, this did not make sense to Dave. Surely his acceleration couldn't keep accelerating? If that happened, surmised Dave, he would soon be travelling so fast that he would break the sound barrier.

Dave heard a thunder-like boom as his speed passed Mach One. He was now travelling faster than his own screams of excitement and fear. Seconds later Mach Two came and went - twice the speed of sound. Mach Three and Four occurred so close together that they were barely distinguishable, and after that Dave's acceleration was so rapid that his passing of the sound barriers became a blur, imperceptible in this great void of whiteness.

Considering that he was travelling many times faster than the swiftest hoverjet, Dave felt incredibly comfortable and coherent. The speed, and even the acceleration, seemed harmless. *If this keeps up much longer,* thought Dave, *I'll soon break the light speed barrier.* However, after a second's further thought, he reassured himself: *I've got nothing to worry about ... it's* impossible *to go faster than the speed of light ... at least I remember* that *from physics class.*

Suddenly, the space around him exploded, rupturing into a sea of impossibly dark whiteness as Dave accelerated passed the 'Mach One' of light. Seconds later there was another explosion, as another flash of infinitely dark brightness signalled that he had passed the 'Mach Two' of light.

I'm glad I didn't listen at school, thought Dave. *They had it all wrong anyhow.* He made a mental note to correct Mr Grobfister, his former physics teacher, the next time they met.

Yet Dave kept accelerating. Soon, the 'Mach' explosions of light became a strobe, which reminded Dave of a discotheque, popular back in the 2020's. Thankfully, the explosions soon became so rapid that they blurred together, becoming one continuous burst of ultra bright light.

For want of something more constructive to do, Dave tried to analyse his situation. He concluded that because he was travelling many times faster than the speed of light then he should be very safe. Nothing could catch him, not even light rays. What danger could possibly befall him out here? Satisfied that he was secure from harm - in fact he was feeling quite comfortable - Dave began to relax. He yawned, stretched, and even contemplated grabbing a quick nap.

Suddenly, without warning or fanfare, Dave reached C^2 - the speed of light squared. It was the unknowable 'Mach One' of physical existence. He smashed violently into a wall of nothingness, which stopped him more softly than a rain cloud would nestle a feather, yet more surely than a pavement stops a falling watermelon. He lapsed instantly into unconsciousness.

Chapter 27

Dave gingerly moved his fingers. They worked. Good. He firmly pinched himself, and felt the pain quite clearly. So this wasn't still a dream. He pinched himself again, even harder, to check. Ouch. Definitely not a dream.

Slowly, he opened his eyes. Where on Earth was he? Not daring to move his head, Dave used all of his senses to scout for clues as to his own whereabouts. He was pleasantly surprised to discover that he was lying on a bed - a *wonderful* bed. The linen was crisp and fresh, the pillows were perfectly fluffed, and the feathery doona was keeping him warm and cosy. The air smelled crisp and fresh like a rain shower, and he could hear no sound at all. He decided that, despite the fact that he was alone, he had never felt more sensational while lying in a bed.

Dave dared to move his eyes, and saw that he was in a spacious room with white walls. Feeling braver, he moved his head, giving himself more scope for vision. On the far wall, he noticed a large white door. It was closed.

That simple vision opened a Pandora's Box in Dave's mind, flooding his consciousness with a cavalcade of unanswered questions. He quickly disregarded the serenity of his surrounds as he tried to comprehend the day's unlikely train of events. Dave remembered waking with a severe headache, what now seemed an eternity ago, in Morgan's office. Perhaps the bump on the head had caused him to have strange delusions? Was he still in Morgan's headquarters?

He recalled taking a large green pill off a young man named Hopgood. Perhaps it had been a hallucinogenic drug. Conceivably, it could have adversely reacted with the 19 or so bottles of Neptune Gold that he had consumed. Perchance he had been intoxicated and had imagined the whole experience, although he had drunk far more beer on previous occasions without DNA, baby imaginings and big white spaces flashing before his eyes.

The meeting with Morgan drifted through his memory uneventfully, as did the media interviews. The newsfeed headline *'Dave to have a Few Quiet Beers with God'* tickled his memory. He recollected looking over the massive crowd, and being deafened by their booming chant of *'We Want God'* as he stood atop the stairs at Hieshler Towers. His last clear memories were of Hieshler and God shaking his hands, Morgan pulling at his cap, and of....

Dave winced. Alexandra.

Now she had gone again - or more correctly, he had gone. But where *was* he? Where was *she*? Would he ever see her again? Dave began to lose his composure. Nothing was making sense. His stress level escalated each time another unanswerable question popped into his mind. He could think of only one way to alleviate his anxiety. Open that door.

But just as he sat up, something happened that instantaneously changed his mind.

The door handle turned. Someone, or something, was entering the room.

Chapter 28

The door creaked slowly open. A hand appeared on the jamb, which was the first clue to the answer that resolved all Dave's questions and conundrums. Its fingers were gnarled and bony, and its skin was wrinkled and loose. The calloused knuckles were conspicuous, as were the thick yellow fingernails. Its large structure showed that it was clearly that of a man and that it could once have delivered a bone-crunching handshake. Overall, the hand's appearance suggested that it belonged to a careworn, aging man who had toiled long and hard in a more impressive age.

The owner of the hand stepped through the door. Even with the bow in his back, he stood head and shoulders above Dave. The man was a giant. His shoulders were structurally broad, but sagged a little from the weight of the world that they had obviously carried for many years. Sparse whiskers dotted his chin, and his head was bald save a patch of whitened hair above each ear. Yet his most outstanding feature was an energetic, merry twinkle that sparkled in his eyes, easily penetrating past his drooping eyelids.

"I'm sorry to have kept you waiting. Would you believe that I almost forgot our appointment altogether?" The old man spoke in a wavering, croaky voice, and strung his words together quickly, almost absently. "It's been getting worse lately, this forgetfulness. Appointments and dates just don't stick in my mind like they used to. Perhaps I'll start writing them down. Anyway, all's well that ends well, as you've arrived here safely. Oh, I am very sorry about your companions. My aim must have been a little bit astray. I mean, I really only wanted to talk to you, but I must have accidentally hit them as well. They must have been standing close to you. Or were they touching you?" The old man paused, and looked down at Dave.

Dave was dumbfounded. Was he supposed to answer? He didn't know where to start. The old man had already raised a thousand questions to add to the thousand that already existed in Dave's mind. Unable to sort his befuddled thoughts, Dave stared dumbly back, nodding absently.

"Ah, touching you, were they? I figured as much. I accept that my aim isn't always perfect, but to hit *four* instead of *one* is most unlikely. My eyes aren't that bad - I knew that they must have been touching you. Anyway, enough about that. Did you have a good trip here?"

Dave dumbly nodded again.

"Great. I hope you enjoyed the early part - I'm quite proud of it. It took me dozens of attempts to get it right, yet I rarely get any genuine appreciation for it. I have almost forgotten how I did it; it was so long ago ... so long ago...."

The old man breathed a deep sigh, as memories of a long-gone age returned momentarily to him. After another sigh, he looked up, mildly startled.

"Oh, I'm sorry. I lost myself for a second or two. Almost forgot you were here. It's difficult to keep my concentration these days. I used to find that kind of thing easy, but now, even after a few minutes, I seem to lose focus."

Dave, who was now more confused than the time he had tried to assemble a do-it-yourself shelving unit by following the instructions, simply kept nodding his head, occasionally adding an empathetic 'Ah-huh' as the old man continued his monologue.

"As I said, it's becoming difficult to keep track of things, like our meeting this evening, for example. I was so busy that I almost missed it. There I was, doing a bit of maintenance work, when I received a report that some people were calling for me. So I did some quick investigations and checked the local news feeds. Sure enough, I had completely forgotten our meeting. Sorry about that Dave, but as fate would have it, I was reminded just in time."

Huh? The sound of his own name jolted Dave back to his senses. How did the old man know his name? He needed some answers.

"Excuse me, Sir," said Dave as the old man paused to draw breath.

"Yes?"

"Would you please tell me where I am," asked Dave, deciding that was a reasonable question with which to begin.

"Oh, I am so sorry, how inconsiderate of me," said the old man. "There I was, telling you *my* troubles, and the whole time you were wondering where you were. Well, let me welcome you, Dave, to my headquarters."

"Your headquarters?"

"Well, part of my headquarters, at any rate. It's quite a big place."

"In that case," replied Dave as politely as he could, "would you mind telling me who *you* are."

The old man looked down at Dave with a wrinkled brow. He had assumed that Dave already knew his identity.

"I'm sorry," said the old man. "I presumed that you knew who I was. After all, we did have a meeting planned for this afternoon."

Dave's mind spun like an old carnival raffle-wheel. He strained his brain for any meetings or dates that he may have forgotten, but to no avail. He only had one meeting planned for this afternoon, and the old man was most definitely *not* Juan Carlos Manuel de la Espirito.

"I'm sorry," said Dave, "but I just can't remember our meeting, or even recollect your name."

The old man looked surprised, but only fleetingly, as he quickly assumed an expression of welcoming conviviality.

"Then allow me to introduce myself," said the old man as he extended his hand in friendship. Dave reached out to return the handshake, but didn't quite make it. He had not yet grasped the withered hand when the next two words that the old man uttered knocked Dave out cold.

"I'm God."

Chapter 29

Dave tentatively opened his eyes. He was in the same white room as where he had first met the old man, and was laying in the same amazingly comfortable bed. This was simply too incredible to be true. Was the old codger *really* God? If so, how could he prove it?

Just as Dave sat up in bed, the old man entered the room.

"Quite easily," said the old man nonchalantly.

"I'm sorry, I don't understand," said Dave. "What do you mean 'Quite easily'?"

"I mean," replied the old man, "that I can prove that I am God quite easily."

"How could you possibly do that?" asked Dave, not realising that he had not even verbalised the question.

"Well..." considered the old man, "if I said that you were about to say the words 'but it could just be a trick', would you believe me?"

"But it could just be a trick," said Dave, before his jaw dropped in amazement.

"What about if I predicted that you were about to ask 'How did you do that'?"

Dave was still amazed from the previous trick.

"How did you do that?" he asked.

"I told you so."

Dave was dumbstruck. Twice the old man had predicted his words, and twice he had been correct.

"That was amazing", thought Dave, "but he's going to have to do better than that to convince a cynic like me that he's really God."

"You're not really a cynic," replied the old man to Dave's thought. "You are simply being sceptical rather than cynical."

"What's the difference between scept ... hang on, how did you know what I was thinking?"

"I'm God. I know everything," said the man. "Or at least I used to. I keep forgetting things these days."

Dave eyed the giant man with an unusual gaze, one with equal parts of reverence and suspicion. Several very bizarre incidents had recently taxed Dave's sensory and logic systems, so he felt within his rights to question the validity of the old man's claim. Just because a bloke had a few lucky guesses at what someone else was thinking, well, that didn't automatically make him *God*, did it?

"All right then," articulated Dave with the manner of a lawyer about to question a shonky witness. "If you think that you know everything then tell me what I keep in the bottom drawer in my bedroom?"

"Two pairs of dirty underpants, a half-eaten packet of crisps, three emergency tins of generic brand lager and some rotten orange peels."

"Wrong!" shouted Dave with a superior type of glee.

"I'm sorry?" said the old man, obviously a little perplexed.

"Wrong," said Dave. "Completely wrong."

The old man paused for a second, thinking.

"Were you referring to your wardrobe drawers or your bedside table drawers?"

"Er, my bedside table drawers."

"In that case," corrected the old man, "I assume you are referring to a photograph of your hero, Elvis Presley."

"Er, correct," said Dave meekly.

"You have another picture of him taped to the cupboard door in your bathroom, next to a very alluring hologram of a certain Ms Honeydew Melons."

Correct again. Dave's jaw dropped again, as his attitude vaulted from scepticism to stupefaction. This guy was incredible. Perhaps he *was* God.

"I can see that you are starting to believe me," continued the old man. "Perhaps this next demonstration will help quell your doubts."

From nowhere he produced a glass, filled with a clear liquid.

"Taste this."

He motioned the glass towards Dave, who, never being one to refuse a free drink of any sort, obediently took a sip.

"It's just water."

"Correct," said the old man. "Now taste it again."

Dave obliged, and after taking a sip, lifted his eyebrows almost through his hairline in amazement.

"It's beer!" spluttered Dave.

"Neptune Gold, to be precise," added the old man as he gave Dave a cheeky wink. "A bit more up to date than the old water-into-wine trick, eh?"

"That's awesome," said Dave, while thinking *I wonder how he did that*.

"I told you before, I'm God, I can do anything," the old man replied to Dave's thought.

Anyone who could make beer from water was obviously very special. Dave, with his scepticism now reversed, finally returned the old man's handshake.

"Nice to meet you, God."

"Delightful to see you again, Dave. You're undoubtedly one of my better jobs."

"Why thank you," said Dave, as he gulped down the glass of Neptune Gold.

*

Ten minutes later, Dave was laughing with unabashed glee. He had just drained the glass for the fourth time, and was watching joyfully as it refilled itself to the brim with ice-cold Neptune Gold. He wondered whether it would be too rude to ask God if he could borrow it. Just for a while. Say, 70 or 80 years.

"I always thought Heaven would be like this," said Dave.

With a twinkle in his eye, God looked at his visitor.

"I've got some news for you Dave. This isn't Heaven."

"Not Heaven? Then where are we?"

"This is my house, Dave, my headquarters. We're in the guest's chambers of the northern wing, to be exact."

"Really? This is your house?"

"Yes it is," replied God, before proudly adding "and I've just finished some renovations."

"What did you do?"

"Oh, nothing major. Changed the carpet, updated the wallpaper in the dining room, and whitewashed the guests' rooms, that sort of thing."

"How long did it take you?"

"Just nine million years, give or take a few centuries," replied God with a sense of pride. "Although I must admit that I thought I'd have it done in two."

Dave was beginning to understand why so many of his friends on Earth only ever half-finished their renovations.

"If these are your private rooms," asked Dave, "then where is Heaven?"

"Just down the hall," replied God matter-of-factly.

"Really? Heaven is just down the hall?"

"Well, yes. It's in the other wing, of course."

"May I see it?" asked Dave, quickly becoming more excited than a vandal in a china shop.

"Of course. Follow me," said God as he hobbled off down the hall. Dave took one last large gulp of the never-ending beer, and although he was usually loathe leaving a drinking session without finishing his glass, he decided to make an exception just this once. He pursued God with an immense feeling of anticipation.

The unlikely duo headed down a long corridor. Dozens of doorways, most of which were closed, punctuated the hallway's stark white walls. God and Dave walked the entire length of the corridor before arriving at a T-junction, which led them into another similar walkway. They traversed this as well before eventually coming to an intersection that had even more corridors running off each axis.

After turning a few times and pacing along for a minute, God hesitated. He reached out for a door handle, and then paused again. Before withdrawing his hand, he turned around and counted how many doors they had passed. Then he shook his head, moved a few further doorways forward, and again reached for a handle. He opened the door and peeked inside.

"D'oh!" said God brusquely.

He paced more quickly towards the next doorway and opened it abruptly. This portal appeared to be a correct choice because God motioned to Dave to follow him through. The door opened into yet another long white corridor, similar to the hallways they had just hiked. Now God was walking more heavily, perhaps even stomping. Dave sensed that God's mood had deteriorated slightly.

They walked in silence for a few minutes before God again stopped. He pushed open a few doors, and then traced his steps back to the start of the hallway, flung open the first door, and gruffled to himself as he marched off down the hall. Sensing that God was now definitely irritable, Dave stayed a respectful pace or two behind. Dave's impression was confirmed a few minutes later when, after yet another wrong turn, God blew up an innocent solar system.

He wondered what had upset God. Dave was about to ask God if he would like to discuss anything, but reconsidered. He felt that it might seem impertinent for an unemployed lout from Earth to be offering advice to the Creator of the Universe. Then it occurred to Dave that as God could read his thoughts, he already knew that his grumpiness had been noted. Not only that, but God already knew that Dave had decided not to ask. Therefore, if he had been impertinent, God already knew about it, so he may as well go ahead and ask it anyway.

"Is something the matter, God?"

"What makes you think that anything is wrong?"

"Well ..." said Dave slowly, trying to be as tactful as possible, "... those planets you just destroyed gave me a hint...."

God paused for a second and breathed out slowly, counting to ten as he did.

"My mother told me to do that if I was ever angry," explained God as he calmed. "It really does work."

"Your mother? I didn't know that you had a mother."

"Of course I have a mother," replied God incredulously. "Where did you think I came from?"

Dave tried to think of a reasonable reply to this question, but couldn't. He instead made a mental note to follow it up later, and reverted to his original query about God's exasperated state of mind.

"Are you sure that you are all right? You just seemed a little bit upset before."

God paused, allowing his thoughts to organize themselves.

"Well, I must admit that I do get a little irritated at times."

"Oh?"

"It's a hard job, administering all the universes. Not that I take much of an active role in running them on a day to day basis anymore; I've scaled down my commitments to a consultancy level. But the early millennia took their toll. They were tough years, really tough. The stress of the pre-big-bang era really affected me, and I just haven't been the same since."

"In what way?" asked Dave.

"My mind ... just isn't focused anymore. I know a man can't expect to stay at his peak much past a couple of googolizillion years old, but my mind is definitely starting to slip. I keep making simple errors."

"What sort of slips? What sort of errors?"

"Oh, just simple things, nothing important really. But it is the basic gaffs that I find are the most irritating. For example, I forgot to include gravity waves in a universe I created the other day. Damn near ruined the whole thing. It was like trying to bake a cake without butter; it just kept crumbing apart. Another example is these doors. I used to know what was behind each of them, but now I can hardly remember where to find the stairway to Heaven. As I said, not major things, but it does exasperate me when I continually forget details."

"So what do you think is causing this memory loss?"

"I'm not certain, but I think," said God as he lowered his voice to a whisper, "that I'm going a little bit senile."

"Senile?" repeated Dave doubtfully, comparing God's relative togetherness with his blithering Earthly neighbour, Old Mr Smiggins. "I don't think that forgetting a simple thing like gravity waves necessarily qualifies you as senile. That type of thing is easy to forget ... I do it regularly. It sounds more like a case of simple absent-mindedness to me. What makes you think that you're going *senile*?"

"Our meeting was the final straw, Dave. I completely forgot about it. If it had not been for that crowd of people calling for me from Earth then I never would have remembered it at all. In fact, I still can't recall making our appointment in the first place. Never before has such a complete level of forgetfulness afflicted me. The fact that I can't even remember *making* the booking proves I'm becoming senile, rather than just a little bit absent minded."

Dave hesitated. He wasn't sure how to break the news to God.

"Break what news?" questioned God. Dave forgot that God could hear his thoughts as if he had broadcast them on GTN or HHTV.

"Well..." hesitated Dave. He didn't want to tell God the truth, as he may have to leave without seeing Heaven if he did.

"What news?" repeated God.

Dave decided - wisely, considering whom he was dealing with - that honesty was the best policy.

"I wasn't really supposed to be meeting you this afternoon," he confessed.

God looked at him, bemused.

"I was supposed to be meeting a football player, Juan Carlos Manuel de la Espirito. His nickname is God."

God looked down at Dave with an indescribable expression on his face, one that Dave interpreted to be a mixture of boiling fury and mild amusement. However, he could not decipher which was the dominant emotion, although a rule he had once learned in Sunday school about not using God's name in vain suddenly vaulted into his mind. He lamely attempted to excuse himself, and then continued his confession.

"I hope you don't mind the nickname ... it wasn't my idea ... I only use it sparingly. Anyway, it was the *other* God, the football playing God, for whom the people were calling. I suppose that I should have mentioned earlier that it was him, not you, whom I was supposed to be meeting."

Dave nervously watched God's face for a response. He had never experienced the wrath of his creator on a personal level, and after observing what God had done to the innocent solar system a few minutes earlier, Dave had no desire to provoke him to even the 'mildly cheesed off' stage. God looked at him steadily, without a hint of changing emotion.

"Are you telling me that we didn't have an appointment this afternoon?"

"Er, well, no. We, er, didn't," replied Dave, now very nervous and showing it. God looked unwaveringly at him again.

"Are you telling me that I bought you here, even though we hadn't even booked a meeting?"

"Er, in a sense, yes, you're correct. We didn't have a meeting booked, but in my defence I...."

Dave did not get to finish his plea of innocence. He didn't need to. God was too busy laughing, and dancing a peculiar version of the Highland fling down the hallway, to have listened.

"I didn't forget, I didn't forget," God sung aloud. "I'm not senile, I'm not senile."

Dave stood back and stared open mouthed as God, the Lord of the Universe, the Creator of Life, and the All Powerful Master of Everything, twirled merrily around the hallway singing a ditty. Dave had seen some odd sights in his thirty-four years, but this, without doubt, was the weirdest.

A minute or so later God began to tire. He leaned against a wall, resting.

"I'm sorry for acting so immaturely," puffed God as he caught his breath, "but your confession has lifted a huge weight off my mind. You see, I've been forgetting small details for a while, but ever since you arrived I've been worried that I was really cracking up. No matter how hard I tried, I couldn't recall making our appointment. Now it turns out that I didn't make it in the first place! It was all a simple misunderstanding. What a relief."

"Well I am really pleased to hear that you're okay," said Dave, gratified not only that he had escaped God's wrath, but also that the universe was still in capable hands.

"Why thank you, Dave. I'm glad we've cleared up that mess. Thank you very much for coming, your visit has been most interesting."

Dave's disposition took a sudden dive. "Does this mean that I have to go back?"

"Of course it does, Dave," replied God. "It would be against the rules for me to keep you here."

"Which rules are they?"

"The rule that says that a createe cannot enter my premises without an appointment."

"But I am a human, not a createe," said Dave, his mind swimming with visions of Martian monsters.

"I am the creator," replied God by way of explanation, "and you are a createe."

"Oh," said Dave. "So everything is a createe, including me."

"Correct."

"But couldn't you break the rules, just this once? I promise that I won't tell anybody."

"What would be the point of making rules if I didn't even follow them myself?"

"Because you didn't want to?" suggested Dave weakly.

God shook his head.

"What it boils down to, Dave, is this. My unfortunate mistake of bringing you here without a genuine booking has created damage in your space-time envelope that is going to be very difficult to repair. The longer that you stay here, the more bothersome the job becomes."

"Could I book an appointment now?" asked Dave hopefully.

"Only if you wanted to stay here forever, and take your chances at the sorting compound," said God. Then, realising from the shape of Dave's eyebrows that he had again used an unfamiliar concept, God provided a brief explanation.

"The sorting compound is where we assess each createe regarding a universe transition. Probably the simplest way for you to visualise this area is to picture it as the gateway to your human concepts of Heaven and Hell, which although not precise terms, will do for now."

"So you are saying that if I want to stay here, then I have to take my chances at the Pearly Gates like everybody else."

"That's a fair summary."

Dave thought back through his life on Earth. This was actually a simple task, as it had passed through his mind *in toto* only about an hour previously. On reflection, he decided that he was probably only a line-ball candidate for Heaven; although he had never done anything seriously evil, he had never performed any heroically good feats either. He then realised, with a sense of regret, that he had never done anything much at all. Not unless drinking beer, eating pizza and telling jokes at the Stranglers Bar counted as something. However, another factor ultimately swayed his calculations.

"If I stayed, would I ever see Alexandra again?"

"Not until she died," replied God, "and even then you would have to hope that she was assigned to the same alternate universe as you."

Resolving his dilemma was now easy for Dave. An eternity in Hell would be pretty dull and dreary, but to never see Alexandra again would be unbearable. Although he dearly wanted to see Heaven and to hang with God, Dave's love for Alexandra tilted the delicate balance Earthwards. It was a depressing decision, but Dave accepted he had to make a choice.

"Beam me down, Scotty," said Dave ruefully.

God chortled. He enjoyed watching *Star Trek*, particularly the early episodes, and Dave's comment had tickled his memories of the show. Dave poked his index fingers up behind his ears, imitating another *Star Trek* character, Doctor Spock.

"Estimated chance of returning here one day, 100 percent," mimicked Dave.

God chuckled at the near-perfect imitation. Dave, on a roll, switched to his Scottish accent, precisely capturing the speech pattern of first mate Scotty.

"Aye, captain. We have a problem in Solar System 2-B, Planet Earth."

"Why is that, Scotty?" asked God, joining in the game.

"The humans are confused, Sir."

"What are they confused about, Scotty?"

"They've just discovered that male sperm is an excellent sexual lubricant, Sir."

God laughed again. Although he felt that Dave's one-liner was very ordinary, he enjoyed the clever impersonation.

Dave sensed a glimmer of an opportunity. Maybe this was his passport to Heaven. Or at least a temporary entrance visa. He went for broke. With one nostril flared and both eyes crossed, Dave poked his tongue at an acute angle, pulling the funniest face he could create at short notice. As rolled one eye around in circles, God broke into a hearty cackle.

Sensing that he still had a chance, Dave launched in to a comic cavalcade. He hit God with a few standard one-liners, and then continued relentlessly with the full series of A-Man-Walks-into-a-Bar jokes. Despite having heard them all before, God couldn't help but howl even more. After ten solid minutes of mirth, Dave ceased his silliness. God was clutching his aching ribs, and his bronchitis was starting to play up. After allowing God to catch his breath, Dave made one final, beseeching solicitation for God to permit him to stay.

"Please can I stay a while," begged Dave, shamelessly dropping to his knees. "Just a little bit longer. Pleeeease. Puh-leeeese." He switched on his 'lost puppy dog' expression. God looked at him thoughtfully.

"You're certainly terrific company," he said. "Sometimes it is a bit boring up here, and your lively sense of humour has been a welcome change."

Dave felt a sliver of optimism.

"The saints and angels are wonderful people, but they become very predictable after a few million years. Simply, they are not as much fun as you regular, mistake-riddled humans. In fact, it is your abundance of flaws that makes you so interesting. I would dearly love you to stay for a while, but unfortunately, rules are rules. You have to go back to Earth."

Dave was devastated. In desperation, he made one final effort to convince God to let him stay. Luckily, he had saved his two best routines for last.

"Knock knock," said Dave.

"Who's there?" asked God....

*

It worked wonderfully.

The knock-knock joke, which Dave had initially heard at kindergarten, had tickled God into another fit of giggling. Then, just as he was starting to laugh uncontrollably, Dave gave him his king hit: his impersonation of Elvis Presley eating a bucketful of deep-fried chicken, while singing an abridged version of one of his classics - Dave's own composition - entitled *Jailhouse Chook*. God had laughed so hard that he had almost cracked his sternum.

Now God was doing the begging. He was pleading, between laughing seizures, for Dave to stop. Tongue in cheek, Dave threatened to continue his cannonade of comedy unless God permitted him to see Heaven. He was surprised and thrilled when God, after only slight further hesitation, agreed.

Heaven! He was going to Heaven! This was nearly as good as winning a lifetime supply of Neptune Gold.

Chapter 30

Dave's initial excitement was now heavily diluted with fatigue. They had been walking for what felt like hours. God realised that Dave was tiring, and offered him some words of encouragement.

"Keep going, Dave. We're nearly half way there."

Dave stopped in his tracks.

"Half way?"

"Almost," replied God. "Are you getting weary?"

"Well, I must admit when you said that Heaven was 'just down the hall', I didn't expect a corridor this long."

"It is a very big place."

Dave grimaced.

"Would you like to use an *Instaport* instead?" inquired God.

"I could answer that a little more accurately," said Dave, "if I knew what an *Instaport* was."

"It's one of these," said God, as a large mirrored door appeared in front of them. "It will take us anywhere on the premises, instantly. I used to operate them all the time, but these days I prefer to walk for the exercise. I'm fairly sure I can remember how it works, although I must admit that I haven't used one for a few millennia."

"It's got to be easier than walking," suggested Dave, who had long been regretting that his most demanding form of exercise on Earth had been playing virtual darts at the Stranglers Bar. God opened the Instaport door, and they both entered without delay. There was a flash of blackness, after which they emerged on the other side of the door. Dave looked up to see another corridor, similar again to the one they had just exited.

"Whoops," said God. "We got off a stop too early. We're in the Collections Wing."

"What's the 'Collections Wing'?"

"Oh, that's just a little nook where I keep my collections," replied God. "I like collecting as a hobby. It helps me relax and pass the time."

"Really?" asked Dave, momentarily distracted from his desire to see Heaven as soon as possible.

"Would you like to see them?" asked God, secretly hoping that Dave did. "I'm rather proud of them."

"You bet I would."

God beamed like a new father as he led Dave into his major collection room.

They entered a parlour, which was grand in both design and size. The room's decor was ornate in every sense of the word: the skirting boards were intricately carved from precious stone, wallpaper of glowing thread covered the walls, and chandeliers fashioned from what looked like massive diamonds hung from a ceiling that was so high that Dave could not see it. The floor space was crammed with thousands of cabinets, each expertly constructed from finely-worked timber. Each cabinet had six shelves, and was fronted by a paper-thin sheet of crystal that was polished so meticulously it was almost invisible. Each shelf had, neatly laid out and labelled, rows and rows of God's collectables. His pride and joy.

Pens. Just pens, ordinary biros, and pencils.

"Where did you collect these from?" asked Dave, trying to feign interest in what was possibly an even duller collection that his boring cousin Adnor's 'Photograph's of bicycles I have ridden' collection.

"Oh, I just keep my eyes open. Usually they are not difficult to find. They just tend to pop up in all sorts of places: loose shirt pockets, the bottom of ladies handbags, second drawers in kitchens...."

"They're lovely," lied Dave, and seemed to get away with it.

"I'm always on the lookout for new and interesting writing implements, so if you do ever come across any, be sure to let me know."

"Consider it done," said Dave.

"Guess what else I collect?" asked God, who was excited at having a visitor to show his wares.

"Socks?" ventured Dave.

God's face fell into a pout.

"How did you know?"

"Just a lucky guess," replied Dave, while making a mental note to apologize to Old Mr Smiggins for accusing him of stealing socks from their communal clothes dryer. Dave's tour of God's pen and sock collection mercifully ended about an hour later. As God finally summoned the Instaport, Dave realised one piece of knowledge that had previously eluded him for his whole life: he now knew why there was never a pen around when you needed one.

God and Dave stepped back through the *Instaport*. This time God steered it correctly, and managed to land both Dave and himself in the target area, the Separating Compound - eternity's waiting room. The room didn't look like Heaven to Dave - because it wasn't - but it was infinitely more interesting than a row of *'Early Graphite\Boxwood HB-HHB'* pencils, so he strolled contentedly for a few minutes, simply observing the room and all that was in it.

Despite the walls of the room appearing to be straight, it seemed to Dave that it had no corners. The walls seemed to go on forever. It soon dawned on him that this was true, as the room was round. However, it was so enormous that it gave the illusion that each section of wall was straight, just as the Earth's horizon appears flat rather than round.

The Separating Compound was, like most things in this part of the universe, extremely large. It was so large that, to anyone who understood the language of Ancient Gayak, it could accurately be described as GHjh!as#bid.

In the distance, a massive crowd of people was packed into what Dave assumed was the centre of the room. Instinctively, Dave headed towards them. God seemed happy to tag along, as his thoughts appeared to be elsewhere. As they approached the crowd, Dave became surprised, then puzzled, then progressively more amazed as he observed their behaviour. This, it was clear, was no ordinary crowd.

The characteristic of the crowd that so intrigued Dave was the complete lack of any form of sexual activity. There was no lovemaking, nor was there any kissing or cuddling. Dave found this both amusing and unlikely, primarily because no one was wearing even a shred of clothing. The only other times that Dave had seen this many naked people together was on naughty STOVE movies, so he automatically associated mass nudity with naughty behaviour. But these people not only seemed uninterested in lovemaking but in everything else around them.

At first they appeared to Dave to be intermingling haphazardly, almost as if milling after a Sunday church sermon. However as Dave approached them he noticed that they were not really walking. They were all standing very stiffly, and only occasionally taking small steps forwards. Nor were they talking. Their faces were motionless, expressionless, and like most of their owners, wrinkled. They looked as if they were dead.

Which, it soon occurred to Dave, they were.

He soon deduced that the people were standing in a long queue, which gradually spiralled inwards as it circled the room. Dave's eyes followed the line of people towards the centre, where a towering staircase corkscrewed its way upwards.

I wonder if that's the Stairway to Heaven, Dave thought as he turned to God, expecting an answer. However God was still busy listening to another thought, and did not answer him. The nature of that other thought, and God's preoccupation with it, soon became apparent. He turned to Dave with a concerned look on his face.

"I'm sorry Dave," he said quietly and quickly. "I'm going to have to leave you for a while."

"Is something wrong?" asked Dave, becoming instantly uneasy.

"Hopefully nothing that's not fixable. I've just received reports of some trouble in an experimental universe on which I've been working. The new fundamental energy units are spontaneously de-inertialising."

"Oh!" exclaimed Dave with a perplexed look on his face. "Spontaneously de-inertialising. Is that dangerous?"

"Only if you existed in that universe."

"Does anything exist there?"

"A few prototype bacteria, some basic animal life, and some low configuration humanoids."

"What will happen to them?"

"I'm not exactly sure," said God. "It appears that yet again I have forgotten to include a vital physical force of some kind, so two conceivable outcomes are possible. The first possibility is that the inhabitants slowly roast themselves to death as their fundamental structure decays. The second is that the entire universe will suddenly cease to exist altogether. I'm hoping that they merely roast themselves. I'd hate to lose the whole thing as it was coming along quite nicely. The new fundamental energy particles were terrific and made afterlife transitional phases so much easier. However it looks like I've got a few glitches to iron out before I can use them to upgrade any other systems."

Dave was taken aback. Fundamental structure decay? Afterlife transitional phases? Roasts? He suddenly found himself thinking yet another thousand questions. However, these thoughts all remained unanswered, because God was already stepping back through the Instaport.

"I'm sorry I can't explain everything more fully," said God as he began pulling the door closed behind him, "but I'm in a bit of a hurry."

"What will I do?" asked Dave.

"Just have a look around. I'll be back in about a quadmegazillion daddoseconds." God paused, then clearly added *"Don't go anywhere without me"*, closed the door, and vanished from sight.

Dave stood in the middle of the enormous room, surrounded by thousands of naked dead people, completely alone. Utterly confused yet again, he tried to collect his thoughts. How long did God say that he would be away? Was it a quadmegadaddo zilliseconds - or a quadzillidaddo megaseconds? What the heck was a daddo?

After some rough mental calculations - based on what he could remember from high school mathematics classes and making up the rest - Dave deduced that God would be away for sometime between two minutes and eighty billion years.

He decided that he might as well explore the room while he waited. Continuing his walk towards the centre of the room, he mingled amongst the undead corpses. They did not acknowledge him, speak to him, or even look at him. Even worse, they did not even attempt to cover their nudity. Dave took quite some time to become used to the sight of naked octogenarians. He decided that when God returned he would personally thank him for inventing modesty.

Dave wound his way gently through the throng, being careful not to bump anyone lest he disturb his or her countenance. To be walking amongst the dead was a feeling beyond strange, beyond eerie. As Dave looked at their wasted, wrinkled bodies, he couldn't help but think of the amazing richness of memories that must still exist, even in death, in the twisted physical matter of their brains. Each person's entire chronology of emotions, experiences and knowledge was somehow stored away in a lump that physically resembled nothing more than a mouldy pawpaw. If only all of that knowledge could be sucked out, processed, and somehow tinned.

Cutting deftly across the flow of the zombie queue, Dave honed in on the staircase at the centre of the room. After some nimble footwork and lots of unnecessary apologising, he arrived within reach of his goal: The Stairway to Heaven.

Standing within twenty paces of the stairway's base, Dave felt dwarfed by its majestic height. The steps spiralled their way upwards for what looked like a mile and then stopped abruptly at a small platform. Hundreds of men, women and even some children, all dead, slowly clawed their way upwards like ants up a flagpole. Painstakingly they plodded higher, each heading doggedly for their destiny.

Dave squinted, affording him a less blurred vision of the platform high above. Each new arrival at the zenith stepped over the ledge like a bored lemming, but instead of plummeting to (another) death, they simply vanished. Dave surmised that the ledge was something like an Instaport: a one-way valve to eternity in Heaven.

Becoming dizzy from looking up, Dave refocused his attention to ground level, where two things caught his attention. First, another stairway, which was identical to the other in almost every way, except one vitally important difference: it went down. The stairway to Hell, Dave logically concluded.

Second, Dave observed an old man sitting at the junction of the two staircases. He distinguished himself by wearing a long white robe, which was the only other item of clothing in the room besides Dave's jeans and lucky shirt. The old man sat facing away from Dave, behind a mammoth desk. After edging closer, Dave noticed that the desk supported the most colossal book that he had ever seen.

The book was as large as the desk itself, and had so many pages that new roman numerals must have been invented just to number them. It contained so much paper that forest-loving environmentalists would have been completely justified in protesting against its publication. The computer age had obviously not arrived in Heaven.

The old man had not yet noticed Dave, as he was busy in a discussion with a woman who seemed to have suddenly developed consciousness.

"I'm sorry, Mrs. Zoupowski, but you know the rules," the old man was saying. "You should have thought about all this before you swallowed those dress pins."

"How was I to know?" she asked.

"It's not my decision, Mrs. Zoupowski. Up you go."

The lady acceded to this final command. Whatever it was that she was arguing about was now inconsequential. Perhaps, Dave guessed as he watched her begin the lengthy trudge up the stairs, she had some unfinished business on Earth.

The next person in the queue stepped forward. The old man gently placed his hand on the new arrival's forehead, which animated the corpse out of its trance.

"My name is Saint Barnabas," said the old man in the robe. "I am filling in for Saint Peter, who is on long service leave. May I start with your name, please?"

"Theodore Aloysius McLaughlin."

Saint Barnabas raised an eyebrow.

"Theodore *who* McLaughlin?" he asked.

"Theodore *Al-lo-ees-ee-uss* McLaughlin. A-L-O-Y-S-I-U-S," came the well-rehearsed reply.

Saint Barnabas began leafing laboriously through the pages of the gigantic book, muttering something to himself about Russians and Sri Lankans as he did. A few minutes later he stopped, and ran his forefinger down what Dave guessed to be a column of names.

"Date of birth?" he asked.

"The 3rd of October, 1967."

Saint Barnabas scrutinised some fine print.

"Yes, here you are," he said after a while. "Theo McLaughlin. Died of pancreatic cancer, aged sixty-seven."

"Correct," replied Theo. "It hurt like Hell, too."

Saint Barnabas raised his eyebrow again, this time at Theo's poor choice of expression, before returning his gaze to study some details in the book. Theo waited patiently until his natural curiosity eventually intervened.

"Would you mind telling me what caused the cancer?" he asked.

"I suppose I could," replied Saint Barnabas dryly. He hated those types of requests. In fact he detested this entire public service position. The hours were long, it was always busy – 150 000 new arrivals every day - and it really cheesed him off having to tell some people that they had to spend the rest of their existence in Hell. He tried his best to be patient and understanding, as these people had recently died and most of them were still feeling a bit depressed about it. Nevertheless he secretly could not wait for Saint Peter to get back, although he was loathe to think that his return was still a few million years away.

Patiently complying with Theodore's request, he studied more of the fine print in the large book.

"The cancer-causing cells entered your body from a portion of duck liver pate which you spread on a cracker biscuit at your sixty-second birthday party."

"Damn!" said Theo. "I knew I should have stuck to my diet plan." He thought for a few moments, before asking "Was it anything to do with my cigarette smoking?"

"Not really," replied Saint Barnabas after again consulting the book.

Theo smiled. "Thank goodness I never quit."

Both men had a wry laugh at the cruel irony of life, which was quite easy to do when you were dead. However the mood soon turned sombre as Theo realised that he was about to learn his final destiny.

"Well, I guess this is the moment I've been waiting all my death for." He paused nervously. "I tried to live an honest life. Tell me, Saint Barnabas, what is my fate?"

Saint Barnabas looked at his interviewee with mild insouciance.

"I think you know that just as well as I do." He turned, and pointed down the stairs.

"Down you go."

Unceremoniously, Theodore McLaughlin shuffled off, and began plodding down the long stairway. Dave shuddered. How could the man be so subdued at such a wretched moment?

Dave watched and listened intently as the next corpse stepped up towards the desk. It belonged to an obese man, who looked lucky to have survived to his very advanced years. He looked even older than Old Mister Smiggins. The man's hair, which was thick, dark, and slicked with oil, was incongruous with his wrinkled, bloated, bulging body. Saint Barnabas laid his hands on top off the hair, which miraculously drew life into the waddling corpse.

"Why thankya. Thankya very much," drawled the awakened body.

"My name is Saint Barnabas. I am filling in for Saint Peter, who is on long service leave. May I start with your name, please?"

"Why sure ya can," drawled the obese old man. "It's Presley."

Barnabas began the difficult process of turning the pages of the book.

"First names?"

"Elvis Aron - that's Aron with one 'A'."

"Date of...."

Saint Barnabas stopped mid-sentence, and looked up, startled. "Elvis! Elvis Aron Presley! You're here at last. We've had people asking about you for sixty years."

"The double deep-fried bacon and peanut butter sandwiches had ta get me eventually," replied Elvis. "Although it didn't stop me from gittin' to 99 years ol'. Just a few more months I was gunna make 100. Mighta even thrown a party for ma fans."

Dave, who had been looking and listening to the whole session with great curiosity, was inexpressibly excited. Then, before he had even breathed again, a depressing shock overcame him, as the sighting threw him into emotional turmoil. He was excited to have seen his hero in, well, the flesh, but juxtaposed with this joy was the grief of knowing that Elvis was dead. *Officially* dead. Never again would the King of Rock'n'Roll sing a new song, although, Dave admitted to himself, he hadn't performed any during the last six decades anyhow. As his mind vaulted from exaltation and excitement to despair and depression, his emotions finally settled on a thought: perhaps he could meet with Elvis in person?

Dave looked up just in time to see Elvis heading up the stairs. He thought furiously as he desperately wanted to meet with Elvis, just to talk with him, and maybe even discover where he had been during the 'missing years'. It also wouldn't hurt to check if Elvis had any unpublished demo tapes lying around in a drawer somewhere back on Earth. With minimal time to appraise the situation, Dave could think of only one method of getting to Elvis: he had to get permission from Saint Barnabas to walk up the stairs. After quickly assessing his chances, Dave could see only one way that he was going to obtain that authorisation. Pretend he was dead.

Stripping himself naked, and even removing his shoes and smart-watch for authenticity, Dave slipped surreptitiously into the queue about a dozen places from the front. Saint Barnabas was too busy arguing with his latest interviewee about the definition of the term 'malfeasance' to notice. Wearing nothing except a bland expression on his face and a piece of flesh-coloured tape that was unfortunately still stuck around his shin, Dave moved steadily along the line.

As he neared the front of the queue, Dave became increasingly nervous. Pretending that he was dead was going to be a difficult task. How did a dead person act? For inspiration, he thought back to a few conversations he had endured with his dead-boring cousin Adnor, and soon worked up a suitable persona.

However, he then realised that he hadn't really thought through the logistics of his plan. Saint Barnabas had the relevant information on all human life and death literally at his fingertips, and could easily expose Dave as a fraud. Dave toyed with the idea of trying to explain the whole situation from the beginning, but dismissed it quickly; the old man sounded irritable. He also thought of, and then rejected, the idea of waiting around for God. He might still be away for a few billion years.

Dave increasingly wished that he had never attempted the queue-jumping exercise. However he was now almost at Barnabas's desk, so it was too late to change his mind. He needed a plan. And he needed it very quickly.

Just as his nerves began to belly dance, Dave conceived a workable idea. Perhaps he could pretend to be someone who had just died - a false identity. But who? He scanned the queue behind him looking for a familiar face. Although he had thousands of people to choose from, with another couple of corpses arriving every tick of the clock, his efforts were in vain. Ahead, another person clicked through the metaphorical turnstile at the top of the queue. Dave was now only one person away from disaster. He had no plan, no ideas, and no hope.

Then, just as he was about to drop to his knees and plead to Saint Barnabas for forgiveness, a minor miracle saved him. Across the room, at the far end of the long, circular queue, a new arrival appeared - a new soul on the forked road to eternity. The corpse was not handsome; in fact it was hideously ugly. However, to Dave it was the second most beautiful sight (after Alexandra) that he had ever witnessed. The body had the unmistakable features of his senile, deaf, and now obviously departed neighbour, Old Mr Smiggins.

So the old bastard has finally croaked it, thought Dave.

He looked back towards Saint Barnabas, just as the last interviewee tramped off down the nearby stairs. Dave, now with a hint of an opportunity, dutifully stepped forward. He had spent years campaigning for an interview - admittedly this wasn't a job interview, but it was an interview all the same - and he wasn't about to blow his chance. Standing more rigidly than a London Tower Guard, Dave stepped in front of the old man. He maintained a blank, emotionless expression on his face as he fought a powerful urge to cover his exposed genitalia. Saint Barnabas, who by this stage was almost due for afternoon tea, barely looked up as he laid a hand upon Dave's forehead.

"My name is Saint Barnabas. I am filling in for Saint Peter, who is on long service leave. May I start with your name, please?"

"Smiggins," replied Dave, faking a croaky voice.

"First name?"

"Er...." Dave paused. He had never heard Old Mr Smiggins' first name, and he didn't have a clue what it was. Impetuously, he blurted out the first thing that popped into his mind.

"Old."

Barnabas looked down at the book, despondently shaking his head. This afternoon had been very onerous. He would have to do this one by birth date.

"Year of birth?" he asked impatiently.

Dave thought furiously. If he slipped up here he was in trouble, deep trouble. How old was Old Mr Smiggins? Furiously, he harkened back to his Earthly conversations with his neighbour. He was ... he was ... he was eighty-six! Doing his second piece of mental arithmetic for the hour, which he considered above a healthy limit, Dave struggled to quickly subtract Old Mr Smiggins' age from the current year.

Borrow ten, makes the three into a two. Eleven minus six is five. Three minus eight, no, two minus eight is, shit, borrow ten, twelve minus, how many, um, eight is four....

"Year of birth," repeated Saint Barnabas, this time far more taciturnly, completely interrupting Dave's train of thought. Time was up.

"Nineteen forty-eight," blurted Dave, forced to call on a mathematical estimating technique he had developed over years of scoring dart games in the Stranglers Bar. Perhaps because he was wearing his lucky shirt, Dave was very fortunate. By some fluke of fate, and with some help from his well-honed pub math skills, he guessed correctly.

"Ah-huh," said Barnabas cryptically as he found and studied Wolfgang Adolf Smiggins' personal history in the large book.

"Hmm," he added thoughtfully as he rubbed his chin.

Dave's pride in his mathematical prowess rapidly deteriorated into a sickening worry as he observed the Saint's body language. So far, he had not even considered the prospect that Old Mister Smiggins may have not led a wholesome life. In fact, as he spewed over the relevant facts in his mind, Old Mister Smiggins clearly led a completely amoral, perverted existence. What if, as was highly likely, his destiny was an eternity in Hell?

Dave was about to break down and confess the whole charade when Barnabas spoke.

"It looks like it's up the stairs for you, Smiggins."

Dave was overjoyed. The words had barely left the lips of the wizened Saint before Dave began bounding up the stairs, chasing his hero.

"Strange man," muttered Saint Barnabas as he headed outside for a cigarette and a coffee.

Chapter 31

Elvis Presley had established quite a start on Dave, who was doing his best to make up for lost time as he leapt from step to step with uncharacteristic vigour. However, the slowly moving traffic hampered his progress. The other stair climbers, most of who were aged, toiled very sluggishly. In addition, the staircase was unusually narrow, so overtaking was difficult. Dave tried to be polite.

"Excuse me, madam. Could I just squeeze past? Er, sorry sir, if you wouldn't mind letting me through, I'm in a bit of a hurry...."

However, his pleas fell on unresponsive ears. The corpses seemed to be in a trance-like state; not complete unconsciousness like when they were in the circular queue, but more of a Parisian-to-a-tourist-like ignorance. Their faces seemed even more twisted in desperation than previously, and some even muttered mild expletives at Dave.

He could not fathom why they were all so dull and depressed. All the reports he had heard, although he admitted that they were only unconfirmed rumours, suggested that Heaven was a wonderful place, with free beer and pizza and lots of beautiful happy people. Why weren't these people smiling, laughing, and generally celebrating their sublime dates with destiny? Dave quickly realised that he would require more than just politeness to get past these dead-heads. This situation called for *nous*. Luckily, he had plenty of that.

Using a dexterous combination of hip, elbow and shoulder movements which he had perfected through years of trying to get quicker service at crowded bars, he managed to worm past a few people with minimal disruption. He began to gain on Elvis. But after a few further minutes of pushing, shoving and stair climbing, Dave began to tire. He was still exhausted from his earlier hall-hiking expedition with God, and he had long since exceeded his self-imposed maximum daily exercise quota.

To add to his problems, Dave noted that the next person on the steps was exceptionally obese, and would be difficult to pass. Dave slowed to a steady plod, enabling him to regain some strength for the upcoming passing manoeuvre that would require considerable effort.

He took the opportunity to check on Elvis's progress. The corpse of the King of Rock'n'Roll had steadily ascended the steps, and was now about half way to the top. Three people still separated him from Dave. Judging that he remained on schedule to catch Elvis a few minutes before they reached the ledge, Dave apportioned himself a further minute at the slower pace.

Then, with renewed vigour, Dave attempted some passing manoeuvres on the fat man. First, he tried a standard shoulder edge, a technique that involved slipping his arm in front of the fat man's shoulder and trying to slide past him. However the man was simply too large, and Dave was forced to try the addition of a hip nudge. Yet again he failed to make any impression, even when he added a difficult inwards-sliding knee roll.

Dave was taken aback. That particular combination had never failed him at any bar on Earth. He tried the same combination on the man's other side, this time with a double helping of deftness. Yet he remained stuck behind the fat man; like a Ferrari on a freeway behind a little old lady in a Lada. Despairingly, Elvis was now climbing further away from him. He tried his complete set of body leveraging, barging and charging techniques, none of which helped his cause. The human roadblock barely flinched. In desperation, Dave tried crawling through the man's legs, but scored only a bruised nose for his trouble.

The physical approach was not working, so Dave decided to change tactics. Perhaps a verbal approach would work. First, polite requests. No response. Then he invented a few lies to increase the apparent urgency of his need to get past. However if the man actually believed that Dave had a bowel problem then he did not acknowledge it. Then Dave tried, in order, threats, pleading, begging and then finally in a final act of desperation he resorted to the truth.

"Please, sir, you've got to let me pass," Dave begged. "I've got to talk with that man ahead on the stairs. You may have heard of him, his name is Elvis Presley. No? Well, he is a legendary Rock'n'Roll performer from the 1960s. He's been a hero of mine since I was a child. I will never have the opportunity to talk with him again. So, please, Sir, I am begging you, please let me past."

The fat man, on hearing Dave's final impassioned plea, stopped completely, and slowly turned his head around on his triple-chinned neck. Perhaps, Dave hoped, he had finally penetrated the man's empathetic side. As the man's face came into view, Dave felt that he looked familiar. However he could not place where he had met the man before, and had no recollection of the man's name. The fat man spoke.

"Bugger off."

Then he slowly rotated his head to the front, and continued his slow plod.

Dave bristled with instant indignation. He had just opened his soul to the fat man, who had told him to 'bugger off' in reply. Dave felt his fingers curl into fists but stopped before swinging a punch. As he counted backwards from ten, like God's mother had espoused, he realised that physical force was useless against a man of such stature. Even when fighting against an inanimate papier-mâché piñata at his cousin Adnor's eighth birthday party, most of the uncles declared that Dave had only just won with a split points decision. He clearly did not have the arsenal to trouble the giant in front of him.

Repressing his vindictiveness, Dave returned to his original problem of how to catch Elvis. He clearly was not going to get any cooperation from the human beanbag in front of him, and going around or under him was futile. That left only one possible way of getting past. Over.

Dave halted, both to gather strength and to let the man get a few steps ahead. Then, with every ounce of power that his tired muscles could muster, he leapt up the stairs, first individually and then two and three at a time as he gathered speed. Unleashing a fearsome howl, Dave launched himself into the air.

His leading foot came down at the level of the man's derrière. Thinking instinctively, Dave jammed his toes into a roll of fat in the man's lower back. Using the fat like a rung on a human stepladder, he vaulted even higher, like he had learned to do while playing Australian Rules football as a teenager. After flinging one ankle across the man's shoulder and grabbing his pudgy ears, Dave pulled himself up and over in one not-very-smooth motion. With a distinct lack of grace, he landed in a heap in front of the fat man. Mission accomplished!

But Dave had no time to celebrate, as he immediately realised that he was not yet out of danger. A size fifteen foot weighing about a quarter of a tonne was bearing down towards his head. He rolled sideways and then quickly scrambled up the stairs, just managing to avoid being trampled like a dried cowpat as the fat man continued his unyielding progression.

Now out of immediate jeopardy, Dave hauled himself up and, pausing only to give the fat man the rudest finger sign he could create with two hands, he headed up the staircase at double speed. Elvis was now nearing the top, and Dave still had two people to pass. He darted around the next man, who was mercifully thinner, with ease. As Dave continued up the stairs, his mind sent him a memo: *that thin man also looks familiar*.

Dave afforded himself a quick glance over his shoulder. The man, even in death, was very neat. His fingernails were manicured, his hair was neatly slicked back, and his teeth were whiter than hospital linen. He looked to be in his mid-fifties. Dave looked at his eyes for a response, but they, like every other pair of eyes on these stairs, were strangely distant and desperate. Dave, unable to place the face, ignored the neat man, and concentrated on his own progress.

Now only one person - a well-muscled, good looking, athletic young man - separated Dave from his idol. With adrenalin pumping through his veins, Dave charged past him, barely stopping to apologise. Elvis, who now was only a few steps from the platform, was in his sights. Bounding three stairs at a time, Dave soon reached him, and breathlessly called out.

"Elvis," he hollered.

His hero did not respond.

"Elvis!" Dave repeated, this time even more loudly.

Not surprisingly, there was still no response. In Dave's excitement, he had not considered the possibility that Elvis would ignore him, even though no-one else on the stairway had said anything any more jovial to him than 'bugger off'. Still, Dave was not going to allow this minor distraction to deter him. He had invested too many calories to give up now.

"Excuse me, Mister Presley. Could I just say hello?"

Dave might as well have been talking to a bucketful of refried chicken nuggets, which were, as far as modern science had determined, completely deaf. Elvis simply refused to acknowledge Dave at all. Like everyone else on the stairway, Elvis seemed completely preoccupied with his own post-mortal thoughts. Dave, too, was now starting to experience despair-type emotions as Elvis stepped onto the platform. He followed the large corpse, and would have begun urgently tugging on the back of Elvis's shirt had he been wearing one. However as he was naked, Dave began madly tugging on a large hairy mole that covered the area over which Elvis's left kidney presumably resided.

"Please, please, please, Mister Presley," begged Dave, "at least tell me where you've been for the last sixty years."

Elvis silently stepped onto the platform.

"*Please,*" beseeched Dave. "Just a quick word or two."

Elvis turned, and for the first time made eye contact with Dave.

"I get so lonely..." he said in a deep, sing-song voice.

Dave was stunned. He had no idea why Elvis had suddenly opened up to him in such a soulful manner. Elvis continued.

"I get so lonely...." he repeated.

"Well, Sir," mumbled Dave. "I'm sure if you, just, er, went out a little more. Er, no. That wouldn't help ... er, maybe if you...."

"I get so lonely I could DIE!" sang Elvis, with pointed emphasis on the last word.

Dave suddenly realised that these were the final stanzas of his favourite Elvis ballad *Heartbreak Hotel;* the song that had been playing in the Stranglers Bar when he had first met Alexandra.

Dave was flabbergasted. Shocked. And completely thrilled. The King of Rock'n'Roll, the world's all-time most legendary performer, had sung his last words to him. Of all the people who had ever existed, the King had chosen *him* to witness his ultimate performance. This was not like those rock stars who didn't know when to quit, clinging to the last scraps of adulation through dozens of "last performance ever" shows and repeated comebacks. This was it. Finito. Kaput. Adios. No comebacks guaranteed. The last *ever* Elvis show.

What an honour! What a privilege! His grandchildren - presuming that one day he would marry Alexandra and have children with her, who would in turn mature and find partners with whom *they* would have children - would one day hear of this historical occasion.

Milking the opportunity for all it had to offer, he continued chatting excitedly to his now dead idol.

"How about an autograph?" he asked, pointing to the pen which was still conveniently taped to his shin. Elvis looked at it, and then at Dave. Slowly, Elvis's aging, forlorn countenance changed, and grew to one of sinister sarcasm.

"Why don't you ..." Elvis began, as he broke into a cackling laugh.

"... go ..." he continued as he stepped forward on the platform.

"... to ..." he cackled as his rising voice reached fever pitch.

" ... Hhhhheeeeelllllllllllll!"

Elvis screamed as he stepped over the ledge, fell into eternity, and disappeared.

Dave stopped. This was not the Elvis he had grown to know and love. How could this wounded creature be the person who had sung *Love Me Tender*? Now that he thought about it, those last few lines of *Heartbreak Hotel* had been performed with a certain degree of cynicism as well.

What was wrong with Elvis? Why was everyone on this staircase so aggravated? They were all about to enter Heaven, but not one of them had a smile, a kind word, or even a seasonable comment to make. Had these people spent all of their goodness on Earth? Sure, they were all dead, but was it *really* that bad? Did they have to be so blunt and rude about the whole situation?

Dave sat on the edge of the platform, feeling rejected. The thrill of his first exchange with Elvis was rapidly evaporating. He had expended a lot of energy on his hero, but was now feeling hurt; all he had received in return for years of faithful worship was a curt few bars of *Heartbreak Hotel* and a maniacal 'Go to Hell'.

The well-muscled man interrupted Dave's thoughts as he stepped onto the ledge.

"Pardon me," apologised Dave as he moved to one side. "I hope I'm not in the way."

The man either didn't hear Dave or chose to ignore him as he stepped over the ledge to his destiny.

"Lucky bloke," said Dave as he watched him disappear.

Dave felt that if these morose, rude people had been sent to Heaven, then it should be an easy gig for a fun-loving bloke like himself. This thought led him to wonder if he could possibly pop in to Heaven for a few hours or so. He mulled over the positive aspects of his suggestion for a few seconds. First, he had walked all the way up the stairs for very little return, and felt that he deserved to see Heaven as a reward. Second, Elvis would probably be in a more receptive mood once had had settled in to Nirvana. And third, God had instructed him to 'Have a look around', hadn't he?

Dave briefly tried to think of some countering arguments. He only just managed to avoid acknowledging a few of the more pessimistic predictions that popped into his head. While his subconscious was neatly suppressing the fact that God had expressly told Dave not to go anywhere without him, Dave paused to allow the well-groomed man, who was now on the platform, to take the plunge. Then, after a further two seconds of deliberately avoiding any negative thoughts about his proposed visit to Heaven, Dave made his decision.

Mothers of Heaven, lock up your daughters. Here I come.

He stood up on the edge of the platform, shivering with nervous anticipation. He was just considering whether he would enter Heaven with a triple somersault or a one-and-a-half flip with a reverse twist, when he was forcefully struck. By a thought.

Hieshler.

Dave froze. The man who had just jumped was Harry Hieshler. As he quickly analysed and evaluated this new shred of knowledge, an entirely new paradigm formed in his mind. Hieshler, as everybody knew, was a selfish, greedy and conceited man. Not a good candidate for Heaven. The despairing faces of the stair climbers began to make sense, as did Elvis's final twisted remark, and Old Mister Smiggins' unexpected destiny. This was not the stairway to Heaven at all. That must make it the stairway to....

He had to get back down those stairs. Fast.

Dave turned to see the obese frame of the Morgan W. Morgan bearing down upon him. He panicked. While he dodged to the left and danced to the right, Morgan simply continued his methodical march forward. Dave hopped sideways a few more times, before he was forced to retreat to the edge of the narrow platform like a pirate walking the plank. He had only centimetres between his left foot and an eternity in Hell. In desperation, he tried to jump over Morgan.

He missed.

PART THREE

Chapter 32

A pungent odour filled the air, smelling like a combination of rotting eggs, sewer gas and expensive aftershave lotion. The stench was so strong that it roused Dave from his deep sleep. He groaned, pulled the twisted sheet off his legs, and then threw his lumpy wet pillow onto the floor. Slowly, very apprehensively, Dave opened his eyes.

The first thing that he noticed was that the ceiling was very dirty, even by his standards. The paintwork was cracked and peeling, and water marks stained half a dozen areas including a spot directly above Dave's head, which emitted a regular drip. As Dave watched, a rat scampered out from a hole in one corner of the ceiling, scurried down the wall, and disappeared behind a decrepit wardrobe. Dave heard a screech as the resident rat family welcomed back a parent.

Dave sat up to better survey the room. As he moved, the bed creaked and groaned rudely. It did not like being disturbed. Despite the obvious mess, Dave felt a strange familiarity about his surrounds, so he warily decided to explore them further. As his feet reached the floor, they touched something foreign and instantly recoiled.

Vomit. A puddle of mouldy vomit.

Dave wiped his toes on the sheet, but it was not much cleaner than the floor. He retched as he realised he had just slept on such disgustingly dirty linen. Then he retched again as he realised that he had just slept in such a disgusting dirty room. A rapidly escalating urge to escape from the room enveloped him. However he was naked and his ignorance of what was outside reinforced Dave's desire to dress at least to the point where he wouldn't be arrested. Hopefully, the old wardrobe had something, *anything* that he could wear.

The path to the wardrobe was uninviting. The floor was strewn with discarded food, beer bottles, and all manner of unidentifiable mould and stains. Holding his nose and inhaling as sparingly as possible, Dave gingerly stepped along what he felt was his safest path. He winced as some unidentifiable brown goo squelched between his toes.

Mentally thanking the architect for making the room quite small, he soon arrived at the wardrobe. He pulled at the doorknob, which fell off in his hand. So he tugged at the door, which fell off its hinges. A rat screeched aggressively it scuttered for cover, as did a very angry looking dung beetle.

It was Dave's *lucky* day. Lying indignantly in a soiled heap on the bottom of the wardrobe was a soiled pair of jeans and a stained brown shirt. Knowing that he had no alternative, Dave cringed as he brushed down the jeans and shirt, and gingerly pulled them on. Strangely, both items were exactly his size.

An eerie feeling began to gnaw at the back of Dave's mind. Apart from the filthy state of the room, something felt very wrong. The feeling fuelled his urge to escape from the room as quickly as possible. He stepped his way across towards the main door, opened it, and then discovered why it had been closed. A huge pile of rotting garbage was blocking the way. Momentarily taken aback, Dave retreated, and sat back on the bed, which collapsed under the sudden strain, sending him sprawling sideward. His cheek squelched against a mouldy, unidentifiable stain that smelt of rotten cheese.

At this point Dave was close to breaking. Who would live in such a pigsty? What type of person would allow a room to degenerate to this vulgar state? Where the hell was he?

The gnawing thought at the back of Dave's mind continued to grow steadily. As he looked across the room, his gaze fell upon an empty pizza box, and then some empty beer cans. A frightening realisation snuck its way into his consciousness.

No. It couldn't be.

Trembling with dread, Dave rolled onto his side. He saw exactly what he had hoped that he would *not* see. Next to the bed were the remains of a very dejected-looking but familiar bedside table. With visible emotional pain, Dave reached down, and pulled open what remained of the bottom drawer. Staring back at him was a tattered, fading photograph of Elvis Presley.

This was *his* room.

How? That was the only notion that Dave's mind would consider. He contemplated every possible 'how' imaginable, concentrating on two in particular: 'How did I get here?', and particularly 'How do I get out of here?'. Unfortunately for Dave, all the answers that his mind provided were either very unlikely or unthinkably awful.

He rolled the alternatives to the first question over in his mind, and narrowed them down to the two most likely scenarios. He had just woken in his own bed after an incredibly long sleep either, during which time he had experienced a wild, vivid dream about God, Heaven and Elvis, or.... No!

Dave picked up the dirty bed sheet, and used it to scrub some built-up film from the small window above his bed. The rag did not clean very efficiently, but it managed to wipe away enough grime so that Dave could see through a small portion of the glass. What he saw did not please him. On the pot-hole strewn road outside was a car: an old-school, non-hovering, petrol-engine car with four wheels, four doors and a windscreen. The vehicle instantly confirmed Dave's worst fears.

Dave had hoped that the entire experience of Heaven, God and Elvis had been a bizarre dream. If this were true, he reasoned, then he had to assume that the mess in his room on Earth had simply festered and grown of its own accord. This was not entirely unbelievable, as it often seemed to do this, even when he was awake. He could have sworn that the mess multiplied itself while he was sitting at the Stranglers Bar. If this theory was correct then the world outside should have remained in *status quo* while he was asleep. Even presuming that he had thrashed his sixty-hour Mexican sleeping record, the rest of humanity should not have changed to any great extent in the interim. But the car....

On Earth, petrol driven vehicles had not been sighted on the roads for at least 10 years. Advancements in nuclear energy and aero-spatial engineering had long since provided a far more economical, quiet and more efficient means of transport, the Hovercar. Ordinary cars had been banned for over a decade. Sighting the petrol car was solid proof to dispute his 'wild dream and self multiplying rubbish' theory. This left only one possible solution in Dave's mind.

He was in Hell.

He sat amongst the rubbish and the rats for hours, ruing his predicament. How did one get out of Hell? He had only vague feelings that it involved Morgan, Hieshler and Juan Carlos Manuel de la Espirito, but apart from that he had developed no firm thoughts, no plan, and no real direction. He assumed that it would be a tricky task. In the absence of any better ideas, Dave went to the Stranglers Bar to think.

Chapter 33

Dave pulled a rancid piece of unidentifiable garbage out of the hole, revealing a welcome flicker of light. He was tunnelling through a massive pile of rotten rubbish that was blocking his front doorway, and the glint meant that he was almost through.

"Interesting security concept," mumbled Dave as he burrowed even further into the tunnel. After widening it to a suitable diameter, he wormed forward through it. After much sliding, squeezing and wriggling, he finally popped his head through into the world outside. Any lingering doubts that Dave had about whether he was in Hell or not instantly evaporated.

His once cosy front yard now looked like a battlefield. The small picket fence at the bottom of the garden was constructed from tall iron bars, with rolls of barbed wire on its top and skirting its base. His original magenta and turquoise Fashion-Turf now looked like a cracked concrete car park, and was strewn with broken bottles and potted with pools of putrid water. The air was thick with pollution, and its smoky odour almost choked Dave as he inhaled. Sounds of nearby gunfire rattled his ears, and the cries of miserable children spread across the landscape like smog. Unmistakably Hell.

Yet despite its obvious gruesomeness, the whole set up of Hell struck Dave as rather non-classical. There was no Fire-and-Brimstone, the Devil was not running around with a pitchfork, and he could not hear any elevator music in the background. Hell was nothing like he had previously imagined. This Hell had buildings, roads, cars, and even a few forlorn plants. In fact it looked very much like Earth, except more primitive. And *exceedingly* less hospitable.

Dave decided to make one last reality check: Old Mr Smiggins. After extracting himself from the garbage pile, he walked across to the old man's apartment and knocked on the door. Unfortunately, nobody answered. Dave knocked again, but much to his dismay, there was still no answer. Old Mr Smiggins obviously hadn't arrived yet.

Unbeknownst to Dave, Old Mr Smiggins was presently about half way along the queue in the Separating Room, and was about to enter the fight of his life with a very disbelieving Saint Barnabas.

Dave looked through the window of Old Mr Smiggins' apartment. He did not see what he expected to see. He anticipated that Old Mr Smiggins' room would be covered in garbage, like in his own. What he saw instead was not a filthy mess, but, in a grotesque way, was even more disgusting. Pornography.

The entire apartment was wallpapered from skirting to cornice with vile pornographic pictures. Dave was not a prude - he had been known to slip into the Babe-O-Matic at the Stranglers Bar on the odd occasion - but what he saw repulsed him. The photographs depicted every fetish of which Dave could conceive, and plenty that he couldn't. The images were nauseating.

On a shelf were dozens of old-style videotapes, all with lewd titles bursting with cheap innuendo. The whole place was so devoid of morality that it was un-liveable. How could anyone wake up in the morning and face a cesspool of sin like that? thought Dave. He turned away from the room before he was sick. Even the garbage pile at his own front door was more inviting than Old Mr Smiggins' decrepit apartment.

Dave's thoughts returned to his task at hand: getting to the welcome familiarity of the Stranglers Bar. A quick check of his pockets revealed $6000 in old fashioned cash in his jeans; not a fortune, but hopefully enough to buy a few beers and a pizza for dinner. He walked across his yard – one small mercy was that the cracked concrete was less nauseating than the garish FashionTurf that insulted his yard on Earth – and then climbed through a hole that had been blown through the security fence. He walked warily down the vaguely familiar street.

He passed several more dwellings, all which stirred distant feelings of recognition. It seemed to Dave that God had modelled Hell on the Earth, but why? He made a mental note to clarify that point when he spoke to God again. *If* he spoke to God again....

After a few anxious and unpleasant minutes of walking, Dave approached a steeply rising section of road. He had never noticed that a hill lay between his apartment and the Stranglers Bar before, probably because he had always flown over it in a Hover-taxi.

A gang of extraordinarily obese men congregated at the base of the hill. Perhaps, Dave mused, they were too unfit to walk up it. However, he quickly elected to keep this thought private, as he noticed that the men all carried a variety of primitive lethal weapons such as nunchakus, knives and machetes. Moreover, they all wore leather jackets emblazoned with patch *'The Fat Fighters & Bikers Club'*.

Dave decided that on the balance of probabilities that it would be safer if he avoided even talking to the fat men, lest they take offence at inconsequential words such as *fat*igue, *fat*uitous or *fat*ality. Staring blankly at the ground, he passed nervously by the gang, praying that they did not try to kill or maim him.

A short time later, puffing heavily from the unaccustomed exercise, Dave arrived at the Stranglers Bar. After ducking under a flying dagger that had strayed from a knife fight in the car park, he went inside for a drink.

'Not very convivial' was his first observation; Dave was, on occasion, a master of understatement. The ramshackle bar area reeked of vomit, and was spattered with blood stains, some of them clearly recent. Simultaneous fights were occurring: one between two men armed with broken pool cues, while the second involved a woman who was beating up a man, who by this stage had a broken nose. Dave sat self-consciously at the bar and waited for service.

And waited.

And waited some more.

After five full minutes of inaction, he whistled quietly to the bartender, who seemed to be making himself busy doing nothing. The only response that Dave discerned was that the barman tried to make it even more apparent that he was busy, which was difficult as he was still not actually doing anything. Realising that he was in hostile territory, Dave decided to take a considerate, careful approach to the situation, and continued waiting calmly.

A tough, ragged looking woman with an empty bottle in her hand stepped up to the bar beside Dave. She smashed the bottle violently down on the bar, sending glass splintering in all directions. The bartender looked up absently, as if stirred from a daydream.

"Get me a beer," growled the woman.

The bartender did not acknowledge the request, but eventually skulked off to pour the beer. The rough woman looked across at Dave.

"It's the only way to get service around here," she snarled.

Dave was beginning to believe her. He was also getting thirsty, so he decided to test her theory. When in Rome.... Picking up a nearby empty bottle, he smashed it down hard onto the bar. It didn't break.

"Arrgh. You're a big wimp," scorned the woman, ripping the bottle from Dave's grasp. "You do it like this."

She crashed the bottle down hard. Onto Dave's head.

Dave's immediate thought was to hope that his skull was stronger than the glass. Thankfully, it was.

"Oh," said Dave as his watering eyes focused back on the woman. "I can see the technique now. It's all in the wrist."

"That's right," said the woman. "Here's another demonstration so that you don't forget." She picked up another bottle, and smashed it viciously across Dave's face.

"Why thnank-nyou very mnuch," said Dave through a bloodied nose and lips as he struggled manfully to hold his temper. "I'll renender thnat for nenxt tine."

The bartender returned with the woman's beer.

"Get another one for sauce-face..." commanded the woman. Dave felt pleasantly surprised - perhaps this was her way of apologising.

"... he'll pick up the tab for both."

Dave didn't think much of the apology, but did not have either the courage or stupidity to protest. Besides, the woman had already sculled the entire bottle, and had stomped off in search of another victim. The bartender eventually returned with a beer, which Dave gratefully accepted. He had been looking forward to this. He opened his mouth and poured the beer down his parched throat. The fluid barely touched his tonsils as it headed straight for his stomach. However his tonsils copped a battering a second later as the beer, for want of a better term, reversed its journey.

"Arrgh," gagged Dave, fighting for breath as the warm, foul-tasting liquid belched its way out of his mouth. "What was that?"

The barman looked at him with disdain.

"That was a beer, you loser," said the barman. "And you owe me for two of them."

Dave's faced flushed with instant anger. Beer was a subject that was very dear to his heart, and he was not going to let some lazy two-bit barman lecture him on the topic.

"I'm not paying for that," insisted Dave, forgetting his earlier vow to be considerate and careful. "That drink was disgusting. How long since you've cleaned the pipes? Or the glasses? There was some dried tomato sauce and a cigarette butt on the bottom of mine. And the beer, or whatever it was, was watered down. What's more, if you insist on serving something that tastes like...."

The barman had heard enough.

"Security!" he yelled.

Before the sound 'Sec' had left the barman's lips, two hostile men pounced on Dave. One had no hair, no shirt, no neck and no brain, while the other had big muscles, big tattoos, a big beard and a big attitude problem. The bald bully tried to separate Dave's foot from his shin, while the bearded one attempted to rotate Dave's head through three hundred and sixty degrees, giving new meaning to the name "Stranglers Bar".

"What 'ave we got 'ere?" asked the guard with the smallest brain and the least hair.

"A loser," replied the barman.

"A loser, eh?" repeated the guard, as if he was trying to remember what the word meant. He was.

"Yes," continued the barman. "First he threw up all over the clean floor, and then he accused me of watering down the beer. He even had the ignorance to say that the security guards were pathetic weaklings."

"What does pathet ... he said *what*?"

"He said that you guys were pathetic weaklings," lied the barman.

That was more than enough provocation for the two maniacs who voluntarily acted as security guards at Hell's Stranglers Bar. Before Dave could even begin to protest his innocence, they set upon him with a ferocious series of kicks and punches. Dave rebounded helplessly between the thug's boots like a pinball as they launched into him without pausing for mercy.

Two terrifying minutes later, the attack abated. Dave lay on the floor, feeling not only very bruised, but also lucky. It's not every day, Dave thought, that two vicious thugs from Hell attack you, and you are *lucky* enough to survive. However, in assessing his own degree of luck, Dave hadn't taken into account one salient fact: the guards weren't finished with him yet.

"That was for the 'pathetic weakling' comment," said the bearded thug. "Now you're going to pay for the beer."

The bare-chested thug upended Dave by the ankles, and jangled him up and down like a giant tea-bag. Six thousand dollars - Dave's only funds - fell from his pocket. The bearded bully scooped it up.

"How much for two beers?" he asked the barman.

"Er, about four thousand dollars," replied the barman, who had watched Dave's flogging with alarming indifference.

"What about a tip?"

"Why of course," replied the barman sarcastically. "How stupid of me to forget. Two beers will actually cost you...."

"Six thousand dollars?"

"Yes, six thousand dollars, that's it," echoed the barman. "Six thousand dollars and we're all square." He took the money, put a thousand dollars into the till, and slipped the rest into his back pocket as he made another wisecrack at Dave.

"That's not a very big tip. I hope you're not expecting service with a smile next time you drink at the Stranglers Bar."

Dave wasn't. Nor, he vowed, was he ever drinking at this bar again, not even if it was the only place on Hell that served beer. He might buy some take-aways, he conceded, but he would never drink here again.

The bald thug released his grip, dropping Dave like a kid's school-case onto the muck-laden floor. Dave decided that this would be an opportune moment to quietly leave, and began crawling towards the exit. He did not get very far.

"You're not going anywhere," said the bald thug as he cruelly stood on Dave's little finger, "until you clean up this mess...."

"I guess that's reasonable," surrendered Dave, before adding that he thought it was a tiny teeny weeny little bit unfair that he had to clean up everyone else's mess as well.

"... with your tongue," added the thug.

Before Dave could utter another word in protest, he felt something like a dingo trap clamp onto the back of his neck. He was even more terrified when he then realised that it was a not an animal snare, but the bearded bully's hand. Dave tried to break free, but it was utterly useless - the man's grip was far too strong. He felt as impotent as a kitten trying to escape from the jaws of a Pit Bull Terrier. Then the bald bully joined the assault. He grabbed a fistful of Dave's hair, and knotted it through his own fingers. Then, millimetre by agonising millimetre, the thugs forced Dave's head downward towards the vile floorboards.

Dave resisted with all his might, but the harder he pushed, the more firmly the thugs pressed back, and the louder they laughed. Soon a small crowd of hecklers gathered to watch Dave suffer the indignity that only licking a mouthful of someone else's vomit from a filthy bar floor can impose.

Dave broke into a sweat. He expected Hell to be tough - a bit on the hot side perhaps, and the occasional jab of a pitchfork to contend with - but this was unbearable. Slowly, torturously, the floor became closer, and its nauseating aroma filled Dave's nostrils. He gagged. Anger flooded his bloodstream, and he resisted with every ounce of strength he could muster, but his efforts were futile; the thugs' hands were so strong that it would have been risky for them to masturbate.

They continued to press his head downward slowly but agonisingly surely, and soon it was almost touching the floor. His moment of filth arrived as he heard the words he had been dreading: "Stick out your tongue."

Dave, defiant to the death, refused. He wanted to shout 'NO' but dared not open his mouth. He tried to shake his head, but could not move it. So he just kept silently kneeling, one thug on each side, the whole time thinking furiously. His neck was aching and his eyes were watering and his gut was retching, but his brain was working overtime. He steadfastly remained motionless, except his arms, which he began to imperceptibly slide forward.

"I said," repeated a thug - Dave didn't know or care which one - "to *stick out your tongue*."

Dave again refused, as the bullies delicately rubbed the tip of his nose into something that looked suspiciously like diced carrot. He moved his arms forward another fraction. If he could just slide them one more centimetre....

"This is your last warning, punk," commanded the thug in a very, *very* intimidating voice. "Lick that floor. Now. *Or else*."

Dave hoped his arms were in the right position, and played his last card. With one almighty lunge, he flung both elbows backwards.

Some people, in desperate or life-threatening situations like a car crash, feel as though they are experiencing the action in slow motion. Dave felt as though he could have gone for a cup of coffee and a sandwich as his last-ditch play unfolded. Milliseconds ticked by like minutes as his arms flung upwards. Adrenalin surged his veins like hot oil as his elbows searched desperately for their targets. Farther backward they thrust, as far as he could drive them, but still, they contacted nothing but air. With a final heroic play, Dave forced his shoulders back so far that they almost popped out of their sockets, giving his elbows one last arc in which to strike. With this decisive lunge, Dave's elbows simultaneously hit their bull's-eyes: their hard bony tips each rammed into two warm, soft, and cuddly lumps.

Testicles.

Dave felt the grips of his attacker's hands slacken. Without pausing to say goodbye, Dave was up like a racing cheetah out its starting box. He shot towards the door, with the howls of two very angry thugs ringing in his ears.

Dave ran harder than he had ever run before. He pushed himself with even more determination than the time he heard that a free beer promotion was on at the mall. Simply, he ran for his life.

The two guards, after ten vital seconds recovering from Dave's well-aimed blows, pursued him with vengeful rage. Luckily by this time Dave was just out of knife throwing range, which he discovered as he heard one weapon clatter to the ground only metres behind him. He turned out of the Stranglers car park and bolted for home.

His legs and arms pumped furiously as he sprinted down the street, hurdling potholes and prostrate drunks as he ran. He soon began to wish that he had done something more demanding with his days on Earth than drink beer and eat pizza, as his fitness level was already showing its mediocrity. Dave afforded himself a quick glance over his shoulder. The thugs were still 30 or 40 metres behind, but were catching him rapidly. Moreover, they didn't look happy.

"Thank goodness I never smoked cigarettes," gasped Dave to himself, "or by now my life would have been shorter by the rest of it."

A short steep rise in the road loomed in front of Dave like Mount Everest. His lungs were bursting, his legs were burning, and his heart was beating *double allegro*. How was he going to get over the hill? Focusing ahead, he tried desperately to ignore the very clear messages from every cell in his body to stop. If he could establish even a small break up the rise, Dave reasoned, then he could possibly scoot away on the steep downward section on the other side. Hopefully this would give him enough of a lead to make it home and ... Dave wasn't sure what he would do when he made it home. His thoughts turned to a more pressing matter. His legs.

They were stopping; involuntarily, undeniably, and unfortunately stopping.

Dave fought with grit and mettle like never before. He was exhaling air harder than a whoopee cushion at a weight-watcher's meeting, and sucking it in just as ferociously. Every muscle in his body strained to deliver another dash of speed, but they had nothing left on which to draw. His muscles were swimming in a bath of lactic acid, and did not care for further work. Agonisingly, they began to cramp.

Dave looked up. He was nearly to the crest. He looked back. The maniacs were catching him, fast. Their aerobic fitness routine - beating the life out of someone for at least twenty minutes, four times per week - was paying dividends.

He now realised that his flight was worthless. Despite his efforts, he was resigned to the fact that the bullies would soon catch him. Then they would flog him to death and leave him to rot by the roadside amongst the drunks. What a horrid way to die. Dave had always imagined himself dying from too much sex or a similar ailment. Ending his existence as a bitumen smear in Hell was definitely *not* what he had envisaged. What was worse, if he died in Hell then he would never see Alexandra again.

Dave was now almost at the top of the hill, but that fact was small consolation. He was knackered. His legs had seized, his lungs were blistering, and his heart was broken, both metaphorically and physically. As he staggered onwards, he looked despondently ahead down the sweep of road, taking in what would presumably be the last sights of his existence. The vision was of no comfort: filthy potholes dotted the road, rubbish covered the footpath, and ugly graffiti plastered the fences. Even the gang of vicious looking fat men, who were loitering ahead, was nothing more than a blot on the landscape.

Suddenly Dave stopped in his tracks, not just with exhaustion, but also with a chance realisation. *The Fat Fighters & Bikers Club.*

He looked behind to discover that the two security guards were now almost at the crest of the hill. Timing was crucial. Dave quickly took a few steps sideways, and turned to face the group of obese men. Then he did something that would normally have been grossly foolish.

He insulted a gang of men who were carrying very dangerous weapons, and wearing leather jackets denoting that they loved a biff.

"Hey, you bunch of fat bastards! Yes, I'm talking to you, you bloated bags of blubber." The gang became angry.

"You look like a six-pack of cellulite sacks." They became extremely angry.

"You lumps of lard. You huge hippos. You rotund rhinos." Dave wished that they would hurry up and try to kill him, as he was quickly running out of both insults and, more importantly, time.

They obliged.

Dave sprawled forward onto the ground as knives, nunchakus and machetes shot through the air towards him. As the shower of weapons flew at him, Dave dived forward into a large pothole. From its muddy bottom, Dave watched the weapons fly perilously close to his head, some missing him by only centimetres. He turned to see the security guards clear the crest of the hill, and watched as their expressions changed from hatred to fear as they ran headlong into a shower of high velocity lethal weapons.

A nunchaku wrapped itself around the bald one's scalp, while the other guard had a free beard trim courtesy of a machete en route to his throat. Dave felt only a tiny shred of sympathy as his two tormenters writhed in agony on the road. Then he finally allowed himself the luxury of a sigh of relief, and crawled out of his ditch.

He doubled back on his path, and took the long way home. Knowing that he was safe from retribution from the fat men - none of them could run fast enough to catch a disease - he gave them a parting wave. He eventually arrived home feeling extraordinarily sore, still terrified, yet also a little bit proud of himself. He curled up in the softest, driest pile of rubbish he could find, and had a long, broken, uncomfortable sleep.

Chapter 34

Morgan's dream was ending. Distant images of a competition, a big crowd and a hot day drifted out of his consciousness. He had fading recollections of a cap, a deafening chant, and then of a searing pain that scorched through his whole body.

He heard a monstrous noise, and woke with a jolt. Something was wrong. A blaring siren wailed in his ear, almost deafening him, and sending his eardrums into paroxysms of pain. As the wailing continued, he screamed in anguish, which only intensified the cacophony. He leapt up, still stunned and half asleep, to search for the insufferable instrument of torture. He soon found it: an alarm clock.

Morgan did not bother switching it off. Instead he hurled the timepiece violently into the floor, sending circuit boards and electrical transistors ricocheting in all directions. He *hated* alarm clocks. Why hadn't someone invented a better method of waking sleeping people?

After rubbing sleep from his eyes, Morgan focused on his surrounds. He was surprised to discover that he was in his office, not his bedroom. *How strange*, he thought, *I can't even remember nodding off*. Must have been a hard day. He walked across to his workstation in front of the control panel, and sat in his favourite chair. The arm rests felt awkward and maladjusted, and their width was far too narrow. He *hated* it when other people sat in his chair. It was even more unforgivable when they readjusted the ergonomics as well. Morgan grunted an unintelligible series of expletives as he struggled to extricate his huge derriere from between the armrests.

"Whoever committed this sacrilegious act will be tortured and then fired," he mumbled as he delicately rubbed the friction burns on the sides of his hips.

A crackling voice filtered through the intercom speaker on his workstation.

"Excuse me, President Morgan."

Morgan did nothing. The past few minutes had been very irritating, and this innocent interruption gave him an opportunity to improve his mood. He decided to repeatedly ignore and then brutally terrorise the employee who had just tried to contact him on the intercom. Provoking and/or tyrannising workers always made him feel better.

Sitting in his readjusted chair, Morgan waited for the voice to return. He decided that five, perhaps six times he would disregard the interruption, and then soundly punish the owner of the voice for allegedly disturbing his midmorning nap. He waited calmly, anticipating a hint of intimidated nervousness in the voice. The voice remained silent.

"Who is this moron?" mumbled Morgan. "Doesn't he know that I've got better things to do than sit around waiting for him to interrupt me?"

Morgan waited defiantly for five minutes, gradually becoming more frustrated. Why didn't the voice return? What was the message? It could have been important.

"When I find that idiot," growled Morgan, "I'm going to crush him like a cockroach. He will whimper like a whipped dog by the time I'm finished with him. Then, while he is grovelling in remorse ..." Morgan rubbed his hands slowly together, "... I will fire him instantly in front of his colleagues. They will see that nobody, *nobody*, makes Morgan W. Morgan wait unnecessarily."

Morgan waited - unnecessarily - for a further minute, until his impatience skyrocketed so high that he could not contain it. He exploded like a popped champagne cork and cannoned out of his office, across the hall and into the secretaries' typing pool.

Morgan recoiled as he entered the office, horrified by the scene that confronted him. He stared in shock as the vision organised itself on his retina, then travelled along his optic nerve before transmitting itself onto his brain. Other areas of Morgan's brain immediately sent him messages telling him to completely disbelieve what he was observing, as it could not possibly be happening. So he blinked, and looked again, but the same picture registered in his mind.

The scene was complete disgrace. His employees were - gasp - not working.

He paid his staff to work, not to waste time with idle banter and idiocy. Where was the discipline that he had so painstakingly flayed into his employees? Despite the ferocious scowl upon Morgan's face, most of the staff remained ignorant of his presence. They were otherwise involved in more pressing matters, like reading magazines, drinking cocktails, or flirting. Morgan's temper exploded.

"Who was it," he boomed, "that just called for me?"

A couple of faces turned lazily in his direction. One young secretary, who was casually buttoning up her blouse, volunteered some information.

"I think it was Hopgood," she said.

Morgan looked around the office, frothing with wrath. He spied a face that looked somewhat familiar - one that belonged to a bespectacled young man whom he thought was named something like Hopgood.

"Was it you?" he commanded of Hopgood, who was reading an old comic book.

"Was it me who *what?*" sneered Hopgood, annoyed that Morgan had interrupted him just as the Phantom was about to clobber a jungle thief.

"How dare you speak to me in such an insolent tone," said Morgan between gritted teeth. "Now answer my question properly or I will dismiss you from this job, instantly."

He stood over the young man, trying to intimidate him not only with angry words, but with his physical presence as well.

"I'll tell you what," replied Hopgood after a significant and annoying pause. "I'll save you the trouble." He nonchalantly rolled up his comic and placed it under his arm, then added "I quit." He sauntered out of the room, blowing kisses to the typing pool girls as he did.

Morgan had never been so affronted in his life. As he looked at the debauched scene in front of him, he boiled with fury as he calculated how much money he was wasting on this disrespectful bunch of louts.

"Why you disrespectful...." Morgan stopped mid-sentence. He was about to unleash a fearsome verbal attack on the entire staff, but reconsidered. Simple chastisement was an inadequate punishment for this unforgivable display. A far more painful and degrading deterrent was required. Still in a blind rage, he stormed out of the administrative area, back to his own office. He sat at his desk, trying to devise a new discipline program, but he was so angry that he could not concentrate.

Deciding that an eating binge might settle his nerves, he called the catering unit and ordered a tray of his favourite snack: sandwiches with a filling of bacon, chocolate sauce, peanut butter, potato chips and sour cream.

"No can do. We're on lunch," was the curt reply from a nameless chef.

"Do you know who this is?" yelled the irate President.

"I don't care if you're the President of England, mate, we're on lunch. We're not sending you a tray of peanuts, or anything else."

"This is Morgan W. Morgan!" he yelled down the line. "I want some sandwiches, or I'll have your job! Do you understand me?"

Over the next ten seconds, Morgan could not believe what he heard. Nothing. The chef had hung up.

Morgan, now angry beyond emotion, could feel his cranial blood pressure swelling his head to the next hat size. Where had his staff learnt these insolent habits? With a quivering hand, he jotted a short phrase onto a notebook page headed 'Discipline Program'. The message simply read *'cat'o'nine tails'*.

Then, as his anger overrode all other bodily functions, he sat at his desk staring bitterly into space. After ten minutes, he had not relaxed at all. His muscles still trembling and his breaths coming in shallow rasps, Morgan began to comprehend the extreme extent of his rage. From experience he knew that there was only one way to calm himself from such a turn of anger; only one way to soothe his knotted, seething mind. He turned to his favourite source of instant gratification. Violence.

He pushed his chair along in front of the instrument panel, past the remote controls, computer terminals and the laser probes. His eyes focused on the large, gleaming, red button in the centre of the panel. In the face of such overwhelming desperation, it was a beacon of hope. After keying a code number into a security panel, Morgan salivated as the 'BOOM' system flickered into life. This would be fun.

Swiping a smart card through a scanner, he accessed the next security level, and began scrolling through a computer screen to select a weapon. Morgan chose a small nuclear warhead - destructive enough to take out a decent sized city - delivered via a rocket-launched missile. He chose New Zealand as the target, simply because he didn't like rugby.

Shivering with delicious anticipation, he typed a password to access the final level of security. After rapidly rubbing his hands together and quickly licking his lips, Morgan paused for a second to savour the moment. Then with a holler of joy he thumped down the 'BOOM' button with an enthusiastic fist.

"Arrgh!"

His fist recoiled as he screeched in pain. The security system had not released the 'BOOM' button.

He looked at the screen, which was belligerently flashing a message. It read *'Security Password Incorrect. Access Denied'*. After uttering numerous audible obscenities at the machine, he used his good hand to carefully retype his password on the keyboard.

'I - A - M - T - H - E - B - E - S - T.'

Again he pressed the 'BOOM' button, this time more tentatively. However it remained locked in position, with the same message blaring on the screen in front of him.

"This is *impossible*," growled Morgan. Surely, he had not mistyped his password twice? Painstakingly, key by key, he re-entered his egocentric password into the computer, well aware of the consequences that another mistyped letter would induce. Shivering, but now with trepidation rather than anticipation, he timidly touched the top of the boom button.

The noise that the alarm clock had created earlier in the morning was like a lullaby compared to the response of the 'BOOM' system to Morgan's third incorrect entry. Sirens wailed, lights flashed, bells rang and buzzers blared as the anti-tamper mechanism sprung into action. Morgan jumped up in a blind panic. He had activated the self-destruct sequence. In half an hour, one thousand hidden bombs would simultaneously detonate, blowing the building to bits.

Ten mind numbing seconds later, a platoon of soldiers stormed into the room. They headed directly for Morgan, and tackled and bound him like a rodeo calf. Morgan could only writhe about on the floor, howling through his gag in disbelief, as more security officers poured into his office. The fire brigade, the police department, the FBI and a navy unit all appeared within minutes, among them a team of weapons consultants who somehow disarmed the self-destruct trigger.

Fifteen minutes later the Chief of Global Security arrived from the capital. He released the handcuffs from Morgan's arms, unbuckled Morgan's belt from around his ankles, and let him explain his side of the story, which was that the security system was malfunctioning, or words to that effect. After Morgan had exhausted not only his list of insulting expletives but the Chief's patience as well, the Chief tried to inject some level-headedness into the not-too-cordial discussion.

"This was all explained in the memo," he said with a straightforward air.

"Memo?" retorted Morgan. "What memo?"

"The memo informing you that the 'BOOM' system has been suspended."

"Suspended? Suspended by whom?"

"The world government," said the chief in a measured tone, annoyed that Morgan was wasting his time in wanting explanations of universally known facts. "I am sure you have heard about the lobbying by the Human Rights Activists."

The chief's words stunned Morgan. Was this a joke? He looked around the room for secret hidden cameras, half expecting a toothy blow-waved game show host to leap out from behind a hidden screen, complete with canned laughter and applause. Morgan looked back at the chief, searching vainly for a hint of a smile. He could not see one.

"Human Rights Activists?" said Morgan. "Impossible. How could such a pathetic bunch of unemployed, greenie, communist louts have lobbied the government? Collectively the HRA's don't have enough funds to buy a lentil burger, much less influence government policy. That costs billions. Anyway, what rights do a bunch of placard-waving peace lovers have to stop my 'BOOM' system, just because it causes trivial amounts of continental plate damage and occasional insignificant genocide? What about *my* rights? Don't I have rights, as protected by the 169th amendment to the American constitution, to use arms against a perceived enemy?"

"Personally, I think that the HRA's have a valid *raison d'être*," responded the Chief.

Morgan was vilified. Despite not knowing what *'raison d'être'* meant, he had never been so affronted in his entire life - certainly not by the head of what was virtually his own security service.

"Get out!" Morgan shrieked. "Get out before I … before I…." He was about to say 'call security' but realised the folly of such a statement. Caught like a netted fish, he resorted to ranting.

"All of you get out of this office, get off this floor, get out of this building, and get out of my life," he yelled without drawing breath. After waving his fist in the air, he aggressively ground his finger into the Chief's chest. The Chief did not flinch. He stood solidly, staring down at the very red-faced president, silently amused by the way that his jowls bounced as he screamed. When Morgan finished raving, the chief looked at him with a calm smile on his lips.

"With pleasure," he responded. "Men!"

His security staff bounced into line and stood to attention.

"Fiiiiiile OUT!" commanded the chief. The security staff, drilled to the millimetre, turned as one, and marched methodically out the door. Then the captain turned, clicked his heels together, and followed without as much as a goodbye salute for his ex-employer.

Morgan sunk into his chair and buried his face in his hands. What a horrible, horrible day. What had he done to deserve this? So far today he had dismissed a secretarial assistant, the catering unit, and the entire security staff. At this rate, he would soon not have any staff left.

Morgan should not have fretted about staffing levels. He would soon have far greater dilemmas about which to worry. Unbeknownst to him, Hell was watching him carefully. At the moment, it was simply warming up.

Chapter 35

Dave awoke in his garbage pile, desperately needing an answer. Usually if he wanted a solution to a particular problem, he simply went to the Stranglers Bar until the problem went away. If that didn't work then Plan B was to simply take a nap, and hope that when he awoke the answer had simply materialised in his head. Unfortunately on this occasion, despite a long sleep in a rubbish heap, he still had no idea how he was going to get out of Hell.

The only feeling he had —this notion had visited him in his dreams many times the night before – was that he had to find Morgan, Hieshler and Juan Carlos Manuel de la Espirito. Those three bastards had got him into this mess, so they could get him out. But how could he do this? They were presumably in the USA, on the other side of the planet, while he was stuck in an Australian back street with not a cent to his name.

To ensure that he had not missed a simple solution, Dave curled up and had another nap, but was still none the wiser on awakening. Solving this problem was proving to be the intellectual equivalent of beating Harry's Heroes in a football match: almost impossible.

To help bestow some energy into his thought processes, Dave decided to cook himself a feed. He scavenged through the garbage and found enough leftovers to scrape together a passable pizza. After baking the pizza in the fridge, which due to a seriously overheating motor was usefully warm, he guzzled it down greedily. Not bad, he thought. In fact it bore an uncanny resemblance to generic supermarket pizzas on Earth.

As was his habit after eating pizza, Dave switched on the television. Banal soap operas, infomercials and sitcoms helped his digestive system. Dave figured that this occurred because his body had learned to divert its blood flow from the brain, which it did not use when watching such television, to the stomach. The picture was very blurry, and the screen was covered in more snow than K2. This did not faze Dave, as his old-school television on Earth was only marginally better, so he was adept at tuning televisions using nothing more than ordinary household implements. A few minutes later, his 'fork + blender + corkscrew' antenna was merrily receiving snippets of the major local stations.

By rotating the kitchen fork to different angles, Dave channel-surfed for a few minutes. He found about a dozen stations, all of which were, somewhat surprisingly, subsidiaries of either HHTV or GTN. Half of the channels were showing infomercials, while the other half were in commercial breaks. At least, Dave figured, he was unlikely to get indigestion.

 A big-lipped curvy-hipped game show promoter crackled her way onto the screen, promoting a promotion.

"GTN is giving away yet another set of absolutely phantasmagorical prizes in our latest sensational competition. Don't worry, absolutely NO skill is involved, so anyone can win. Now hold on to your hats folks, as I tell you the array of sensational spoils on offer."

Dave didn't have a hat, so he hung on to his head instead.

"The lucky third prize winner will receive an all-expenses-paid around the world trip for two for a decade. Wow! Even luckier will be the second prize winner, who takes home a royal title from any Middle Asian island PLUS all the trappings. Whacko! And the fantastic first prize is ... wait for it ... Madagascar! That's right, you, too, can own your own nation, complete with its own political system, millions of hectares of public housing, thousands of car parks and dozens of wild animals."

Dave was about to change the channel, but took a masochistic interest in the drivel he was watching. The infomercial was like greasy fast food: it was so bad that you just had to have more. Dave fine-tuned the fork, and leaned closer for a better view.

"To enter, simply send a box filled with cash to GTN headquarters. The person who sends us the most money will be declared the winner. It's so simple that even the kids can enter!"

Dave scoffed. Hell had no tact. Nor did it have any finesse, style, or subtlety. At least, Dave felt, they could have asked viewers to 'send the most coupons' or even 'make the most telephone calls' rather than simply 'give the most money'. Although, Dave conceded, the net effect was much the same.

By tinkering with the corkscrew, Dave again changed channels. As he settled in to watch an infomercial for a very ugly pair of sunglasses, he forced a weak smile at the irony of the situation. Here he was, sitting in a beer-less apartment room, watching television commercials scheduled by the two bastards who had synergistically dragged him here in the first place. Even in Hell, Morgan and Hieshler were probably making a quadzillionmegadaddo dollars. But how in hell could he get to them?

Chapter 36

Hours passed. Slowly, a feeling of gnawing resentment grew inside Dave. As he monotonously flicked from one commercial to the next, the resentment gradually spawned an extended family of related emotions. Sitting amidst the squalor, with a half-baked pizza curdling in his stomach, Dave's countenance spiralled downwards as the hopelessness of his situation enveloped him.

Hell was a big place. It had no exit door, nor could he hit the 'escape' button. He couldn't jump off Hell's bus at the next stop, or slam a door in its face. No matter how far or fast he ran or rode, he couldn't possibly outpace Hell.

His loneliness magnified the hopelessness of his situation. Dave had no one to whom he could turn; a family of rats was his only acquaintances. Even a visit to Old Mr Smiggins was out of the question. For any person, living in Hell was awful beyond description. However, for Dave it was even worse, for unlike Hell's other residents, Dave *knew* that he was there.

In this part of the world, ignorance was bliss. All of Hell's other residents were joyfully unaware that they had to endure eternity in this most godforsaken of places, so despite the debauched and evil nature of their surroundings, they were able to continue their lives without completely capitulating. But Dave did not have this luxury. He was fully aware of the consequences that his own stupid actions had engendered. This knowledge was an unbearable burden. In short, he was without *hope*.

"I am a complete nincompoop," said Dave to himself, as his thoughts lamely led him through a guided tour of his own shortcomings.

He was lazy, that much he readily admitted. If he had studied harder at school, or tried with more determination to score a job, Morgan's computer would never have chosen him to 'win' the competition. Perhaps fewer days spent in the Stranglers Bar would have equipped him with more common sense and worldliness, which he now realised he had sadly lacked in the lead up to his win in the *Date with God* competition.

If only....

That phrase rebounded around his thoughts a thousand times. If only he had told the truth to God from the start. If only he hadn't lied to Saint Barnabas. If only, *if only* he had controlled his own impulsiveness and not chased Elvis up the stairway. Dave sunk another notch.

The pain of self-realisation grew too powerful to subdue any longer. Dave buried his head in his hands, and for the first time since he had dropped a half-full bottle of bourbon, he cried. The tears flowed freely down his cheeks, where they rained upon the cockroaches that were trying to nest in his chest hairs. At least, thought Dave, I can't get any lower.

As he nursed that sentiment, a rat tried to nibble on the end of his little finger. Dave was too spent to flinch. At least I am of use to someone, he lamented. The only other person who ever really believed in me was Alexandra.

The mere thought of Alexandra initiated something that Dave didn't think could possibly happen: his mood turned for the worse. The memory of his distant loved-one imbued a more powerful, even deeper melancholy within him. Not only was he stuck in Hell, but was without Alexandra. His tears flowed even more freely as he thought of the grief that he must have caused her. He painfully recalled their second and final meeting. It was the swiftest and sweetest of his life's defining moments. As he had glanced into Alexandra's eyes, he realised that his life had a purpose: he realised that he had to be something - *something* - for her.

Alexandra was a wonderful girl, so beautiful, charming, and intelligent. She had tracked him across the globe, and found him despite no doubt overwhelming adversity. How had she done it? *His* efforts to find *her* had been embarrassingly ungainly by comparison. Then again, Dave admitted, most of the planning for his various operations had been done over a half a dozen beers at the Stranglers Bar, which he now realised was a poor environment for hatching well-laid plans.

As Dave mulled and churned through his life, he gradually realised that he had rarely planned anything at all. He had just drifted through life, waiting for it to affect him. He had lived like a pinball, reacting to others, bouncing off their lives and ideas. Sure, he occasionally had plans for the future, but they were always fantasies, far-fetched dreams or half-baked schemes.

He resolved that if he ever returned to Earth that he would *make* his life worth living, instead of *hoping* that it turned out well. He would study something useful, gain some skills, and work at least a bit harder. That way, Alexandra would have something to love besides a bloke who knew a few jokes and could do nifty impersonations. His sense of humour could carry him through another evening or two, but after that....

He had to get back to Earth. He was *going* to get back to Earth, if not for his own pathetic sake, then for Alexandra's. She did not deserve her anguish.

He shooed away the rats, brushed himself down, and picked himself up. Task One: find Morgan and Hieshler.

Dave knew that this was not as simple as it sounded, and even more difficult than if he was on Earth. So far it was clear that Hell had no advanced technology, and therefore probably no Horizontal Displacement Units. Even if Hell had planes and trains, he had no money for a fare. This first part of his plan, he could see, was not going to be easy.

What resources did he have? What talents could he apply to this situation? The respective answers - a massive pile of garbage, and a penchant for long naps - were thin pickings with which to travel to the other side of the planet. Nevertheless, Dave vowed to find a solution come Hell or high water. At least he was comfortable with the *lack* of technology around him. A wry smile coursed to the edges of his lips as he realised that amongst all people he knew, this old-school environment suited him better than most; even Alexandra would be like a fish out of water without Einstein55, STOVE systems and LifeMovie replays on which to rely. In contrast, his watch Elvis had barely worked and his experience with his old television had already proved its worth.

Even better, he had no beer. There were no spirits, liquor, nor even half a bottle of cheap wine. Nor did he have enough money to buy any supplies. Dave was sober. His usual method of solving a problem – having a few beers until the conundrum disappeared – was useless, so on this occasion he would have to think his way through and attack his multiple issues head-on.

No more floating. No more excessive drinking. And he vowed not to sleep again until he had a solution. Dave turned his entire being to solving the problem. Just an hour later, he had an answer.

He mended a large, sturdy crate that he had scavenged from the garbage pile, and then packed some of the least disgusting food and drink that he could forage into a bag. Carrying this equipment, he hurried off downtown. He was going on a journey. In a very unusual vehicle.

Dave puffed up outside an office building and rubbed the grime and dirt off the nameplate on its rusting letterbox. It read what his memory told him it would read: *Australian Postal Service.* Excellent. After walking up to the door, he let himself into the empty lobby. The service desk was unattended; a sign on the counter said that the clerk was on lunch, and would be returning at noon. Dave looked at the clock above the counter, which it read 12.20 pm. Using typical public service averages, Dave figured that he still had at least 10 minutes before the clerk returned.

He looked along the service desk for a pen. Half a dozen thin wire chains hung from the desk; at one point in their existence they had tethered ballpoints to the desk, but now they hung pen-lessly across the counter. His plan had hit a snag at the outset. Why was a pen never around when he needed it?

He sat forlornly, but at the same time determined to solve this problem. Where could he procure a pen in this most inhospitable of worlds? Suddenly the answer came to him. Yes! That's right! Perhaps the only act of sensible preparation he had ever undertaken was about to pay him back.

Dave bent forward and loosened the tape that was still around his ankle. Completely ignoring the pain of a thousand simultaneous defoliations, he wrenched the blue and silver biro free. For once, a pen *was* around when he needed it.

After scrawling the words 'MADAGASCAR COMPETITION - GTN HEADQUARTERS - USA' on the side of the crate, he underlined them for emphasis. Then he jumped into the chest, pulled the lid down over his head, and set out to re-break his sleeping record.

Thirty seconds later he pushed his way out of the container, and took out his pen to make some optional additions. He drew a large downward-pointing arrow on the side of the box, and then printed 'THIS WAY UP' upside-down beside it. This beautiful piece of reverse psychology, Dave predicted, would at least ensure that the crate was not carried with him on his head. Satisfied with his preparation, he taped the pen back onto his shin, climbed into the crate, pulled the lid tightly down, and set himself mentally for a very unpleasant journey.

*

Thirty hours later, sporting a very bruised head, Dave finally became aware that his movement had ceased. He had been flipped, thrown, rolled, battered and banged as he had been transferred from van to plane to train to car, but now all was still. He was tired, bruised and sore beyond belief. He had no idea where he was, or what was going to happen to him next. What was waiting for him on the outside? Hell had been mightily nasty so far; even on Earth he would have been scared in this situation, but here in Hades that fear was greatly magnified. But he also decided, with newfound determination, that he could not possibly learn anything while lying in a cramped crate. Despite his overwhelming fear, Dave knew that there was only one way to find out what Hell had in store for him; only one way that he had any chance, however slim, of seeing Alexandra again.

He took a deep breath, and, with great trepidation, loosened the top board of the crate. But just as he began to force open the lid, he heard the sound of footsteps approaching. The horrifying memory of the thugs at Hell's Stranglers Bar jolted into his mind like it had been hit by a falling brick. Now even more terrified, Dave remained motionless and silent as the footsteps came nearer.

Chapter 37

Juan Carlos Manuel de la Espirito was doing something very unusual. He was working out: bench pressing, shoulder flexing, lat pulling, and knee curling the heaviest weights he could move. For most elite sports stars, a session in the gym would not fall under the definition of 'unusual'. However, for God to be exercising was very peculiar, for despite his unrivalled athleticism, everybody knew that God never trained. Training was below him. Practice drills, skills sessions and fitness workouts were for those not as gifted as he. God felt that he could succeed on talent alone, and to be fair to him, so far he had. Spectacularly.

The media were naturally stunned when God announced via a press release that he was in heavy training. The finals were still two weeks away, and everybody who knew anything about football knew that Harry's Heroes were a certainty to win their twenty-sixth straight title. Even without God, the HHTV bookmakers would have installed them as narrow favourites. With the greatest player in the history of the universe on their side, they were unbackable certainties. Even the opposition coach ruefully accepted that winning was out of the question. So why was God training?

"Because I want to be in the best shape possible for my team mates," he had told the media.

The media lapped it up. 'Doing it for my team' they headlined. The television stations, particularly Hieshler's channels, commissioned endless documentaries on God's new dedication and work ethic. His new approach inspired his team mates, and made Coach McConichie a very happy man. They really believed what God had said. Every lying syllable of it.

The real reason that God was training was not for the finals, or for his teammates. It was for himself. He wanted his body to look even better in the victory photographs.

Had he been aware that he had died and that he was, in fact, in Hell, God would not have worried about the victory photographs. He would have known that Hell had even better aim than he did. Like it did with all of its other residents, Hell was simply sitting back, detachedly letting him brew a poison of his own weaknesses. Then Hell would calmly watch and snigger as it allowed him to drink the entire vile cupful.

Chapter 38

The red line on the monitor continued to rise, while the adjacent blue line persisted with its free fall. A dozen pairs of eyes were fixed upon both projections as the blue line teetered dangerously close to zero, while the red line blipped relentlessly towards 100 percent. A dozen well-dressed executives sported wide grins: they were clearly supporters of the red line. The two innocuous dashes travelled further and further apart, until finally it happened: full divergence. One hundred percent and zero percent respectively.

The executives hollered and whooped and cheered. Their company, HHTV, now had a complete domination of the television market share, while the blue dash of GTN flat-lined on zero.

Harry Hieshler sat back and smiled. Victory tasted so sweet. Money was now unlimited, virtually infinite. The world's finest luxuries were his for the picking.

"Life," he mused to his excited executive committee, "doesn't get any better than this."

Unfortunately for Hieshler, he was correct. Although he did not realise it, Hell was busy with him, too. It was simply giving him enough rope with which to hang himself.

*

"Life," grumbled Morgan to himself, "can't get any worse than this."

Unfortunately for Morgan, he was wrong.

He had just endured, without doubt, the most despicable day of his existence. The disobedience and vulgarity of his staff earlier that morning now seemed like a mild lover's tiff compared to his tortuous afternoon. He had only had one meeting: a three-hour discourse with the President of England. He *hated* that woman. She had arrived in her wheelchair, and had made no effort whatsoever to mask the dark colour of her skin. She even had the gall to present him with a petition, signed by a mere five billion people, calling for him to end his war-for-ratings programming policy and promising a global boycott of GTN until he complied. After she had eventually wheeled herself out of his office, he had summoned a bulldozer and a backhoe to remove the offensive document from his office.

Attempting to resurrect some semblance of sanity from his day, Morgan eased back into his favourite chair to read the mid-afternoon newspaper. The front page headline, however, did not help his cause.

"HARRY HIESHLER IN TAKEOVER BID FOR GTN"

Morgan did not read the rest of the article. He did not have time. His instincts were screaming at him, telling him to purchase every remaining free share in his own company. If he could just buy a controlling share then he could retain some power; power he could not lose. Power to Morgan was like oxygen to other non-Morgan life forms – it was his air. He needed it every minute of every day, and he would do anything to keep even a tiny breath of it alive.

Flinging the paper aside, he lurched for the telephone and quickly dialled his stockbroker, Jonathon Jenkins. He prayed that he was not too late to ward off any major loss. Mercifully, the telephone was answered promptly on the third ring.

"Get me Jenkins," said Morgan immediately.

The receptionist paused momentarily as she reorganised her greeting.

"Yes, Sir. Good afternoon, Sir. Welcome to...."

"Cut the small talk," interrupted Morgan. "I'm in a hurry. Just get me Jenkins."

The polite voice paused again before replying.

"Certainly Sir, I will attempt to find Mr Jenkins. Please hold the line."

Morgan held the line. He also tapped the desk, bit his fingernails, and wriggled his feet as precious seconds ticked past. His mind, whirring along in an adrenalin charged rush, interpreted every moment as a minute. His imagination taunted him with images of Hieshler's stockbroker in full flight, calling "Buy! Buy! Buy!" at every click of the tickertape as his power base drained away like filthy water down a bath's plug hole. Finally, after an hour's wait of thirty seconds, Morgan heard some activity on the other end of the line.

"Hello, this is Jenkins," the voice stated.

"This is Morgan."

"Who?"

"Morgan. President Morgan W. Morgan from GTN, you idiot. Now pay attention, because I only want to say this once. I want the lot. Everything. I'll pay any price, just as long as I get the lot. Understand?"

Jenkins hesitated.

"Er, I think so. You want the lot."

"Correct."

"That shouldn't be a problem, particularly if you are prepared to pay any price."

"That's fine," said Morgan, visibly relaxing - finally something was going right.

"I'll get on to that order right away for you, Mister Morgan."

"Good."

"I just need to know one more thing."

"What?"

"Would you like it pan-fried, or thin and crispy?"

"Huh?"

"Your pizza."

"What pizza?" yelled Morgan in a voice that was so scorching it almost melted the telephone receiver.

"Your pizza with the lot," replied Jenkins, who by now was starting to become irritated by this rude stranger. "That *was* what you ordered, wasn't it?"

"Who the hell is this?" seethed Morgan.

"My name is Jenkins," returned the voice. "Sammy Jenkins. You asked for me by name, so stop playing games. Do you want this pizza or not?"

Morgan hung up.

"Jerk," added Sammy Jenkins down the unoccupied line, and felt better for having said it.

This time Morgan dialled more deliberately. He had already wasted valuable time with one wrong number, and he was not going to repeat his mistake. Another lost minute could mean the difference between fiscal slaughter and financial survival. This time he dialled correctly and, after a frustrating pause, a voice answered in the manner he expected.

"Good afternoon. Welcome to Smithers, Cypherson, Sandfield, Serenay and Jenkins, Certified Stockbrokers."

Now sure that he had the right number, Morgan did not fritter away any spare seconds on pleasantries.

"Get me Jenkins."

Morgan was about to specify "*Jonathon* Jenkins," when the voice interrupted him.

"Unfortunately we are on lunch at the moment...."

Morgan interrupted.

"I don't care if you're on your honeymoon, luvvy, just get me...."

He stopped before finishing his sentence. The voice continued without wavering.

"... leave your name and number after the tone, we will return your call as soon as possible."

A recorded message.

His entire empire was on the verge of being stolen from under his nose and his stockbroker was at *lunch*. At 3.30 in the afternoon! Limply, Morgan dropped the telephone receiver to the floor and let his chin drop forward in despair. He had no more anger to expend on this diabolical day: it had beaten him. The whole world seemed to be against him, despite everything that he had done for it. He stayed in his melancholic posture for over ten minutes, lamenting all the rotten luck that his life had dealt him.

If only he hadn't stumbled into war reporting then he would never have created the enormously successful television station that now burdened him. What a dud hand to be dealt. He could never have become a journalist in the first place if he had not attended such a good school as a child. The pain of this irreparable misfortune ate at his soul. Damn his parents! And as for those ungrateful staff members – they should be thankful that he even permitted them to work for him, much less pay them the ludicrously high minimum wages. It had been an awful day. What else could possibly go wrong?

Morgan received his answer almost immediately. His office door flung open and he looked up to see Harry Hieshler and his hangers-on marching triumphantly into his office.

Chapter 39

It was half time in the 34th game of the 35-game finals series. Harry's Heroes were playing the Oriental Raiders, a gritty team of determined Chinese footballers. The first team to reach 18 wins would be crowned the Global Club Champions. Although they were leading by only 17 wins to 16, everyone considered that Harry's Heroes were certainties to win the title, as their star player had not yet set a foot on the field.

However if Coach McConichie had his way, God's nonappearance policy was about to end. The final series had been in progress for over a month, and despite sixteen humiliating losses, God was yet to make an appearance. Sure, his team remained firm favourites, but Coach McConichie felt that God was letting down both his side and his fans by leaving his first appearance until the last possible game.

The nervous coach knocked on the door to God's private gymnasium. As usual, God ignored him. Coach McConichie knocked again, this time with more authority, and yelled to his star player.

"This is Coach McConichie, God. Please open the door."

God, who was on his tenth repetition of his tenth set of shoulder presses, ignored the voice. Just one more repetition and his whole session would be complete. He strained every muscle fibre in his body as he tried to raise the bar above his head. With trembling, fatiguing muscles, he edged the bar higher. Just one ... more ... centimetre....

"Hey God! Let me in!"

Coach McConichie's loud yell startled God, and he lost concentration. The barbell fell from his spent hands, and thudded to the floor. He had missed the last repetition, and had failed to complete his routine. He was livid.

"Aaaarrrrrgggghhhh!" God let out a scream of frustration. In anger he took a kick at the barbell that had defeated him and then charged to the door. Frothing at the mouth, he yanked the door handle open.

"Why thanks, God," said Coach McConichie, unaware that his innocent interruption had just caused irreparable damage in player-coach relations. "We really need you again. It's half time in the thirty-fourth game, and we're down by three goals. Now I know that you've been working hard for the...."

The coach stopped mid sentence as his eyes met those of his star player. God's eyes were boiling with anger - his black pupils had opened so far that they almost consumed his irises, and his blood vessels were pumping a violent red. Every part of God's eyes screamed 'I hate you!' at his startled coach.

"I ... I ... er...." stammered Coach McConichie. "Ss ... ssorr ... sorry, er, God, Sir. Am I, er, interrupting something?"

God's eyes widened even further, more than adequately answering the coach's question. Coach McConichie meekly stepped back and closed the door.

God screamed again. The coach quickly retreated to the relative sanctity of the playing arena, where he had only 11 players and 100 000 fans to whom to deliver the bad news. God would not, er, be playing today. Again.

Sulking in a corner of his gym, God could not get over the fact that Coach McConichie, the arrogant bastard, had interrupted his gym routine. He could not believe that his own coach had the gall to knock on his door without first obtaining his permission to do so. How dare he! Now his workout was in tatters, and he would look substandard in the victory photographs. This was an unforgivable impost. He summonsed a group of scantily-clad models into his hot tub to help him forget about this tragedy.

Chapter 40

Hieshler was enjoying himself. It had been a good week. Not only was his team about to win the final of the Global Club Championship, but he had just performed a very pleasant duty. In fact, he had just experienced the most gratifying moment of his life.

He had demoted Morgan. To assistant mail boy. The lowest post in the massive organization that was GTN.

With this job came not only complete disrespect from every other employee, but a dirty existence of scurrying around in the storerooms in the bowels of the building. The thought of even an hour in the infamous 'dungeon' made Hieshler squirm. Then the same thought gave him a warm erection as he realised that he had just compelled his most despised enemy to endure it for a lifetime.

Hieshler knew that he could have simply sacked Morgan. But that would have been far too quick and simple. Why slice off Morgan's fingers with a sharp knife when he could bludgeon them to a pulp with a meat tenderiser? Why burn Morgan's fingers with a match when he could slowly roast them over hot coals? No, he would not grant Morgan any mercy. He would make him grovel and serve and crawl for a while, and then watch as Morgan's power-hungry psyche painfully self-destructed.

Sadistic pleasure flushed through Hieshler's veins as he commandeered Morgan's office. The renovating was a task that he had performed with relish. The grey businesslike sterility of Morgan's era was quickly replaced by the outlandish over-the-topness that Hieshler adored. Mirrors were affixed to the walls, ceilings and floors. Rare animal skins, complete with heads, were laid as floor coverings. All the office fittings, from file clips to furniture, were plated in gold, while the initials 'HH' were monogrammed onto every surface. Very Harry Hieshler.

He had even ordered the construction of a giant strut between the twin towers of his new headquarters so that they now resembled a giant 'H'. He planned to build a clone of the complex next door, and then plate both buildings with gold. Then his initials would shine like the sun above the miserable, drab landscape of the world outside.

Then, for no apparent reason, it happened.

Hieshler had just completed a call to his left foot pedicurist when a tiny red spot caught his attention. The red spot was a reflection in a mirror.

Of a pimple.

Hieshler could not believe what he was seeing. A *pimple* - on his own chin! He looked down at the floor, which was also a mirror, for confirmation. Again he saw the unmistakable suggestion of a blotchy red spot on his chin. He rubbed at it to check that it wasn't simply a lipstick smudge or a beetroot stain, but it didn't budge. He delicately ran his fingers over the mark to see if it was raised - it was.

The horror! Acne!

His heart thrashed around his chest cavity for a few anxious beats, and then sank. This finding had completely ruined what was otherwise a perfect day. From the mirror, the pimple defiantly stared back at him from his own face. Hieshler had seen some ugly sights in his life, but none of them - not one - had ever been in a mirror. How grotesque. He couldn't let anyone see him like this, lest he instantly and permanently lose their respect.

He pushed the intercom and summoned his secretary, Miss Dingwell.

"Yes Mr Hieshler?"

"Cancel all of my appointments for the next month."

"Er, yes Sir."

"I do not want anyone to disturb me until September."

"Not at all, Sir?"

"Not under any circumstances."

"Yes Sir."

"Except," added Hieshler, "for Doctor Schmidt."

"Your plastic surgeon?"

"Yes, my plastic surgeon," replied Hieshler in a hushed tone. "Get him on the phone for me immediately."

Chapter 41

"When you've finished polishing my boots, you can go outside and scrub my bike. I noticed some dirt on the handgrips this morning."

"Yes Sir, right away Sir," came the forced reply.

"Don't forget to wax the saddle, and blacken the tyres."

"I won't forget, Sir."

"Good lad, Morgie, good lad." The senior mail boy sat back in his chair and nonchalantly lifted his feet onto the old milk crate that served as a desk. Morgan removed the size seven gym boots from the mail boy's feet, and sulked his way down to the far reaches of the store room to clean them.

"Double time, Morgan," ordered the mail boy to his new assistant. "You've got the eastern tower deliveries to finish before lunch."

"Yes Sir," replied Morgan, quickening his pace for a few steps until he was out of his superior's line of vision. "Grimy little freckle faced bastard," he mumbled under his breath.

"I heard that," echoed a prepubescent screech from the mail office. "Consider yourself on report, Morgan."

The new expanded HHTV empire, which had just subsumed GTN, employed approximately 211 945 669 people. Morgan, on the scale of power and authority in the organisation, was currently ranked 211 945 669th. Or, to state his position more succinctly, last. The two people whom he most particularly despised in the overawing hierarchy above him were vastly different people. One was ranked 211 945 668th; he was sixteen years old, had gawky thick glasses and wore a football jersey to work. Morgan was about to begin the task of cleaning his sneakers.

His other most-despised adversary was ranked first; Morgan was currently being utterly and entirely humiliated, intimidated and humbled by him.

It would have pleased Morgan to know that so far Hell had merely been toying with his major nemesis: Hieshler's foxtrot with fate was about to begin.

Chapter 42

"Yes, I think that it is time." Doctor Schmidt spoke in a tight, nervous voice that was coloured with a thick German accent. "Yes. Definitely time for the bandages to come off."

"Are you sure the scar would have healed by now?" said Hieshler, his words muffled by many layers of facial bandages.

"I am certain," replied the tall, bearded doctor with confidence. "The spot removal was over three weeks ago."

"What if it my tan has faded?"

"I trust you have been taking the tanning pills I prescribed?"

"Of course," said Hieshler. "I've got them here in my drawer."

"Fine. Then you don't have anything to worry about. I can assure you that your face will look so tanned and smooth and suave that no one will ever know that you had a pimple."

"Are you positive of that?" asked an increasingly nervous Hieshler – he had been worrying about this moment for weeks.

"Of course I'm sure. Trust me. I'm a doctor."

"That's good to hear," replied Hieshler, reassured by the confidence of his surgeon. "I couldn't bear the shame if anyone discovered that I had suffered with acne."

Doctor Schmidt placed a reassuring hand on the shoulder of his highest-paying client.

"Let's take off these awful bandages, shall we?"

Hieshler nodded. He had received the best care that modern plastic surgery had to offer, so he had nothing to fear. Without further discussion or ceremony, Doctor Schmidt began to unravel the long silk bandages that encircled Hieshler's face. Gradually the thickness waned until only one layer of bandage covered his features.

"Now for the final unveiling," pronounced the proudly expectant surgeon.

As the doctor slowly peeled off the final layer of silk, a horrified expression flooded over his face. As he pulled off the last strip, he gasped in horror. Then he bolted from the room, blithering unintelligibly.

Hieshler gripped his chair in terror. What had happened? He opened his eyes, which were blurred and hazy, and looked towards one of the many nearby mirrors. In this instance his clouded vision was a blessing. Had he been able to see himself clearly he may have gone into a permanent coma instead of just passing out.

*

Hieshler awoke on the floor of his office in a cold sweat. It was dark. Had it all been a dream? Switching on a light, he tentatively shifted his gaze toward a nearby mirror. He saw his own reflection, felt instantly nauseous, and promptly passed out again.

*

Hieshler awoke on the floor of his office in a cold sweat. It was dark. Had it all been a dream? Switching on a light, he tentatively shifted his gaze toward a nearby mirror. He saw his own reflection and dry retched.

To phrase it in the kindest possible way, he looked non-beautiful. To be less kind, but more precise, he looked *vile*.

His skin had been eaten away from his face and neck, exposing the underlying muscles. What remained of his skin was patchy, scaly and flaking. Mucous oozed from the wounds. His hair had fallen out, as had his eyebrows, and his eyeballs protruded way too far from their hollow sockets. Jutting out from the point of his chin, adding to the irony of the situation, was a huge, red, blistering, pimple.

Feeling more shaken than a James Bond Cocktail, Hieshler crawled to his desk. On it he saw a handwritten note, obviously from Doctor Schmidt. However even after ten minutes of painstaking squinting, he couldn't decipher the doctor's atrocious handwriting. Just as he was wondering where he could find a pharmacist to help him translate the scrawl, he noticed a light flashing ominously on his answering machine. He flicked the replay switch, and heard a voice that was flavoured by both a German accent and a very guilty tremor.

"*Good morning President Hieshler. I believe we may have made a tiny little boo-boo with the tanning pills. I think that instead of prescribing one tablet every six hours for half a month, we may have accidentally prescribed six tablets every half an hour for one month.*"

Hieshler groaned. An overdose. By over 1400 percent.

Doctor Schmidt's voice changed to an official, medical-sounding tone.

"*Unfortunately at this dosage the medication has a high level of toxicity, which engenders an efficacious decomposing effect on the epidermis, superficial melanin layers and subcutaneous tissue structures. While there have been reports in medical literature of rare satisfactory outcomes following such toxicity, the condition has a more likely prognosis of continuing in status quo. Intervention has been found to be benign, and a stagnant course is your condition's most likely resolution.*"

Doctor Schmidt's voice paused meaningfully, before continuing.

"*I'm going on a long holiday. I'm not sure when I'll be back. Goodbye.*"

Hieshler moaned again. He had not understood a word of the diagnosis, although he sensed from the long-winded nature of the doctor's message that most of it was bad news. With the aid of a medical dictionary, Hieshler painstakingly translated Doctor Schmidt's message. He eventually summarised it in one simple, clear sentence.

The skin had rotted off his face, and could never be repaired.

As the full impact of the doctor's message hit him, Hieshler became nauseous. His limbs felt weak, and a cold chill went through him. The pimple burst. This was, by far, the worst singular moment of his existence.

Hell knew Hieshler's weak spot, and had let him hit it with unerring accuracy. Hieshler's physical appearance was now, and would always remain, hideous. No amount of money could fix him, no surgeon could repair him, and no clothes could disguise the horrible ooze that was presently doing a poor impersonation of facial features.

It was more than Hieshler's self-obsessed ego could bear. His entire existence had been for the purpose of flattering himself, and posing vainly with the adornments of his wealth. Now that all of those trappings were useless, Hieshler's mind could see no reason for living. Meekly, without a hint of courage, he surrendered. He decided to go in to hiding for a while - perhaps, say, the rest of his life.

Where could he go? The Earth was such a small planet. He could not possibly hide at home, as someone would eventually call. The thought of seeing employees, family, or associates was unthinkable, as was the possibility of taking public transport. He had to isolate himself somewhere - somewhere nearby - somewhere with food, shelter and water. Then he could simply wait for the passing years to take their toll. All other avenues were useless, unachievable, and futile. Without his looks, he was nobody.

After but a few minutes thought, Hieshler could only think of one place that satisfied all of his criteria. He staggered across to the elevator, stepped in, and headed down to his new home.

Chapter 43

The crowd was restless. *His* appearance was imminent.

It was the last game of the finals. The Oriental Raiders had managed to square the series at 17 wins apiece, so the winner of the present game would be declared the champion team. With only five minutes to go, the scores were level at nil all. Surely God was about to appear.

The television stations switched to their highest-paying advertisers as Coach McConichie used the last of his requisite 150 timeout calls. However, for once he had not called this break simply at the request of a television station. This was a tactical call, and was vital to the outcome of the game – nay, to the rest of his life. He would require every precious second of this timeout to coax his star player onto the field.

Inside the dressing room, God was undertaking the last of his preparations for the game. He had timed everything to perfection - the script could not have played itself out more perfectly if he had written it himself. The series was even, the game was tied, and the whole world was waiting for him. God self-indulgently imagined his entry to the ground. The crowd would be chanting wildly in anticipation of his arrival. As he strode on to the field, they would suddenly stop screaming, and would simply gasp in wonder at his huge muscles and well-cut body.

His preparations for this day had been painstaking. He had swallowed or injected every physique-enhancing substance that he could buy; he had not only taken a range of steroids, growth hormones and peptides, but protein supplements, herbal extracts and Chinese medicines as well. He had also worked hard in the gym. Now his body was lean, mean, and frighteningly muscled. He was primed to ignite the crowd into a frenzy of delighted awe.

God looked at his watch. Only ten minutes to go. A casual glance at the monitor in the corner of his private dressing room told him that the score was still nil-all. He began his pre-game preparation in anticipation of the knock on his door that he knew would soon arrive. Despite still being furious at the coach, God had decided that he would play anyway. The adoration, victory parties and festivities would be worth the humility.

Carefully he washed and brushed his hair. Then he rubbed oil over his toned muscles like a body builder before a pose-show, and pulled on his jersey. What a jersey it was! He had designed it himself, especially for tonight. Except for two stripes bearing the Heroes' club colours, the jersey was transparent to afford his fans a clearer view of his tanned, muscular chest.

After practising his humble-country-boy smile in front of the mirror for a few minutes, he plucked a few hairs from his eyebrows and then shaved for the second time of the day. After running over a few lines from his victory acceptance speech, he laced up his white baby-platypus-leather, gold trimmed, mink-lined football boots. To complete his preparation he tucked a tightly rolled pair of football socks down the front of his jock strap. All parts of him had to look in 'proportion'. Nothing could be left to chance.

Then he had a final check of himself in the mirror. His hair was slick, his smile was radiant, and his shorts looked suitably well endowed. And his body! His body was so fantastic it almost gave him an erection. Just as he finished his preparations, he heard the expected knock on the door. He opened it relatively quickly to see a very meek Coach McConichie standing, hat in hand, with his head bowed.

"I'm very sorry about...."

"Out of my way, you ignorant fool," commanded God as he swiped his contrite coach aside. Then, with his chin held high and his chest out as far as he could puff it, God strode out through the dressing room and into the players tunnel. Already he could taste the sweetness of the victory champagne.

His earlier visualisations were uncannily accurate. The crowd, sensing that he was about to arrive, had boiled themselves into a fever pitch of hype and hoopla. Then, as they recognised his familiar gait in the tunnel, they went berserk.

"We want God! We want God!" boomed the familiar chant.

The nearer their idol came to the playing surface, the louder the chant became. As God reached the end of the tunnel, the earth on which he stood literally shook to the beat of the crowd. God had been waiting and planning for this moment all his life.

He stepped proudly onto the playing field, for the first time giving the crowd an unencumbered view of his new physique. He thrust both arms out, flexing his massive biceps in a pose. The crowd stopped chanting; the only sound was that of 100 000 jaws dropping simultaneously. It was followed by 100 000 people sighing simultaneous *oooohs* before following with a massive chorus of *aaahhs*. Half the crowd - the women - either became faint or cried, while the men simply looked upon their hero with unabashed admiration and awe.

God's ego almost exploded. His vanity grew so big that it warranted its own postcode. He took a low bow, signalling to the crowd that he now permitted them to cheer again. They obliged.

Ten minutes later the cacophony began to fade, so the referee moved to centre field and blew time-on. Now all that remained was for God to score a goal so that he could start celebrating and partying.

Harry's Heroes kicked off. This galvanised the crowd into a heightened frenzy of violent vocality as they screamed for their idol. Much to their delight, the ball was immediately passed to God. With great showmanship he tweaked the ball into the air and caught it on his nose, spinning it like a seal. Then he flicked the ball further into the air, and headed it over an incoming defender. Nonchalantly he trotted down the sideline, weaving in and out of the Oriental team with consummate skill. He soon closed within striking range for goal.

However instead of shooting for goal immediately, God decided to ham it up a bit instead. After all, this was the last grand final of this series. Circling back down the field, God laughed and waved to the crowd, barely looking at the ball as he headed, dribbled and flicked it around the opposition. Occasionally he would dribble the ball between an opponent's legs, just to further underline his superiority. A few times he condescendingly stopped and goaded the defence like an ego-driven boxer.

After a few minutes of prancing, God looked up at the clock. The game had less than 20 seconds to go. Time, he decided, to put those Chinese pretenders out of their misery. He clapped his hands above his head, to which the crowd dutifully responded with a synchronised beat. Show time.

God juggled the ball with his feet a few final times, then spun out through a ring of desperate defenders and accelerated goal wards. Playing the ball better than any other player could even dream of doing, he approached top speed at the halfway line. His blistering pace quickly left the entire defensive line-up in his wake. Soon only one very nervous goalkeeper stood between him and the victory party.

The ball exploded off his right boot. Like lightening it sped towards the goalmouth. The keeper dived to the ground and covered his head with his hands in a defensive ploy - the last keeper to stand in the way of one of God's power strikes was still in spinal traction. The ball scorched towards the undefended goal. Open mouthed, the crowd stood as one to watch its progress.

Suddenly, a loud wail rang out across the pitch, sounding unmistakably like a fat lady singing. An instant later, the ball crossed the goal line and scorched through the back of the net. God's shot, although a fine and hard strike, was one second too late. No goal.

The game was a draw.

The crowd was stunned. God's teammates were vilified, and Coach McConichie was rampant. Everybody looked at God for a response. Was he upset? No way. He would win it in a penalty shootout instead. The extra few minutes would give him some extra posing time.

While his teammates and opposition took nerve-wracked shots from the penalty spot, God entertained the crowd with a series of muscular displays. After ten minutes of prancing and preening, the referee interrupted by calling God for the deciding kick. As a parting pose for his adoring army of fans, God pulled his shorts up high, and flexed his hard, toned buttocks. The crowd went into unrestrained raptures at this audacious stunt.

God stepped confidently up to the ball. He signalled for quiet, and the crowd responded as though their batteries had been disconnected. The stadium was hushed as all eyes focused on God. As he stepped back to line up the ball, God felt something loose in his jockstrap. He surreptitiously rubbed his groin to check what was wrong.

Oh, dear. The rolled pair of socks had worked its way loose.

It must have happened, God realised in a panic, when he bared his buttock muscles to the crowd. What could he do? He was in the middle of a huge stadium being intently watched by 100 000 people, so he had nowhere to hide. He couldn't possibly reposition the sock, as millions of television viewers worldwide were analysing his every gesture and movement with slow-motion replays. God could only hope that the socks stayed in his jocks for just five more seconds. Then thousands of fans would swamp him and his secret would be safe.

Nervous and awkward for the first time in his life, God lined up the ball. With a lilting, sideways gait, he started the run-up for his kick.

Chapter 44

As Morgan scoured the dirt and dung from the doles of the head mail boy's sneakers for the seventh day in succession, a feeling of burning resentment billowed inside him. His own ex-employee had, over the past week, continually belittled and intimidated him. The humiliation had steadily penetrated through Morgan's many outer layers - his arrogance, his power-lust and his superior air - and was now cutting to the core of his soul.

"It's an outrage," he muttered to himself. "I am supposed to dish out the degradation, not receive it."

Morgan had plummeted from the planet's most powerful man to its lowest life form; he had shrivelled from Emperor of the Earth to scraping poo off shoes. As his fingernails worked into the tread on the sneaker's sole, Morgan's psyche imploded. His ego simply could not tolerate the ignominy any longer.

"Morgan W. Morgan does not take orders from anyone," he blurted aloud, mutinously casting the shoes aside.

This flagrant act made Morgan feel emancipated, but only fleetingly. He knew that if he reported back to the senior mail boy without completing his assigned duties then he would be disciplined again. This was not a feeling that he relished, as his butt was still smarting from the previous occasion. Worse than that, the mail boy would report his indiscretion to Hieshler. The mere thought made Morgan's stomach churn.

He had to escape this Hellhole. Morgan tried to abscond by taking an elevator ride to the lobby, but someone - presumably Hieshler - had invalidated his security pass. Even frantically pushing the elevator button a hundred times did not help. Furthermore, Morgan possessed an intimate knowledge of the building's layout - he had designed every square centimetre of it himself - so he knew that no other exit from the basement existed. His enemies had him trapped, without any route of escape, like a rabbit down a burrow.

Bereft of viable alternatives, Morgan turned in the other direction. He headed down the maze of stairways and corridors that he knew only led deeper into the bowels of the building. His gait was very deliberate. He had, as far as he could figure, plenty of time.

For hours Morgan wandered, stopping sporadically to curse his bad luck, rail against Hieshler, or beat his head against a wall in frustration. As he trudged deeper down through the multi level basement, the atmosphere became danker and darker. Every step carried him further into territory that had remained almost untouched since the earliest days of his empire. Very few of his employees had ever ventured this far into the 'dungeon'. It was like travelling through a time warp as he opened doors that had been closed for decades. Dust covered the floors, and spiders' webs enigmatically sealed many of the boxes that were piled high in the massive storerooms.

Caring not what he found ahead of him, and feeling only hatred towards everything that he was leaving behind, Morgan roamed even deeper down the corridors and stairwells, and soon he had only rats and roaches as company. Over the next week, days and nights ceased to exist as Morgan lived under the perpetual dull glow of ten-watt light bulbs. He slept in holding bays and ate food from long-forgotten catering supplies as the humiliating macrocosm of GTN and HHTV became a weeping scab on his memory. Eventually he reached the lowest basement, where he made a crude camp, and stewed in his own hatred. Vowing retaliation on the outside world, he began to plot his revenge.

Chapter 45

Nothing was moving except Dave's heart, which was thumping at triple its usual rate. He lay curled in his crate, motionless, as the sound of footsteps moved closer. Dave dared not even blink lest the noise reveal him. Hell had been mightily inhospitable so far, and he had no desire whatsoever to see a Hell prison block from the inside; nor, as he painfully recalled the Stranglers Bar, did he wish to chat with any security guards. So despite a growing claustrophobia, a throbbing headache, and a burning desire to find out where he was, Dave stayed put.

The footsteps came closer still.

Please keep going, begged Dave silently. *Whoever you are, please just pass by.*

The footsteps approached. As they did, Dave realised that two separate sets of feet were walking side by side. Visions of two horrible, nasty security guards flooded into Dave's mind, replacing the vision of a single, horrible, nasty security guard.

Dave gulped as the footsteps walked within a metre of his crate. They stopped. Dave held his breath.

"This is the trailer load I was tellin' you about." The voice belonged to a cockney-accented female.

"When'd they come in?" replied the second voice, which also came from a female - a very gruff, rough sounding female.

"Yesterday afternoon. They've been sitting 'ere since, cause I don't feel like opening 'em."

Dave gave a quiet sigh of relief. Thank goodness for laziness.

"What if Hieshler finds out?"

Huh? thought Dave. He expected to be in GTN headquarters, not Hieshler's HHTV. But at least he was now a step closer to the truth.

"Hieshler won't find out," continued the cockney woman. "He ain't been seen for weeks. Even Dingwell, his assistant, ain't heard from him."

"I wonder what he's up to?"

"I dunno. But there's a rumour that he left the country for a homosexual affair with his plastic surgeon. Nobody's seen either of 'em for ages."

"Really?"

"So they say."

"Isn't that what they said about Morgan?"

"Probably. Nobody's seen him for weeks either."

"Good riddance to both of them."

The women paused as they digested the previous conversation. Dave's mind, too, was trying its best to comprehend the information, but was doing a very poor job. He was still trying to decipher in which of the presidents' buildings he was hiding, when the women said something that completely surprised him.

"What about God, eh?"

"Funny, wasn't it?"

"I could've killed myself laughing when that sock fell out."

"He calls himself a Greek god - must be the god of small sausages. Why else would he resort to puttin' rolled socks down the front of his jockstrap?"

"Or the god of missed penalties. His shot was the worst attempt that I've ever seen. I don't think that I've ever seen anyone take an air-swing at a stationary ball before."

"I reckon he was trying to grab the sock as it fell, and lost his concentration. What a prat, losing the whole series for his team like that."

"I always thought that he was overrated."

"Me too."

Dave was shocked as he listened to the story. God, Juan Carlos Manuel de la Espirito, had missed a penalty to lose the title for his team. It sounded like a *very* embarrassing error. Socks down his jocks? How amateurish. Hell had obviously taken a flying kick at the egotistical superstar.

The women recommenced their earlier conversation, each proffering lame sets of self-excusing reasons for not opening the incoming pile of deliveries.

"Let's leave the parcels. It would take far too much effort to open all these, and I just ain't got the energy. Besides, it's only 40 minutes until lunch, and by the time we get back here after the break we'll barely have time to start before afternoon smoko. Then it's not long till knock-off, so there's no point in even trying to start."

"Yeah, it sucks anyway. I hate sortin' parcels. Let's leave 'em."

"But what are we going to do with 'em? There must be 'undreds of 'em."

"I dunno."

"Well, we can't just leave 'em here."

"Why don't we just move 'em?"

"Where to?"

"I dunno. Maybe we could hide 'em in the dungeon, and then get rid of 'em later when the heat is off."

"Yeah, the dungeon. Good idea."

"Let's go."

Dave heard a click, and then the grumbling of an ill-tuned motor. He then became aware that he was moving - presumably on a parcel trailer to 'The dungeon'. He was not altogether happy with that notion, but, realising that he had no choice in the matter, he remained in his box, anxiously nibbling on a piece of stale pizza crust, wishing that his claustrophobia would disappear. About half an hour later, the engine clattered to a halt.

"They will *never* find 'em down 'ere," he heard one woman assert. "Nobody's been down 'ere for fifty years." The women sniggered as they entered a nearby elevator.

When Dave was sure that the room was deserted, he began to work his way out of the delivery pile.

Chapter 46

A plastic pipe ran down the far wall of the room. Morgan could not take his eyes off it. If that was the pipe that he thought it was....

So far, his revenge plan had progressed very slowly. In fact, it still didn't exist. Every time a suitably evil scheme developed in his mind it hit a snag, and the drawback was always the same: he would have to leave the dungeon to execute it. No matter how monstrously delicious Morgan found his fantasies, they all required that he return to the outside world to execute them. He was just beginning to lament that his goal of complete vengeance against humanity was unfulfillable when he spied the pipe - a tangible link to the outside.

He lumbered to his feet and waddled across to examine the tubing more closely through the dim light. He tapped it knowingly, trying to recollect the architectural plans that he had designed for this building many years previously.

After some fierce mental retrieval, aided by some sketches that he scratched into the dusty floor, he decided that yes, this was it; this was the pipe that housed the electrical and communication wires that ascended into the main building. His lips twisted into a thin smile as a horrific idea spread like a purulent virus through his evil mind.

With renewed purpose, Morgan rummaged through a few storage boxes. He soon found a suitable tool for his purpose: an old tin of sardines. Morgan tore back the tin lid, and then, using the lid's sharp edge, he began sawing patiently through the plastic casing of the pipe.

Revenge would soon be his.

Chapter 47

Dave, after cautiously checking that he was alone, discreetly pushed his way out of his box. It felt *sensational* to stretch his muscles for the first time in days. He decided that a good stretch was generally undervalued, and he now rated it higher than bad sex, which was a concept he would have scoffed at only days earlier.

The light, although very dim, initially hurt his eyes, which had become accustomed to complete darkness. As his vision adapted, Dave noticed that he was in a dank, dingy storeroom, where a thick layer of dust covered almost every surface, and spiders' webs lay undisturbed in every nook. A deathly silence consumed the area, except for an eerie siren, which began inexplicably wailing in the distance. Not knowing the significance of the siren, Dave started walking off in the direction that the two conniving mail sorters had travelled. However before he had taken his third step, Dave noticed something that struck him as odd.

A footprint.

Judging by the dust, the impression was recent. However, this was clearly not a footprint left by one of the mail sorters: it came from an extremely large foot, and it was heading in the other direction. A spooky Robinson-Crusoe-esque feeling engulfed Dave, sending armies of shivers marching up and down his spine. Despite his fear, something burned in the back of Dave's mind, imploring him to find the owner of the dusty imprint. Although terrified, his curiosity quickly overrode his consternation, so he headed down the corridor to track down the mysterious owner of the large feet.

Chapter 48

"At last!"

Morgan pulled aggressively at the plastic pipe, tearing away its outer casing. Inside were hundreds of cables and wires, each carrying power or electronic information to the office tower above him. The lines were of varied thicknesses and multitudes of colours; some were grouped into units, while others wound individually up the interior of the pipe like vines up a tree. He began painstakingly sorting through the tangled web, looking for two particular wires.

An hour or so later, he found the lines he was after - a robust orange wire, paired with an equally thick blue wire. He threw his head back, forced his lips into a contorted smile, and squawked an evil cackle.

Using the sardine tin lid, he cut determinedly through both wires and then stripped away their plastic insulation. Then he maliciously juxtaposed their conducting tips.

"Goodbye, insubordinate mongrels. Adios GTN. And good riddance Harry Hieshler," laughed Morgan with perversion as he rapidly twisted the wires' tips together with his fingers. Then he stood back with his hands cupped behind his ears, stilled his breathing, and listened carefully. In the distance, hundreds of floors above, he heard the dim wail of a siren. His lips set into a serpentine smile: the sound confirmed what he had hoped. In exactly half an hour, his revenge would be complete.

Chapter 49

Fish. That was it. Dave could smell fish.

He had followed the footprint trail for hours until it had ended in the storeroom where he was now standing. Upon entering the room, an unexpected yet familiar smell had wafted up his nostrils. Dave's mind had taken a few moments to register this out-of-context odour as 'fish'.

Dave wondered why a deserted storeroom, which was dozens of stories below ground level, should smell of fish. He literally followed his nose to a corner of the storeroom where the answer to this riddle lay innocently on a box: a sardine tin, brimming with uneaten sardines in a light chilli sauce. Hungrily, Dave scooped the oily flesh into his mouth. He had eaten nothing but scraps since he had first woken on Hell, so the canned fish was most welcome.

Dave rummaged inside the box from where the piscine treasure had been pilfered. He discovered dozens of tins, all similarly filled with sardines in chilli sauce. He was about to gorge himself on the entire boxful when two nagging thoughts interrupted him. The first was a distant memory of the horrible week of dysentery he endured the last time he ate too many tins of chilli sardines in one sitting. This notion alone might have been enough to stop him from wolfing down every sardine he could find, but it was Dave's second thought that temporarily saved his bowels. This other feeling was vaguer, yet somehow far more powerful: something was wrong.

What was it? Dave mused over the problem for a minute, but, unable to think clearly due to his ravishing hunger, he began to tear the lid off a second tin of sardines.

Then the answer hit him.

The lid.

Where was the lid to the original can of fish? He searched the immediate area, but without success. The tin top, which someone had removed from the sardines, was nowhere to be seen. Why? Why would anyone walk for hours into a dreary, depressing basement, and take the lid from a sardine tin? Even more enigmatically, the fish was untouched. Why would anyone open a can at all unless he or she intended to eat the contents?

Dave quivered. He was in a dark room of a deep basement, on the bottom of a strange building, in a foreign country, in Hell.

And he was alone.

With a lidless sardine tin.

Dave urged himself to stay calm, and to think carefully and rationally. He failed.

Dave turned and bolted for the door, but did not get very far. The obese form of a very angry Morgan W. Morgan was blocking his path.

Dave was not a very powerful physical specimen. Apart from his fluke victory against the security guards at Hell's Stranglers Bar, Dave's only pugilistic victory had been against that *Piñata* at his cousin Adnor's eighth birthday party. He was no match for the massive bulk of ex-president Morgan, who clamped two chunky hands around Dave's throat and started to choke him.

"You grimy little freckle faced bastard," growled Morgan.

"I ... ont ... av ... eckles," choked Dave.

"I'll teach you to make me scrape dirt off your shoes," snarled Morgan as he tightened the grip around Dave's throat, lifting Dave's feet completely off the floor.

"It ... asn't ... ee," protested Dave through a larynx so crushed that it was incapable of sounding consonants.

"Before I kill you," continued Morgan unerringly "you are going to beg for my forgiveness."

"All ... ight," nodded Dave in agreement as his lips turned a cheesy blue.

"You are going to grovel for mercy."

"Ess," said Dave, his eyes bulging like jam tartlets.

"Then I will kill you anyway."

Morgan hurled Dave backwards onto the hard concrete floor. Rasping for oxygen, Dave landed flat on his back, which winded him so that it was now difficult to even inhale, let alone deliver an apology speech.

"I said GROVEL!" barked Morgan. He landed a vicious kick into Dave's midriff, which cruelly evacuated the last thimbleful of air from his lungs, making the required act of contrition impossible to deliver. Frustratingly for Dave, he had no idea why Morgan was trying to kill him - he had never even mentioned shoes to Morgan, let alone ordered him to clean them. Even worse, Dave didn't have freckles.

He finally managed to suck in a breath of air and began to explain, in the briefest possible way, that Morgan had perhaps confused him with someone else. He was too late. Morgan lost what little remained of his temper, and with one massive hand locked around Dave's throat, he wrenched him off the floor and pinned him against the wall.

"I gave you a chance to apologise," said Morgan in a sinister tone, "but you refused." He paused just long enough to stare directly into Dave's eyes. "Now you must die."

Morgan produced the jagged sardine lid from his pocket. At least Dave now knew where it was. However this consolation was temporary, as Morgan moved the sharp edge deliberately up towards Dave's throat.

"Goodbye, you little scumbag," said Morgan, as he taunted Dave with the feel of jagged metal against his jugular vein.

The thought of his imminent death petrified Dave beyond response. Morgan nicked a vein in Dave's neck and sneered as the blood trickled down over his own hand, and then watched the warm liquid as it coursed down his forearm and elbow and then dripped to the floor. A drop splattered on Dave's foot. Suddenly, the crazed man paused. He looked down more closely towards Dave's shoe, and then, puzzled, at Dave's face. A confused wrinkle appeared in Morgan's brow.

"They're not your shoes," said Morgan, before he glared back into Dave's eyes. "You're not the mail boy," he said, as though Dave had introduced himself as such. "You're not that grimy little freckle face bastard who made me clean his shoes."

Dave did his best to shake his head. Morgan let his grip slacken, allowing Dave the sanctity of one more breath.

"Who the hell are you?"

Dave thought carefully. This was a very difficult question to answer truthfully. After rapidly evaluating a few responses including time-share hawker, staff parcel opener and government fish inspector, he settled on a simplified version of the truth.

"My name is Dave."

Morgan eyed him suspiciously. He had an overwhelming feeling that he had met this 'Dave' before, but simply couldn't remember when or where. The name ticked over in Morgan's head: Dave - Dave - Dave. Why did it seem so familiar?

Then, something awful happened to Morgan. Something hideously horrifyingly awful, something far more painful than any affliction that had befallen him in Hell so far. In fact, it was worse than anything that could ever happen to anybody.

He remembered. He remembered where he had met Dave before. On Earth.

An unanticipated feeling instantly consumed Morgan's soul: confusion, mixed with hatred, fused with fear, and blended with anguish. Morgan realised, after seeing Dave's face, where he was. He came to know the one fact that no person ever wants to discover.

He was in Hell.

Being on Hell was bad enough, but *knowing* that you were in Hell was infinitely worse.

Morgan looked at his captive, who had already adjudged that 'Dave' was possibly not the best answer. By the searing anguish in Morgan's eyes, Dave realised that Morgan had just realised what he, by virtue of his unorthodox non-dead entry into Hell, had been aware of all along.

"You BASTARD!" bellowed Morgan with a fury that only the knowledge that you will spend the rest of your existence in constant suffering can engender. Dave felt the large hand clamp more tightly around his neck as Morgan drew his other arm back, winding up for a massive punch.

Dave knew that he was about to die. He watched in slow motion as the gigantic fist moved towards his nose with skull crushing velocity. Dave's face contorted with fear and grimaced in terror. He could not possibly survive this blow.

Suddenly, from the corner of his eye, Dave saw a strange figure launch itself at his angry assailant. The stranger's timing was impeccable. The collision rocked Morgan just enough to disturb his fist's trajectory so that it only grazed Dave's cheek en route to pummelling hard into the brick wall behind him. As Morgan bellowed in agony, his grip slackened. Dave fell from his grasp, and scampered out of range as quickly as his battered body would carry him.

Still in shock, Dave collapsed like a wet dishcloth. He lay on the floor, feigning a coma, as the mystery man flailed Morgan with a short plank of wood. The stranger screamed with passionate hatred as he brandished his weapon with all the ferocity that his weak frame could deliver. This man clearly despised Morgan with every cell in his body.

"You bastard, you've ruined my life," he screamed between hits. "I'm ruined, completely ruined, and it's all because of you." He continued swinging at Morgan, who absorbed the weakening blows on his forearms. "I hate you, I've always hated you, and now I'm going to kill you, you bastard...."

Morgan had heard enough. He stepped forward, ignoring the feeble swipes from his now exhausted assailant, and grabbed him by the shirtfront. For the first time he saw the stranger's face. He recoiled in horror and retched up his stomach's contents.

The man pounced on this opportunity immediately. Breaking free during Morgan's unguarded moment, he clamoured up a pile of nearby boxes. The mystery man now realised that he did not have the physical strength to beat Morgan, and that he would have to somehow outsmart him - perhaps stab him in the back later while he was sleeping. Dave did not know who Morgan's assailant was, where he had come from, or why he had attacked Morgan. However, he did notice one thing: Morgan's mystery attacker was a very ugly man. He had no hair, a putrid, oozy face and frail, scaly limbs. And a huge festering pimple on his chin.

Morgan regrouped and turned to chase his attacker. The man called upon his best method of defence: he faced Morgan and looked him straight in the eye. It worked. Morgan caught sight of the face and stopped, instantly nauseous again. However, this time he had not halted just because of the expurgating activity of his stomach. He had also stopped in shock as he recognised his attacker: his ugly head, putrid face and contemptible features could not hide those greedy eyes. Morgan would recognise them anywhere. They belonged to Harry Hieshler.

The thought took a second to sink in to Morgan's disbelieving mind, during which time Hieshler clamoured higher up the bank of boxes. The larger man renewed his chase, but his obese frame was not built for such activity. He quickly relented - standing up from a chair was almost too difficult for him, much less climbing a stack of boxes. Now that they were physically separated, the insults and insinuations began flying.

"I'll get you soon Hieshler, very soon," bellowed Morgan with venerable hatred.

Dave baulked at the name. Hieshler? That vile man who had just attacked Morgan was the once impeccably handsome Harry Hieshler? Hell *definitely* had a mean streak. And damn good aim.

"You'll have to catch me first," taunted Hieshler. "There's plenty of food in these boxes, so I don't think I'll come down for a while. And I can't imagine a fat lard like you making this climb."

Morgan laughed loudly. "I don't have to," he sneered. "In five minutes time we're going to be blown to pieces."

"Don't try to bluff me, Morgan."

"I'm not bluffing," replied Morgan. "Listen."

Hieshler and Morgan - and Dave, who was still motionless on the floor, but was taking more than a passing interest in the conversation - listened intently. The thick, musty silence that filled the room was overlaid by the eerie wail of a distant siren.

Hieshler was next to speak.

"You didn't," he stammered.

"I did," said Morgan.

Did what? wondered Dave. This was an unexpected development.

"You couldn't have enabled the 'BOOM' system," argued Hieshler in desperation. "I am the new president. Only I have the new codes."

"It's easy when you know how," boasted Morgan as he swept his hand across towards the communications pipe. Dave cautiously moved his eyes in the direction of Morgan's gesture, and noticed a plastic pipe that was cut and torn open. Hieshler noticed Morgan's handiwork as well, but unlike Dave, he understood its significance.

"We'll all perish," cried Hieshler.

"Blown to smithereens."

"Turn it off!"

"Be my guest."

Morgan sniggered sarcastically as he sat on a box and opened another tin of sardines, trying to eke a few token pleasures from what were presumably his final minutes in Hell.

"Go to Hell," yelled Hieshler.

"I've got some bad news for you," retorted Morgan through a mouthful of sardines. Then he paused before adding, with chilling seriousness, a statement that resonated very uncomfortably through Hieshler's body: "We're already there."

Dave's mind was whirring. Furiously piecing together all the fragments of information that he had gleaned from the preceding conversation, he deduced that Morgan, by altering something in the pipe, had managed to detonate a bomb that would soon explode. He correctly sensed that Morgan was not in the mood to disengage the weapon, and that Hieshler, in his present geographical and mental state, was even less likely to succeed in that task. This, to Dave's logic, left only one person who could disengage the bomb. He began to creep imperceptibly, slug-like, along the floor.

Hieshler's mind, too, had been whirring. Morgan's last comments were haunting him.

Go to Hell. I have some bad news for you. We're already there. Go to hell - bad news – we're already there. Go to Hell - we're already there ... already there ... already there."

Dave had wormed barely a body length before he heard a howl of unparalleled anguish. It was a screech that shuddered Dave to his core. Even Morgan trembled from its tormented ferocity. Hieshler had deciphered Morgan's remarks, which had empowered him with the unenviable knowledge that he was dead, and was, in fact, in Hell. The scream, although delivered from Hieshler's vocal chords, emanated from the very centre of his soul.

Morgan, now laughing like an evil jackal, goaded Hieshler, taking masochistic pleasure from his enemy's pain. Dave, noting that Morgan's own spite was temporarily distracting him, inched more quickly along the floor. He was soon within reach of the pipe and looked up at its tangled core. He grimaced as he saw the hundreds of multicoloured wires that ran the length of the tube. Finding the adulterated wires would be a difficult task under any conditions - lying on the floor in a dimly lit storeroom made the job nearly impossible.

In the distance, the siren changed pitch, screaming at an even more urgent tone. Dave wondered what it meant. Morgan laughed aloud, taunting Hieshler: "Sounds as if we have only one more minute to live." At least, Dave thought, Morgan had answered his question. "Only one minute before you, me and that little runt over there...." Morgan turned to point where Dave had been lying.

Morgan was mortified. He swung his large frame around and looked across towards the communications pipe where Dave was now standing, furiously sifting through the web of wires, searching vainly for a cut end. Morgan barrelled across the room in a rage. Dave's fingers wriggled like epileptic worms as they parted column after column of tightly packed wires. As Morgan charged closer, Dave spied a few cut shreds of blue and orange insulation. He rapidly scanned the pipe for those colours - across, up, and down, his eyes blurred with a mishmash of vibrant hues and tones.

Eureka! He spotted the wires. By now Morgan had reached top speed and was snorting like a wounded buffalo. Dave's eyes followed the pair of wires downwards, where he saw their roughly cut ends twisted together in a sinister embrace. Morgan was upon him. Dave reached out to tear the deadly connection apart....

A quarter-tonne human cannonball crashed into Dave, smashing him off his feet and into the far wall. It was like a freight train hitting a beer bottle. As Dave thudded to the ground, he glanced down at his tightly clenched fists. Had he managed to grab the wires? He uncurled his fingers. They contained nothing but fingerprints.

He had missed.

The culpable wires remained untouched in the pipe, their short circuit sending their destructive message roof-wards, and the deathly sound of the siren continued screaming in the distance. Morgan belly flopped onto Dave as though he was diving into a swimming pool. With Morgan's incredible bulk squashing his torso, Dave was unable to breathe. He gesticulated wildly to Hieshler, who was still cowering in fear atop his box fortress, but to no avail. Dave scrapped wildly, fighting for a precious breath, but the massive bulk bearing down upon his body made any movement impossible.

The feeling reminded Dave of childhood nightmares in which the harder he tried to move or breathe, the more difficult it became. He wished that he would wake up and discover that it was just a dream - a terrible dream. However, it wasn't to be. The ex-president was unmoved and unconcerned; he was angry, cruel and merciless. Dave's muscles spasmed and his mouth began to froth.

Suddenly, the siren stopped. The room was silent, except for the muffles made by Dave as he flapped his limbs about like a dying cockroach. In that moment of clammy quiet, Dave realised that his struggle was futile. Morgan had completely overpowered him. He was about to die. Then, far above, a piercing beep emanated from the bomb detonator, starkly punctuating the foreboding atmosphere. Further beeps followed it at exactly one-second intervals, as Morgan greedily counted them down.

"Nine."

Dave stopped flailing, and let his arms and legs go limp. A strange warmth started to flow through his body.

"Eight."

Dave began to feel calm, and inexplicably disinterested in breathing.

"Seven."

His chest fell still as his heart stopped beating. A deep relaxation lulled him as peace permeated his thoughts.

"Six."

Morgan's increasingly distant voice continued to count down the seconds, as a menagerie of thoughts ran through Dave's crystal clear mind.

"Five."

Hell knew your weaknesses; it presented you with an agony of your own creation.

"Four."

Morgan, the arrogant powerbroker, was now like a humiliated servant in hiding. His greed for power had precipitated his downfall.

"Three."

Hieshler, the greedy narcissistic, was now cowering atop a cardboard castle. His own vanity had occasioned the vile facade that he now called his face.

"Two."

Even God, the ego-driven footballer, and the perverted Old Mr Smiggins had nowhere to hide from their own shortcomings.

"One."

Then again, Dave realised, neither did he.

The beeping stopped. Dave felt clear. He felt wonderful. He felt warm, and he felt ready.

Suddenly there was a tumultuous boom, which was followed by waves of violent shudders. The ceiling cracked, and debris began to tumble down through the crevices. The shaking escalated to a violent pitch, and the hallways capitulated into piles of rubble as dust choked the air.

Hieshler howled as a skull-shattering boom heralded the explosion's thunderous climax. Fragments of a once great empire crumbled into dilapidated piles. The deafening cavalcade continued as floor upon floor collapsed downwards. Sirens blared and alarm systems screamed. Fire sprinklers tried their feeble best to douse the hundreds of fires until the collapsing building crushed them as well. Both ex-presidents shook in terror as the beams creaked and groaned above them, while debris and dust continued to hail down upon them.

Eventually, the booming slackened to a low growl. The shuddering dissipated. Silence, now even thicker than previously, returned. The two mortal enemies, Morgan and Hieshler, sat inanimately, glaring at each other through the dust, unable to comprehend the enormity of their situation.

Somehow, they were both still alive.

Hell had a future far worse than death for the two evil beings. Despite every other floor of the building being devastated by the blast, the storeroom at the very bottom of the basement was spared. Morgan and Hieshler had survived in a little capsule of life. But they had no escape from the room - the explosion had irreversibly barricaded every exit - and therefore no escaping each other. Hell had sentenced each to eternity with his most hated enemy.

They were together, forever, their privilege of death interminably withdrawn.

Dave hadn't taken a breath for over five minutes. He felt serene, calm and peaceful as he blissfully ignored the chaos and turmoil around him. His mind swam with warmth and happiness, just like when he had first entered God's chambers.

He felt like he was going home for a freshly baked meal after a hard day's work. He was putting on warm dry clothes after a winter's rain had soaked him. Alexandra was cuddling him in a soft bed ... the pillow was just right ... it was raining outside ... he was so comfortable.

He was feeling tired ... so tired.

Tired and happy ... comfortable....

... so, so, tired.

PART FOUR

Chapter 50

"I'm not very happy with you, David."

Dave froze. Nobody ever called him David unless he was in trouble. As a result of this truth, 'David' was one of his least favourite words, and the speaker's tone of voice left no doubt that he was in strife again.

"David," the voice continued, "I am talking to you."

Apprehensively, Dave opened his eyes. He saw a familiar scene: a white ceiling, a blindingly white room, and a soft bed. Above his prostrate body stood the terse-voiced person, whose bony hands, sparsely whiskered chin and balding head of white hair immediately identified him as God.

A sea of memories, mostly unpleasant, washed over Dave. He remembered Elvis, Saint Barnabas, and the stench of Hell as he awoke in his own squalid apartment. Painfully he recalled visiting the Stranglers Bar, and his voyage in the box to find Morgan and Hieshler. A chill went through his body as he relived the chaos as the two presidents became entombed forever in a living coffin. Yet Dave's most powerful memory was of the wonderful feeling of warmth that had floated through him as the GTN tower had collapsed overhead.

"Am I correct in assuming that most of your recent experiences were not very enjoyable?" enquired God.

"That," said Dave, "would be an understatement."

"Why did you go to Hell?" asked God, befuddled. "I thought I had humanoids fairly well figured out, but then one of you does something like this and completely confuses me."

"It was, well, sort of an accident".

"An accident? You walked all the way up a towering staircase, and jumped over the edge into an eternity in Hell, and now you are trying to tell me that it was an accident?"

"Well, when you put it that way, I guess it was more of a misunderstanding."

God raised his eyebrows.

"I thought it was the stairway to Heaven," said Dave, now starting to feel very foolish.

"You thought that Heaven was *up*?"

"Well, er, I simply assumed that Heaven was up, and that Hell was, well, down."

"What a peculiar notion," replied God. "I suppose that next you will be assuming that Heaven has free beer and pizza and lots of beautiful women."

"It doesn't?"

God shook his head.

Dave was upset. If Heaven didn't have lashings of beer and pizza, and plenty of beautiful women, then what was the point of going there?

God was taken aback with Dave's thought. He was proud of Heaven. It was, after all, the culmination of quintozegaquillions of years of creation, research and refinement. So he was also a little disappointed that Dave, whom he considered a typical human being, did not care for the beauty of his creations unless intoxicating beverages, fattening food and/or gratuitous sex accompanied them.

Although, God noted after a brief reflection, Dave's ideas weren't that bad. Perhaps he could use some of Dave's suggestions as the basis for a post-life stage in an advanced universe prototype he was presently configuring? Why hadn't he thought of the beer-pizza-sex idea earlier? It was far simpler than the right-wrong/good-evil conundrums with which he had been tampering so far. God's mind was just beginning to flower with hedonistic scenarios for this new Heaven when a question from his human companion interrupted his train of thought.

"May I see it anyway?"

God snapped back to reality, and excused himself for daydreaming.

"See what?"

"Heaven."

"A visit to Heaven would be very difficult to organise," God responded after a few seconds thought. "Your unscheduled stopover in Hell created havoc in your personal space-time continuum. I had to fold your time shell inside out, and then cut and twist the circumference of your existence envelope to extract you."

"Er?"

"I'm sorry. I'm using jargon again. What I am trying to say, Dave, is that I had to tinker with time to get you out of Hell."

"Oh? Thanks for that. Was it a difficult job?"

"Yes, it was a very delicate operation. No one has ever departed from Hell before, as I designed it specifically to prevent anyone from escaping. Even using a time twist, the only way that I could extract you was if your life ended, but this was not as simple as it seems. I had previously configured eternal life into the system to decrease the escalating number of suicides I was observing. So it was a delicate job to warp your space-time continuum, not to mention breaking a few regulations, to retrieve you."

"Oh, I see," said Dave, although he didn't.

"Nevertheless, you can be proud of your own contribution, Dave. Your positive reactions the vibes that I sent to you - to find Morgan, Juan Carlos Manuel de la Espirito and Hieshler - were admirable under the circumstances."

"I wondered why that feeling kept returning."

"In fact, confronting the presidents probably saved your soul. When they saw you in Hell - which was theoretically impossible as you were not really dead - the resultant metaphysical aberration led to a mutant vibration in the fabric of their space-time cones. Once I observed these vibrations, it was a simple matter of triangulating their positions to localise your coordinates. If you had not confronted those two men then finding you would have been virtually impossible for me: billions of souls exist on Hell, and by the time I had sorted through them all it may have been too late to extract you."

Dave mentally patted himself on the back.

"You were also very lucky that Morgan murdered you. Ordinarily, of course, it wouldn't have worked, as dying on Hell is impossible. However on this occasion I was on hand to manually override the system, allowing you the privilege of life termination. This, of course, returned you here."

"I'm still not sure I understand," said Dave as his mind danced with metaphysical envelopes, soul cones and eternal triangulations. "Do you mean that I *died* in Hell?"

"Of course," replied God, matter-of-factly. "Otherwise you would still be up there."

"So am I now *dead*?"

God paused for quite some time.

"That is a very good question, Dave. A very good question indeed. However, on the balance of the technical evidence I would have to say 'No'. As you were not dead when you arrived in Hell then you can't possibly be dead now - that would involve a reverse-entropy de-materialising möbian time loop, which is clearly impossible. So I would say that despite the trivial matter of having died in your past you are still very much alive."

"Wow!" exclaimed Dave. "So I died. Awesome. I wondered what all that warm stuff meant."

"I designed death to be as eustressful as possible," replied God.

"Well, I reckon you succeeded," said Dave, despite having no idea was 'eustressful' meant.

"Why thank you," beamed God, for he rarely received a compliment from someone who had just passed away. The rhetoric ceased momentarily as Dave tried to absorb and comprehend all that God had told him, but he was left feeling confused about a few delicate matters.

"So what happens now to my spacey-continuum thingo?" he asked.

"Well," said God "your time-space cone has, due to your unorthodox escape from Hell, developed a few glitches."

"Glitches? What sort of glitches?"

"It's difficult for me to explain in simple terms," said God. "But because I had to twist your time loops around so far you can never go back to the universe from which you originally came."

"Never?" said Dave despondently. "But I had an unfinished can of beer in the fridge - what will happen to it? And what will happen to my family and friends? More importantly, what about Alexandra?"

"Your beer, family, friends *and* Alexandra will all continue to exist as before Dave. The only difference is that, in their universe, you won't."

"I won't exist?" cried Dave despairingly. "It's hard enough having died, but to no longer exist is a bit rough."

"You will exist, Dave," explained God, "but in another universe."

"What sort of universe?" asked Dave.

"I've developed some terrific new varieties," boasted God. "You could choose any one that you fancied."

"Are any of them likely to spontaneously de-inertialise?" asked Dave, remembering God's earlier dash away from the sorting compound to save a self-destructing universe.

"Er, I have to admit it's an outside chance," confessed God. Having forgotten their earlier conversation, God wondered how Dave knew anything about spontaneous de-inertialisation. Humans weren't due to discover that branch of physics for a few hundred years.

"I don't want to live in a de-inertialising universe. I want to go back to my own universe. Is there any other way?"

God's brow furrowed. He wanted to solve Dave's problem, but this was a radically unorthodox situation. So much could go wrong, and an entire universe - six long days of work - was at stake. Perhaps he had overlooked a simpler solution. Mentally, he strained every alternative approach through his cortical computers. Eventually he was left with only one other possible answer. However, God was not very comfortable with the solution; he had tried a similar operation once or twice before, and it had been a very difficult and tiring process. Nevertheless, he revealed the idea to Dave.

"We could possibly reverse the entire set of time continua for your old universe, which would effectively rewind the history of its existence by, say, a few weeks."

Dave looked at God expectantly as he unveiled his master plan.

"Then," God continued, "comes the tricky part. We could re-release all of the time cones in the forward direction, at which point your being would be displaced back to its original coordinates in your history."

"Not a bad idea," nodded Dave, as though he could have thought of it himself.

"However, you should also consider one other important issue," said God. "If we perform the time reversal, then Morgan W. Morgan, Juan Carlos Manuel de la Espirito and Harry Hieshler would also be displaced back into history."

Dave's mood mellowed as he gained a full appreciation of God's statement and its implications. If he returned to the past, then the Earth - which had been ridded of three power-hungry, egotistic and narcissistic menaces - would again be burdened by their presence. Sure, Dave admitted to himself, a few people would be pleased to see him back again – his parents, a few old mates from the footy club, and, he knew for certain, Alexandra. But was it fair to the Earth if Morgan, God and Hieshler were thrown into his package deal as well? It would take a lot of benevolence on his behalf to match the evil that they would inject back into society; benevolence that he had spectacularly failed to deliver during his first tenure on Earth. Perhaps humanity would be better served if he simply went elsewhere.

But then Dave thought of Alexandra. He recalled the look in her eyes. *That* look.

He remembered experiencing Alexandra's love, just before God's powerbolt cracked onto the stage, accidentally killing both evil presidents and the egotistical footballer. Something stirred at the back of Dave's mind. He repeated his last thought ... *accidentally killing the presidents and the footballer.*

Accidentally. A loophole.

"But those three men were not supposed to die anyway," blurted Dave. "Their deaths were premature and unintended."

God rubbed his chin thoughtfully.

"Hmm. That's true, Dave. In fact if they had not been touching you at the time, then they would still be living today."

"Good," said Dave, with an air of finality. "Let's get cracking with this time reversal thing then, shall we?"

After much research consisting entirely of introspection, God mentally confirmed the steps that would make it possible for Dave to return to his own universe at an earlier point in its history. However God could not ascertain to exactly which point Dave should return, so he left this minor technicality to a last-minute judgment.

Once God decided to proceed with the time reversal, he immediately began implementing it, as any further wastage of space-time simply increased the likelihood of instabilities developing in the system. He surprisingly permitted his human visitor to watch, on the strict condition that Dave did not touch *anything*.

After a long but a brisk walk that included only four wrong turns, God and Dave entered through a door that was marked:

TIME-SPACE ENVELOPES

Prototype Universe 42, Version 13, Batch 666.

Once inside, Dave saw one of the most unusual sights that he, or anyone else, had ever witnessed. Floating inside separate large crystal spheres were three twisted tubes - their coiled, convoluted forms pulsed with an iridescent purple glow. To Dave they suggested three multi knotted pretzels made from mosquito zappers. Their dimpled surfaces emitted soft sparks, which would occasionally leap from the surface of one tube to the next. Their mere presence imbued the room with an austere ambience: these were clearly very important things.

As God approached the middle tube, a small opening appeared in the front of its spherical casing. As God drew nearer to the tube, the opening continued to widen until it was so large that the front hemisphere of the crystal globe became nonexistent. By the time God was next to it, the casing had drawn back so far that it resembled a coin-sized disc, enigmatically hovering behind the purple tube it had once protected.

"This, Dave," said God with a proud sweep of his hand towards the exposed tube, "is the entire collection of living time histories for your universe."

Dave looked in awe at the strange pulsing forms before him, and gulped in astonishment. This was his universe - viewed from the outside. He wondered if he could see his apartment, or the Stranglers Bar. Or, better still, Alexandra.

"They would all be a little bit difficult to find," answered God. Dave, now adept at thought-conversations, wondered what purpose the other two glowing tubes served.

"This one over here," replied God, "is the Universe which humanoid Earthlings commonly call Heaven. And *that* time tube," he continued as he pointed to the other sphere "is where you have just come from, Dave. It's colloquially known as Hell."

Dave's head jerked with surprise. If only he had a *really* high definition camera.

"If you look very carefully at that one," said God, pointing to Hell's time tube, "you may see something interesting."

Dave, still in awe of what he was observing, pressed his nose against the crystal sphere that surrounded Hell. He became dizzy from following the many twists and spirals as he scanned the glowing tube. After a few minutes of meticulous scrutiny, he noticed a tiny speck of darkness, which was the only imperfection on the otherwise unblemished surface. Dave glanced at God with a questioning expression.

"That was you," explained God. "That was the location of your time cone, which I have just extracted. It was a very finicky procedure, and it caused me so much eye strain that it almost gave me a headache."

"Sorry about that," said Dave.

Then, wanting to avoid wasting any more time, God motioned for Dave to stand aside.

"Don't let anything that you are about to see alarm you, Dave," said God. Dave gravely nodded his head. Ceremoniously, God slowly reached forward and touched the throbbing tube.

The reaction astonished Dave. A wave of muscle cramps flowed up God's arm and into his body. Then his limbs flailed violently in random directions. His head thrashed from side to side, and his body jerked as if he had fallen into a blender. Even his face muscles twitched and spasmed, and he fell to the floor where his convulsions bounced him around like a wonky basketball. Dave watched in horror as God's frail-looking body absorbed the punishing ordeal.

Mercifully but slowly, the jerks began to dissipate. Gradually they became twitches, then shivers, and ultimately waned to nothing more than goose bumps.

The time-history tube responded similarly, though less spectacularly. It dissipated its energy in wild pulses, as though a child was flicking its power switch. The pulsing steadily became a duller flickering, and then a physical vibration. Gradually the soft sparks ceased glitzing from the tube's surface, and its bright purple glow faded to a gunmetal grey.

God now lay motionless on the floor, seemingly in a coma. Despite God's earlier advice, Dave was very alarmed. But just as Dave began to panic - had he caused the death of the creator of the universe? - God's fingers began to move. He was alive. Phew.

"I hate stopping time," God croaked as he groggily raised himself to his feet.

Within seconds, God had recovered. He was soon standing upright, and he gave Dave a wink to signify that all was well. Then, reverently stooping forward, God hoisted the lifeless timeless tube in his arms, and raised it aloft. He fell silent, and into a deep meditative state. Dave dared not breathe lest he disturb God's concentration.

With a grip so strong it could crumble cast iron, yet somehow so delicate that it would not dint a water drop, God began to twist the tube. His face grimaced with intense concentration as he worked his hands in opposite rotations, his knuckles whitening with each effort. The tube creaked and groaned as it slowly gave way like an old lead pipe. God's wrist tendons stood out like wire rope, and his muscles shook with fatigue as the tube reluctantly unfurled. After an indeterminable period of concentrated physical exertion, God had uncurled the entire tube. To Dave's eye it now resembled a giant grey calamari ring, rather than a pulsating purple pretzel that had been knotted by a hyperactive troop of boy scouts.

God slumped against a wall, recovering. His arms hung loosely by his sides, regaining strength. After a few minutes break during which neither man spoke a word, God again hoisted the tube above his head.

"That was the easy part," he said. "Next, I've got to reverse the curves." He inhaled deeply, preparing for the bout that was to follow. Then, with muscles that were still tired and trembling, he began to painstakingly twist the tube in the reverse direction. Dave could only stare in awe as a man who looked at least one hundred years old worked a gym session that would put an entire football squad to shame.

After another period of time that Dave could not even begin to estimate, God again slumped against the wall, exhausted but satisfied that the time-tube had reached the correct reverse shape. Dave, realising how fatigued God was, felt compelled to offer help.

"No thank you," said God as he gasped for air. "Could you imagine the consequences if you dropped it?"

Dave's mind spun with scenarios that a fractured-and-glued-back-together time tube would create. While Dave was imagining himself having a beer with a brontosaurus, God carried the reversed time loop back to its original position in front of the hovering disc. Dave snapped out of his fantasy just as God released the tube into mid air, where it floated delicately as if awaiting further instructions.

God obliged. He reached out and softly touched the tube, which produced an effect that was diametrical to the earlier display. The tube flickered spasmodically into life, and was soon glowing with a healthy purple lustre. God collapsed, limp and lifeless, onto the floor. Dave rushed to help, but God feebly waved him away.

"I'll ... be fine ..." he croaked. True to his word, God steadily recovered as life jerked systematically into his body.

"The theatrics were due to energy transfers," God explained as he began to look and act normal again. "At the moment the time cones in your universe are all rewinding. How far back would you like me to take them?"

Dave began to think back through his past, searching for a moment befitting his re-entry to the Earth.

"Consider it done," interrupted God.

"But..."

"You can't change your mind now."

"But I haven't even...."

"I don't want you changing your mind, Dave. Your first decision must stand."

"Er, all right," replied Dave, despite not having, to his own knowledge, even formulated a decision. "How long will it take to rewind?" he asked curiously.

"Well," replied God, "the time scale in your Universe is completely different from the one we use up here. In local time it should take about nine gazzabillizoomseconds to reverse your universe back to your chosen moment of re-entry."

"How long, in my language, is nine gazzabillizoomseconds?" asked Dave.

"In your language," replied God as he smiled a wry grin, "it is about a six-pack."

"Excellent," said Dave. "Let's not waste a single can of it. Seeing as we have ourselves a bit of unexpected free time, why don't we visit Heaven?"

God wistfully shook his head.

"I'm sorry, Dave, but it would be a little too risky at this stage."

"Please."

"No, Dave. Definitely, unequivocally, absolutely not."

Chapter 51

Peering curiously around the Instaport door, Dave saw a house, some trees, a road and a shop. He felt disappointed; he had hoped that Heaven would be far more titillating.

Dave had managed to convince God that they should visit Heaven. It was, after all, where they had been heading before the unfortunate Elvis incident had occurred. Suddenly, God appeared at Dave's side.

"Where have you been?" asked Dave curiously.

"I wanted to take the stairs for exercise."

Dave stepped out of the Instaport, which, as usual, promptly vanished. He was left standing in the middle of a lush patch of grass, outside a smart block of apartments.

"I'll follow you," said God.

"Follow me where?" asked Dave.

"To the pub, of course."

"I've never been to Heaven before. I don't have the faintest idea how to find the pub."

God smiled. Dave hadn't yet realised.

"Look around you, Dave."

Dave did as requested. He saw a white picket fence, which separated the lush green lawn from a terracotta-paved road. A healthy garden fringed a winding path, which led to the homely apartment building. Despite the obvious charm and congeniality of his surroundings, Dave could see nothing irregular.

"It looks like this neighbourhood has a resident who works for the local council planning and maintenance committee," said Dave facetiously.

"Does anything seem familiar?"

Dave looked again. This was clearly a wealthy, well-to-do suburb; the type of place that he usually could not even afford to visit. Then he noticed the steps leading up to the second floor apartments. Hmm. Could this be?

Closing his eyes, he staggered up the stairs, mimicking his own drunken homecomings on Earth. Without so much as missing a step, he lurched along the landing, and, still with his eyes closed, stopped after a few wobbly paces. Turning sideways, he reached forward. His hand landed exactly where he thought it would: on a door handle. Dave opened his eyes, to see that he was standing outside a trendy little apartment.

"This is my place, isn't it?" he yelled down to God, who had been watching Dave's experiment with amusement.

"Correct," said God. "Have a quick look inside if you wish."

"Won't the door be locked?"

"This is Heaven," replied God with brevity.

Dave entered the room, and felt immediately content. This was *him.* He had often dreamed of refurbishing his own apartment on Earth in this fashion, but he never had sufficient funds or, more particularly, enough motivation, to even begin. The decor was tasteful and the fittings were casual. A full sized virtual snooker set stood next to a charming twentieth century jukebox, and tasteful 3-D holograms of Honeydew Melons adorned the walls. Even the kitchen was tidy. Dave turned on a tap, and was only mildly disappointed to discover that it was water - not beer - that flowed out. Nevertheless, the whole place had such a wonderful feel that Dave was loathe to leave, and it was only when God reissued his invitation to the Stranglers Bar that he could tear himself away.

*

"Very convivial," was Dave's first thought as they entered under the carved wooden archway that served as the entrance to the Stranglers Bar. Almost immediately, a vibrant middle-aged woman with deep brown hair and eyes intercepted them, and led them gracefully towards the bar.

"Good afternoon, gentlemen," she purred. "My name is Wendy, and I'd like to welcome you to the Stranglers Bar."

That was incredible, thought Dave. Wendy had just delivered a typical welcoming spiel to new patrons, but she had said it without a hint of duty or insincerity and without sounding like it was a pre-recorded message from the management. Dave actually *felt* welcome.

"What are you here for this afternoon?" she asked politely.

"Just a few quiet beers," said God, winking at Dave.

"What'll it be then?"

"A couple of large glasses Neptune Gold for starters, please."

Dave looked around the bar. Its basic layout and structure were similar to its Earthly counterpart, but the ambience was unrecognisable. This version was so *welcoming*. Sure, Dave liked the Stranglers Bar on Earth, but that was primarily because he was such a regular patron that he felt at home. He already felt like he *owned* this bar.

Wendy returned a few seconds later with two enormous tankards brimming with cold frothy beer. She placed one in front of each of her guests.

"I haven't asked the boss yet," she said, "but I'm sure that she would like these first couple to be on the house."

"Thank her very much," said God.

"Yeah, cheers," said Dave as he emptied the entire contents of the tankard directly onto the lining of his stomach. After all, it was his first real beer for quite some time.

"Wow, you guys must be thirsty," said Wendy as both Dave and God simultaneously clunked their empty tankards back onto the bar. "Another?"

"Yes please," said God, tossing a few coins onto the bar.

God and Dave took their refilled tankards to a quiet table and settled in for a quick session.

"You've done a great job with the design of Heaven, God. I must admit I expected the pleasures would be more obvious - rivers of beer, never ending pizzas, and thousands of gorgeous women queuing up to date me - but this is sensational."

"Thank you very much, Dave. I'm happy with the way that it is turning out."

"This entire visit has been a real eye-opener for me. I despised Hell - you obviously made it an appalling place, so disgusting, dirty and dangerous. But Heaven - this is fantastic: the people, the buildings, even the price of beer is wonderful."

"I think that you slightly misunderstand something."

"What do you mean?"

"Well," explained God, "I didn't set the price of beer on Heaven. I didn't decorate this bar, and I didn't make the people nicer."

"You didn't?"

"No. And I didn't make Hell such a vile, threatening place either."

"If it wasn't you, then who was it?" asked Dave, confused.

"People, Dave. People just like you."

"Are people like me in charge of Heaven and Hell?"

"Yes, Dave. Just as people like you are in control of Earth as well."

"Do you mean the television station owners?"

"I mean everyone: every man, woman and child. You are all in charge of your own destinies, and the futures of your worlds."

"I don't get it."

"It's like this, Dave. All three Universes began with the same structure. They were initially identical to each other, and are different now only because of the actions of their human populations."

This surprised Dave. He could see vast physical differences between Heaven, Hell and Earth. Even the different tastes of the beer were at odds with God's assertion. How could a tiny human variation explain the huge differences between each Earth?

"Well, Dave, I created your three universes quite early in my career. At the time, I was experimenting with various self-aware life forms, and was having difficulty in adjusting the balance of their good-evil/right-wrong decision making processes. Some overzealous do-gooders had just ruined a universe I had spent months on, while some evil humanoids had destroyed my previous construction. I was determined not to repeat my mistake."

"So what did you do?"

"I created your universe as a test case."

"Do you mean that the entire human race - and our planet, solar system and universe - is just an experiment?"

"Well, in short, yes. Still, I've grown quite fond of your universe now, especially you humans. I was originally planning to discard you after collecting my data, but I've since decided to keep you as a hobby."

"I suppose being your hobby is better than being scrapped, or worse still, de-inertialised."

God took the last gulp of beer from his glass, and wiped the froth from his whiskers with the back of his hand. Wendy arrived on cue, carrying two refilled tankards. Dave quickly knocked off the last half of his drink to catch up. After again paying for the round, God patiently continued answering Dave's queries.

"As I said, your universe was created as a testing ground. After setting the Earth's initial physical elements in place, I let the whole system bake for a few millennia. Then, when its life forms evolved into self-aware humans, I introduced a separating procedure after their death. This procedure grouped them according to how they had lived their life on Earth. As they died, I transplanted some humans to one alternate universe, while the rest went to the other. I could therefore independently observe the results of each group's interactions."

"I see," said Dave. "What were the results?"

"One group of humans created the Hell, while the other group created this," said God as he waved his arm around in a wide arc.

"So from what you are telling me," said Dave, extrapolating his understanding of the situation, "Heaven and Earth and Hell are all really identical, except for the actions of us humans."

"Precisely," said God as he drained the last mouthful of beer from his glass.

"But Hell - it seemed so evil, almost as if it had a mind of its own."

"I think your ancient Gayakan population summarised that effect most efficiently. They had a saying: *Mo#mbil^y f!ombil^y ha#bbilat j!abbilat.*"

Dave raised a twisted eyebrow.

"Which, when roughly translated into modern English, means 'The sweet flower of the Sing-Sing tree attracts butterflies, while the antelope's dung heap is home to only flies.'"

"I'm still not sure I understand," said Dave." Do you mean, like, *shit happens*?"

"Er, almost. What I'm really trying to say is that good people and deeds usually generate favourable fortune, while evil typically attracts further wrongdoing."

"So all of the bad luck on Hell - like that which happened to Hieshler, Morgan and God - was because they created it for themselves?"

"Bingo."

"And all of the good luck here on Heaven is because the people earn it."

"That is more or less correct, Dave."

"Even the cheap beer?"

"Yes, even cheap beer."

"Then why *don't* humans on Earth all act like humans on Heaven?"

"I'm not sure," said God. "I was hoping that you could tell me."

Dave simply shrugged.

"We must get going," said God, "or we may miss the re-entry point back to your universe."

"One more beer for the road?" asked Dave hopefully.

"All right," answered God. "But just *one.*"

*

God had worked up a lather of sweat. He had just finished re-twisting the time tube back to a forward direction, and was exhausted.

"My shoulders are killing me," said God.

"You'll need some physiotherapy tomorrow," suggested Dave.

God carefully carried the dull grey time tube back to its sphere, where it hovered in position as God released it. The room fell silent, as both men realised that it was time for Dave to depart. After an awkward few seconds, God issued Dave with some final explanations and instructions.

"While we were visiting Heaven, time in your original universe rewound a few weeks, and is presently at a standstill. When I touch life back into the tube, time will restart, and you will be transposed back to your coordinates at that point in history. The whole future of your time-cone will again be at your discretion. You will remember nothing of your recent future, because technically it will not have yet happened."

"I'll try and remedy a few mistakes," promised Dave. "I might even clean up the house, and get a job."

God smiled, and patted Dave on the back. Dave had profited from his visit, even though it had originally been an accident. He extended the pat into a big, manly hug.

"Seeing you again was wonderful, Dave."

"It's been terrific to meet you, too. The visit was most enlightening," said Dave, at loss for a more powerful reply. "I'm sure that I'll see you again - hopefully when I'm on my way down to Heaven."

As the moment of departure fell upon him, Dave felt a bit ungrateful: God had been very hospitable, and had even shouted all the beers at the Stranglers Bar. He felt as though he should be offering God a gift to show his appreciation - perhaps a nice bottle of wine, or a box of chocolates. But what could you give to the creator of the universes? Besides, he had nothing tangible to give, unless God wanted a dirty old pair of jeans, or a shirt, or a....

Of course. Perfect.

"I've got a small gift for you, God," said Dave, "as a token of my gratitude."

"This is an unexpected surprise," said God, although he could read Dave's mind.

"Close your eyes, and don't peek," said Dave. "Don't read my thoughts either."

"I promise I won't," replied God, as he heard Dave emit a few muffled yelps of pain.

"You can open them now."

God opened his eyes, and looked down at Dave's outstretched palms. Lying on them was his gift. He beamed a broad smile.

God examined his present with obvious pleasure: it was a quaint-looking humanoid construction, adorned by a blue and silver swirl, and crowned with a lime green tip. Undoubtedly one of the finest examples of a writing implement that he had seen for a long time.

"I hope you like it," said Dave sheepishly. "You can add it to your pen collection."

"It's lovely," said God. "I've never seen one exactly like this before."

Both God and Dave again paused awkwardly, as only one simple sentiment remained unspoken.

"Goodbye, Dave."

"Goodbye, God."

It was time to go.

Dave, for want anything more constructive to do, stood formally to attention. God reached out his hand, and slowly moved it towards the hovering time tube. Dave felt his muscles tighten, as he realised that he was about to be blasted millions of miles and about a month away - exactly where or when, he did not know. As God's forefinger moved within a hair's breadth of the tube, Dave saw soft blurry sparks of energy begin to leap across the gap.

God suddenly withdrew his finger.

"I'll be back in two zillidaddoseconds," he said as he started for the door.

The unexpected interruption startled Dave.

"What ... where ..." he stammered.

"Don't touch anything while I'm gone," yelled God as he disappeared through the portals.

Dave had learned his earlier lesson well. He stayed fixed to the spot, not daring to move, and not even thinking about touching anything. A minute later, God returned in a flurry.

"Sorry about the delay, Dave," he panted, "but I just thought of something that you'll need."

He thrust an ordinary looking pencil into Dave's shirt pocket.

"It's only a nineteenth century HHB - nowhere near as lovely as the piece that you just gave me - but you may find that it comes in handy."

"Handy for what?" asked Dave.

"You're about to find out," said God enigmatically. "See you later."

He casually touched the time tube. Dave instantly vanished into a great mishmash of space and time.

PART FIVE

Chapter 52

"Do you promise? Do you absolutely promise to call me?"

"Yes, I promise."

"At six o'clock?"

"Yes. At exactly six o'clock," said Dave earnestly.

"I'll be waiting by my STOVE phone."

"Already I can't wait to talk with you again."

"You had better take my number down."

"Good idea. But, um, my smart watch isn't working very well today."

"What about your LifeMovie contact lenses?" asked Alexandra.

"They are, er, they're not, ah, working well today either."

"Hmmm. What about a pen, an old fashioned pen or pencil?"

Dave absently tapped his pockets as he sometimes did when he was feeling for something that he knew was not there, like a hovertrain ticket when the inspector passed. However this time he received a welcome surprise: he found an old HHB pencil in the top pocket of his lucky shirt. Where on Earth had that come from? he wondered.

After jotting Alexandra's telephone number onto the back of an old hot dog wrapper, he passionately hugged his wonderful new girlfriend and then kissed her goodbye. As they stood in a lingering last embrace, Dave's eyes were drawn towards the starry night sky. As he stared into space, Dave could have sworn that an image of a massive wrinkled eye, topped with a huge bushy white eyebrow, materialised in the Heavens above. The gigantic eye gave Dave a cheeky wink and then disappeared into infinity.

The End

More books by John Perrier
JP Publishing Australia

"Back Pain: How to get rid of it Forever"
- Self help/back pain/self treatment
- Adult/Young Adult readers
- Available as print edition or two-volume E-Book

"Captain Rum – A Wondrous Adventure"
Edited by Prof. H.D. (Bert) Lampluck
- Historical Fiction/Maritime adventure
- Adult/Young Adult readers
- Published by JP Publishing Australia
- Available as print or E-Book

"Campervan Kama Sutra"
Around Australia with a camper trailer, three kids and a dog*
- Travel/comedy
- Adult/Young Adult/Teen
- Available as print or E-Book

"Using Your Brain to Get Rid of Your Pain"
A simple, common sense guide on how to manage stress, reduce pain, and think more healthily.
- Self help/healthy living
- Adult/Young adult
- Available as print or E-Book

You can find more online at
www.JPpublishingAUSTRALIA.com

"Back Pain: How to Get Rid of it Forever"

The title says it all: this book will help you permanently banish your back pain. In three logical sections, it shows you how to feel better.

The first section makes it easy for you to understand your back pain. Using simple, clear language, it explains the structure of your spine, and demystifies many common pain-provoking conditions. The second part offers a unique quiz that will help you to classify your injury into one of four types. In this way, you will learn how to cure your pain, not someone else's.

In part three, the advice flows thick and fast. You will learn clever techniques that will help you to use your spine more efficiently, and discover how to think, eat, relax, and sleep away your pain. You'll also find useful information on exercises, x-rays, medication and muscles, plus some tips on how to choose a spinal health practitioner. Of course, all of the advice will be tailored to your specific problem.

Because the cure uses well-proven techniques, your relief won't just last a few days or weeks. You will feel better *forever*.

*

"The best self help back book I have ever read."

Dr Keith Charlton, Chiropractor, former governor of the Australian Spinal Research Foundation.

"...a regular dose of humour that will undoubtedly help to lighten your back pain."

John Miller, Physiotherapist with a special interest in back pain.

"One of the most informative surveys of back pain to date."

Graham Sanders, President of the Qld Osteopathic Association

More information on Back Pain can also be found at

www.physioworks.com.au

"Captain Rum: A Wondrous Adventure"
Edited by Prof. H.D. (Bert) Lampluck

When an Oxford Professor stumbles upon an old naval Captain's log, he unwittingly discovers what many scholars now agree is one of the greatest maritime adventures in history.

In 1821, Captain Fintan McAdam set sail from London, solo, in search of adventure. During his journey he discovered incredible new worlds, and interacted with their amazing inhabitants. McAdam's voyage also forced him to confront his enemies within, learning much about himself.

Captain Rum, as told in McAdam's own words through his journal, is a tale of discovery, despair and delight. It will keep you enthralled through many a stormy night.

Campervan Kama Sutra
*Around Australia with a camper trailer, three kids and a dog**

This true story tells of one family's hilarious journey through Australia's rugged outback countryside.

Our intrepid adventurers work their way through numerous mishaps, including, but not limited to, an ill-advised river crossing, an inappropriately packed roof rack and some truly horrible singing.

During their journey, they stumble across a motley assortment of characters such as a confused check-in clerk, a grey nomad with an eye for detail regarding torches, and several Crazy Germans.

While reading Campervan Kama Sutra, you'll not only fall in love with Australia's vast, ever-changing countryside, but you'll also delight in the tragicomedy that arrives with unerring regularity.

You'll laugh until something hurts.

*P.S. There was no dog.

Using Your Brain to get Rid of Your Pain
A simple, common sense guide on how to manage stress, reduce pain,
and think more healthily.

This book will help you to *feel better*. You'll not only learn how to reduce or cure your aches and pains, but you'll discover techniques that will help you to relax away the stresses and strains of everyday life.

However, this book does not contain masses of complex psychiatry, nor is it a collection of old wives' remedies. You won't have to use any drugs to achieve amazing results, nor will you be required to burn incense or wear mystical healing crystals in an ankle bracelet.

Instead, you will learn how to relieve your pain using the most natural cures known to medical science. Furthermore, the treatment will have beneficial spin-offs rather than unpleasant or dangerous side effects. Better still, it won't cost you a single penny!

INCLUDES COMPLIMENTARY AUDIO TRACK!
See **www.JPpublishingAUSTRALIA.com** for details

What other health professionals have said...

"This is an easy-to-understand guide to stress and its related symptoms. The author explains these sometimes difficult concepts by using simple, relevant examples, and enlivens the discussion with a touch of humour along the way. Most importantly, it shows you in simple terms how to manage your own problems. I heartily recommend this book to all sufferers of chronic pain."

(Ian McKenzie, Psychologist, Chronic pain clinician)

"What a wonderful, simple-to-read book! It's funny, insightful, and does a magnificent job of combining theory with practical management. Anyone   suffering with chronic pain or stress should read this book."

(Hilary Thomson, Occupational Therapist, Former head of Relaxation Unit at the King Khalid National Guard Hospital in Saudi Arabia)

Connect and Contact

Your comments, criticisms, typos, praise, offers for movie deals, and suggestions are all very welcome. Please contact us by any of the links below.

Email: **JDPpublishingAUSTRALIA@gmail.com**
                (Please note the extra 'D')

Facebook: **https://www.facebook.com/JPpublishingAustralia**

Website: **www.JPpublishingAUSTRALIA.com**

Mail: JP Publishing Australia
                56 Quirinal Crescent
                Seven Hills, Brisbane
                AUSTRALIA   4170